Praise for *Off the Books*

"Guitarist Peter Leitch inched his way out of the Montreal
and Toronto scenes to land in the East Village in the early 1980s,
and has been here ever since. *Off the Books* captures the danger
and struggle of both the city and the scene in that era with
a cast of characters you wouldn't expect in a jazz
book, from the mechanic he shared a car with to
long-gone and much-missed clubs."
—*New York Daily News*

"Leitch's memoir chronicles an impressive career, recalling a
lifetime of stages and studios shared with jazz greats, mapping
the scene from the 1960s onward."
—*Montreal Review of Books*

"A must read for those wanting a glimpse into what it's like trying
to make a living solely as a jazz musician."
—*Jazz Guitar Life*

"*Off the Books: A Jazz Life* is not your usual jazz autobiography.
Every time the narrative threatens to get bogged down in tour
dates or recording sessions, Leitch zings you.... Perhaps owing
somewhat to his Canadian-ness, Leitch is candidly critical
of many aspects of American society.... We get a fascinating
look at the vibrant 1950s and 60s Montreal jazz scene [and] a
thoughtful and ceaselessly amusing tour of New York
as gentrification takes its toll."
—*Lucid Culture*

"A candid memoir by one of Canada's finest jazz expats."
—Peter Robb, *Ottawa Citizen*

"This is an autobiography tl ... arts
and all, along with due ref ...e."
—*Jaz*

T0164424

OFF THE BOOKS

A JAZZ LIFE

Peter Leitch

Véhicule Press

Published with the generous assistance of The Canada Council for the
Arts and the Canada Book Fund of the Department of Canadian Heritage.

Canadä

Canada Council Conseil des arts
for the Arts du Canada

Cover design: David Drummond
Cover photo of author: Chris Drukker
Set in Minion and Helvetica by Simon Garamond
Printed by Marquis Book Printing Inc.

LIBRARY AND ARCHIVES CANADA CATALOGUING IN PUBLICATION

Leitch, Peter, 1944-, author
Off the books : a jazz life / Peter Leitch.
Includes an index.
ISBN 978-1-55065-348-9
1. Leitch, Peter, 1944-. 2. Jazz musicians–Canada–Biography.
3. Guitarists–Canada–Biography. I. Title.

ML419.L533A3 2013 782.42165092 C2013-902817-X

Published by Véhicule Press, Montréal, Québec, Canada
www.vehiculepress.com

Distribution in Canada by LitDistCo
www.litdistco.ca

Distributed in the US by Independent Publishers Group
www.ipgbook.com

Printed in Canada

Contents

For Sylvia

I am always outside, looking inside.
Looking for something that is true.
But maybe nothing is true.

—ROBERT FRANK

PART ONE

Montreal in the 1950s & 60s

"The music poured into us…"
—EDDIE CONDON

I remember quite clearly that moment of self-realization when I became aware of myself as an individual—an individual with the beginnings of an ego the size of New York City, or at least Chicago. I must have been four or five years old—a bright sunny day—it was an exhilarating experience that seemed to last for hours, if not a lifetime. Almost as exhilarating as my first shot of heroin, many years later.

I knew early on that I was not going to relate very well to the rest of humanity. I was an only child, and life at home was pretty quiet: that is to say, repressed. I was born in Ottawa in 1944, and we moved to Montreal when I was about a year old. My first eight years were lived in a ground floor flat in a large house in Point-aux-Trembles, a working-class district, once a city in its own right, at the far east end of the Island of Montreal. An older Irish couple lived upstairs. They would often get falling-down drunk, and we would hear them fighting. Winters were rough in 1950s Montreal. Three, four or five feet of snow were not uncommon, and the streets and sidewalks were caked with thick ice from November through April. The house was situated right on the St. Lawrence River, and I spent many hours at the water's edge, watching the deepwater oil tankers on their way to the oil refinery docks. The town was almost entirely French-speaking and Roman Catholic, and I used to see the Catholic priests come out of their residence in their long black robes, spitting on the sidewalk.

As a child, my natural sense of alienation was reinforced by living in this almost totally French-speaking neighborhood. I would

(Top) The author, No. 2 Ninth Avenue, Pointe-aux-Trembles, Quebec, August 1946.
Photographer unknown.
(Bottom) Delorimier Stadium, early 1950s.
Photo: J.E. Leitch, © Peter Leitch

play on the street with the local kids, and my mother said later that I came home one day speaking perfect French. Well, it was far from perfect, but it worked. I was told I learned to read from comic books and newspapers, long before kindergarten. My father was a baseball fan (Brooklyn Dodgers). In the '50s The Montreal Royals were the Dodgers' Triple-A farm team, and he took me to games at the old Delorimier Stadium.

On Sunday afternoons he would sometimes drive downtown and buy the *New York Sunday News* for the baseball coverage. I loved the color comics (Dick Tracy, Smokey Stover and other strips that Canadian newspapers would never carry), and the black-and-white photographs of car crashes, murders and crime scenes. I still enjoy the great photographs by Susan Watts and the creative, humorous wordplay of the headline writing in the *Daily News* today. And instead of "All the news that's fit to print," they print all the news that fits, although lately the paper seems to be leaning in the direction of *The National Enquirer*.

When I was eight years old we moved to a house in a development called Village Champlain, suburban tract housing built as a bedroom community for the five huge oil refineries and other industries in the east end of Montreal. The houses were identical little boxes, located just south of Sherbrooke Street, near Honoré-Beaugrand. It was still pretty far east.

I grew up in an atmosphere of extreme conformity. My father worked at an office job at the Imperial Oil refinery and my mother was a stay-at-home housewife. She played a little classical piano and had a few classical records, but nothing that really interested me. There wasn't much music in the house in those early years other than the radio. They were good English Protestant Canadians. In the 1950s, even in Canada, the message was: Keep the family together at all costs, and watch out for those damned commies! And keep buying those brand new GE refrigerators and new cars with big tailfins. The shadow of the bomb hung over us, though perhaps the fear was not quite as intense as it was for our neighbors to the south. We weren't digging bomb shelters in Canada. Of course as a child I had no way of knowing that a universe parallel to the mainstream consciousness of the '50s existed, populated by individuals like Miles Davis, John Coltrane, Thelonious Monk, Robert Frank, William Burroughs, Jack Kerouac, the abstract expressionist painters and the makers of film noir. We went to church on Sundays and I was confirmed in the Anglican Church, but I couldn't get with the ceremony, the rites and rituals, and I couldn't quite get a handle on the Holy Ghost. Weren't ghosts supposed to be scary?

Standing out in sharp contrast to the well-kept lawns and cookie-cutter bungalows of my suburbia was a huge, notorious mental institution, Saint-Jean–de-Dieu, run by an order of Roman Catholic nuns. It covered a very large area, extending from north to south all the way from Sherbrooke Street to the St. Lawrence River. A couple of blocks from my house, it was medieval in appearance and, apparently, in its approach to mental health. The huge greystone buildings, with a giant red brick tower looming over them—which according to legend was where the worst cases were kept—were a constant reminder of another reality. I remember seeing a photograph taken inside the hospital of women at spinning wheels, with the nuns standing over them.

Sometimes I would walk along the tall chain-link fence that surrounded the grounds and talk to the inmates behind it, at least those who spoke English. They seemed more sane than a lot of the people on the outside, and their conversation more interesting. Today the hospital is still there, now administered by the provincial government. The nuns got out of the mental health business, and sold off much of the land. The street which ran along the fence by the hospital is now a major highway connecting the Louis Hippolyte-Lafontaine Tunnel with Route 40 to the north.

I found it difficult to forge an identity as an English-speaking Canadian in Quebec. What *was* an English Canadian living in Quebec? We were brought up in the 1950s to believe that our allegiance was to Britain and the Queen. The monarchy was very important to my parents. Even our flag, the old Canadian Ensign, had the Union Jack on it. At school we sang "God Save the Queen" as a national anthem. At the same time, we were bombarded with American culture through the media—radio, movies, television, magazines. In Quebec, throw in French-Canadian culture, and you had a *mélange* of influences that left very little room to develop a cultural or national identity of one's own. I now realize that not having any strong national or cultural identity was useful to me in being able to easily move in and out of different cultural and ethnic situations as an individual, although I always remained an outsider, no matter what the context.

When I started grade school I began to suffer from regular bouts of vomiting—weeks at a time. I would vomit and vomit until nothing came up but spoonfuls of bile. We never found out what caused these attacks. I was taken to numerous doctors, none of whom could find anything wrong. It all cleared up when I left high school and my parents' home. I think there must have been some kind of repressed tension there, and food just didn't ever digest properly.

I wasn't very good at sports, and I used to get beaten up fairly regularly after school, probably because I offered little or no resistance. Today they call it bullying. These weren't even kids that I knew very well. My parents said it must have been my own fault. I learned early on that no one was going to help me or be "on my side." Certainly not people in positions of authority. Fortunately I had a large enough ego to allow me to develop a genuine contempt for most of humanity. This was the beginning of a fatalistic attitude to life, of living "under the radar." I would sweep it all under the rug until later. Eventually I could set fire to the rug. This attitude was helped along by the small-mindedness and downright stupidity of most of the grade school teachers. I had an experience with a teacher in a second or third grade art class which put me off visual art for about forty years. She was openly hostile and condescending in response to something I had done. Instead of explaining why it didn't work, she just said I was stupid.

I would stay up late watching old "B" movies on television. Two of these that made a lasting impression were Elia Kazan's *Panic in the Streets* with Richard Widmark, and Boris Ingster's *Stranger on the Third Floor*, with Peter Lorre—the latter often referred to as the first film noir.

A lot of these films were about white people in America, completely rootless and bereft of moral fiber. They were just victims of circumstance, buffeted by strong winds and downdrafts dragging them through the labyrinth of the noir city. These films gave me first glimpses of a nocturnal netherworld far removed from my suburban life and began to color my world, not that I needed much help in that direction.

In the Montreal of the fifties and sixties children were not allowed in movie theaters as a result of a 1927 fire in a theatre in which many children perished. The Catholic Church and others lobbied for the complete closure of all theatres ostensibly to check the influence of the evil empire to the south, and its English language. However, the government passed a law that only affected access for children. My friend Robert Walker commented much later that this was a cultural deprivation that we never really recovered from. One Sunday afternoon when I was about ten, we took a drive into Quebec's Eastern Townships. In the town of Sherbrooke we saw a movie theater. "Oh, look!" my mother said, "A movie in English! And it's an animal movie, the boy will love it." It was called *Monkey on My Back*, and turned out to be about a junkie climbing the walls with withdrawal sickness. Great! The second feature was about a group of people stranded on a cable car suspended above a vast mountain chasm. The cable was breaking one strand at a time. It gave me nightmares for years.

My father came from Saint-Romuald, a small town across the river from Quebec City. At that time the road to Quebec City from Montreal was along the north shore of the St. Lawrence through Berthierville, Trois-Rivières, Cap-de-la-Madeleine, Donnacona, and Cap Rouge. We would drive there to visit my two spinster aunts, who lived in a flat above a bus garage in Saint-Romuald. This building belonged to the Levis Transport Company, which operated a fleet of small, locally-built, circa 1945 Prevost buses that worked suburban routes in the area.

I was fascinated by the Quebec Bridge—a magnificent, massive cantilever structure spanning the St. Lawrence River, which my father had watched being built, and had photographed in 1917. Several serious accidents occurred during the raising of the center span. I believe it fell twice before finally being put in place, resulting in many injuries and deaths.

I was to go back to photograph it in the 1990s, still awestruck by the huge green girders and "K" and "X" braces, and the way they were put together. This bridge made Montreal's Jacques Cartier Bridge

Raising of the center span, Quebec Bridge, 1917.
Photo: J.E. Leitch. © Peter Leitch.

look like a toy. Even as a child, I could sense a certain European sophistication about the city of Quebec that, with the exception of Montreal, didn't seem to exist in the rest of Canada. More depressing was the annual summer vacation in Port Rowan, Ontario, a very small fishing town on Lake Erie, where my maternal grandparents lived. It was an eight-hour car trip, there being no Highway 401 back then. Leaving early in the morning, driving on old Route 2 along the St. Lawrence River through Brockville, Kingston, Napanee, Trenton and Belleville, we would reach Toronto in the late afternoon. This was before the Gardiner Expressway and the route took us along Lakeshore Boulevard past Woodbine Racetrack and the waterfront. In 1949 I saw the burned-out hulk of the Great Lakes cruise ship *Noronic* resting at its pier. The image is still with me today.

We would arrive in Port Rowan after sunset, and the older folks would turn down the lights and sit around talking in hushed tones of disease and dying. Late on a hot summer afternoon, my father and I would walk on the cracked sidewalks to the local railroad depot, the last stop on the line, where we would watch the tobacco-chewing old men dressed in blue suits and straw hats, standing

17

around on the platform waiting for the newspapers to come in, spitting onto the tracks.

I returned to Port Rowan fifty years later; not much had changed: although the movie house was now a used furniture emporium, my grandfather's house was gone, and the train no longer stopped there; there were the same cracked and broken sidewalks, the same roast beef (cold and grey as a prison wall), in the same restaurant with its uncomfortable fake mahogany-stained booths, with folks sitting around talking about their bowels.

At Christmas, my Ontario grandparents would send us by train, a fresh turkey packed with dry ice in a wooden crate. It was an event to go downtown to pick it up at Central Station. After looking at the giant Christmas tree in the station, I would cross Dorchester Boulevard and stare down into the huge crater-like excavation bounded by Dorchester on the south, Cathcart on the north, University on the east and Mansfield on the west, where Place Ville Marie now stands. The "hole" was there for years. You could see the CNR trains going from Central Station north into the tunnels that ran under Mount Royal.

I have always had something of an aversion to nature. I think I am much more interested in what man has created than in his raw materials. In the 1950s, prior to the construction of the St. Lawrence Seaway, large ocean vessels could only go as far upriver as Montreal. The large oil tankers, mostly from Venezuela, would dock and unload their cargoes of crude oil at the Montreal East refineries. These massive east end industrial installations also included chemical plants, copper refineries and an enormous limestone quarry with a Canada Cement factory constantly spewing cement dust into the air.

Sometimes I would walk home from Montreal East School, located on First Avenue, along a road that would take me through these areas. There would be ditches and little streams of colored phosphorescent liquids—greens, reds, purples—industrial pollution that would drain directly into the St. Lawrence River. I would walk through a jungle of giant oil and gas tanks and spheres, huge catalytic converters ("cat crackers" in the refinery vernacular), polymer plants, snaking pipelines, all girded in gleaming silver metal. Towering above everything were brilliantly burning flares atop tall steel spires, like religious icons, incinerating waste gases and sending them into the atmosphere.

At the halfway point to home, west of the refineries was "The Limits," as in city limits, so called because Boulevard George V was the line of demarcation between the City of Montreal and the town of Montreal East. At the corner of George V and Notre Dame was a large bus garage and a busy transit hub where buses and streetcars would begin and end their journeys west to downtown, and to the east out of the city to Bout de l'Île. "*Terminus! Tous le monde debarque!*" ("End of the line! Everybody off the bus!") the drivers and conductors would call out. There was a cluster of small businesses—a restaurant, a cigar store and a tavern where the refinery workers and bus drivers would gather after their shifts. I was about nine years old when a man who was vomiting spaghetti into the gutter in front of the tavern looked up and told me that these would be the best years of my life. Yeah. Maybe so. I liked it there. There was a sense that *something* was always happening.

For the first couple of years of high school we were bussed from the east end to the High School of Montreal on University Street in the center of the city, as there was no English Protestant high school in our area. Being downtown every day was wonderful and the school was huge with students from all over the city. It was segregated— boys on one side, girls on the other. I made very few friends, and was already beginning to carry, as a defense mechanism, a feeling that I was quite superior to the "mainstream" and its ways of thinking. There was a boy on the school bus who seemed developmentally challenged, who did things like spitting out the window at passers-by. While deep down I admired such hostile and sociopathic acts, I had already learned never to do *anything* which could cause any contact with authority. Even anything positive. There had always been animosity between the French and English, and sometimes when we got off the school bus returning us to the east end, we would be pelted with rocks by French toughs who were waiting for us. I still bear a scar on my forehead caused by one well-aimed projectile. At home I was fooling around with a guitar my parents had bought for me, and I took some lessons at Studio Labelle on

Ste. Catherine Street, just east of Boulevard St. Laurent. I learned to read music and some basic chords, but it was all outside of the context of real music, and I found it impossible to relate any of it to anything I heard on the radio, for example.

After two years at the High School of Montreal, Dunton High School was opened in the east end, north of Sherbrooke Street, close to the Ville d'Anjou town line. I could walk to school, and I often threw up on the way. It was a total drag. I couldn't relate to most of the teachers, the subject matter, or most of the other students. I did meet two other students from the east end who seemed as alienated as myself, who were to become lifelong friends. Robert Walker is a highly respected fine art photographer today, and Paul Heyer is now professor of Communications and Media at Sir Wilfred Laurier University.

We had no girlfriends and no interest in the pop culture of the day. There was one English teacher who seemed to take an interest in the three of us, and spent time in class discussing things artistic with us which were way over the heads of the other students. And there was a music teacher, only a few years older than me, who took an interest in me. She was a very attractive young woman who wore tight, short skirts, and I was just wild about her. But everyone else at school thought we were just weird or uncommunicative, or stuck up. We weren't really learning anything, and we hated every minute of school. In today's world we probably would have been misdiagnosed with attention deficit disorder and prescribed Ritalin or some other dangerous medication, when in fact we were just bored with the curriculum, the other students, and most of the teachers.

In the meantime, somehow, we had discovered jazz on CBC radio (and occasionally on television) and started to buy jazz records. Jazz music was the only thing I had encountered in life so far that moved me in any way. We would sit through music classes singing songs like "Row, Row, Row Your Boat," and then Bob and Paul and I would go to my house at lunchtime and listen to Miles, Monk, and Trane! Paul was learning the trumpet and the valve trombone, and Robert was learning the saxophone. We had sessions in my basement, trying to copy what we heard on records. One of the records we were really into was Bobby Timmons' first trio LP on the Riverside label, *This Here Is Bobby Timmons*, with Sam Jones and Jimmy Cobb. I still go back to it today.

Forty years later I met my former music teacher in Toronto. She came to one of my gigs and we had a couple of drinks. She explained to me that Dunton High had been her first job and as a music teacher there was very little she could do with the kids. At that time the Protestant School Board of Greater Montreal had no budget for music or the arts in east end Montreal. The program was to just get the kids through school and send them to the refineries like their parents. This was one reason why the very small east end English-speaking community had never produced any serious poets, writers, musicians or artists.

Nothing else was happening for me. There were few interesting programs on television, other than old "B" movies and John Cassavetes' *Johnny Staccato*, and a show about New York City social workers starring George C. Scott and Cicely Tyson called *East Side, West Side*. I regularly stayed up to watch a half-hour low budget local CBC program late on Sunday night called *Shoestring Theatre*, which produced the work of local playwrights and an occasional Albee play. I did have a brief flirtation with photography in high school, but it didn't go anywhere, as I became more and more involved with music. Some Saturdays the three of us would go downtown on the bus to look at and buy jazz records, and to just get out of the east end suburbs and see an urban "downtown" culture.

There was a kind of "beat" scene on and around Stanley Street where there were coffee houses, some of which featured jazz groups: The Little Vienna, The Pam Pam, and The Seven Steps, which became the Potpourri and eventually morphed into the Rainbow Bar and Grill, where I was to perform in the late '70s and early '80s. And south of Ste. Catherine on Stanley was the Esquire Show Bar—an old-fashioned American-style rhythm and blues club where I was to play a couple of times in the future. There was also the Café Prague on Bishop Street that had live jazz on Sundays.

Bertrand Disc & Hi-Fi and International Music on Ste. Catherine Street, and Aspeck Radio further west on Ste. Catherine, were the stores that were stocked with all the Prestige, Blue Note and Riverside releases. We would hover over the bins in these stores gazing at the record covers and reading the back liner notes. I learned much jazz history from doing this. There was also a good record lending library at the corner of Crescent street and Burnside (now Boulevard de Maisonneuve) that had a great selection of obscure jazz records. Many of these recordings were produced in the studio of, and engineered by, Rudy Van Gelder in Hackensack, New Jersey, and after 1960, at his larger studio in Englewood Cliffs, New Jersey. I stayed up late at night and after the local radio stations had gone off the air, I was able to pick up jazz radio from New York: Mort Fega on WEVD and Billy Taylor on WNEW. Great music and hip sales pitches. (Tell 'em M.F. sent you!)

I remember hearing Jackie McLean's "Appointment in Ghana" late one night on CBC radio. An epiphany! I was transfixed! There was some kind of "deep song" going on there that I had never heard in any music before. I knew instinctively that Jackie spoke the truth, and in no uncertain terms. I ran out and bought the record (*Jackie's Bag*), and the cover alone was the most amazing thing I'd ever seen. I ran home and played it, and it was the first music I had ever heard that seemed truly "larger than life." Sonny Clark on piano just knocked me out! I also bought Miles Davis' *Milestones*, and Monk at the Five Spot with Johnny Griffin (*Thelonious in Action*). The fills that drummer Roy Haynes played around the melodies of "Evidence" and "Coming on the Hudson" were totally organic and just the hippest thing I ever heard! Well, Philly Joe Jones on drums was pretty hip too.

I bought a Tommy Flanagan sextet album called *The Cats* (Prestige/New Jazz 8217) with Coltrane, Idrees Sulieman and Kenny Burrell. This record showed me how the guitar could be seamlessly integrated into an east coast, hard bop context.

Sometimes I would go downtown by myself on Saturdays or after school and after checking out the record stores on Ste. Catherine Street, continue on foot, going down the now long gone Des Seigneurs Street underpass under the railway tracks, down the hill below Dorchester Boulevard to St. Antoine and points south. I explored Little Burgundy, St. Henri, Côte St. Paul; the area near the railway yards that had formerly been known as Griffintown, and the waterfront district now known as Old Montreal. I was seeing the city, its neighborhoods and what they looked like—their streets, buildings, infrastructures and ethnicities. I was learning to observe.

Bob Walker and I took the bus to New York a couple of times to buy jazz records and hear music. We were blown away by the visual richness and diversity of the city and the crazed energy on the streets. At that point in time there were still characters on the streets like Moondog and the Eternal Drummer. We went to the original Birdland and caught Dizzy Gillespie with James Moody. Pee Wee Marquette, the famous midget, was the emcee. Lester Young had referred to him as "half a motherfucker." Apparently when the original Birdland closed and turned into a Hawaiian restaurant in 1965, he stayed on, hustling customers on the street.

We used to go to a record store on West Forty-Seventh Street just west of Sixth Avenue called The Original Jazz Record Center. The logo was "From Bunk to Monk." It was up one flight of stairs. Painted on the steps were the names of various jazz styles. Starting at the bottom were New Orleans, then Dixieland, Swing, etc. until you reached the top. The top step said "Hard Bop." That told you what you were in for if you stumbled or tripped on it.

It was a golden age of graphic design as well as music. Designers Reid Miles, Tom Hannan and Andy Warhol did covers at Prestige and Blue Note, Paul Bacon was at Riverside, and the legendary art director Marvin Israel (Diane Arbus's mentor) worked for Atlantic Records, using Lee Friedlander photographs and some of his own paintings. I think that the graphics and photographs on these covers impressed us as much as the music, especially the Prestige and Blue Note records. They were really ahead of their time in their creative use of type and colored gels over black-and-white photographs. There was something almost shocking about the interaction of large sans-serif block lettering juxtaposed with smaller old-fashioned serif typewriter script, with just a couple of letters deliberately placed slightly off line or highlighted in strange puke greens or bilious yellows.

For the record companies these ideas and designs were an effective solution to a low budget, but they were a revelation for kids from east end Montreal who had never been exposed to sophisticated art or music, or modernism in any form. It is difficult to describe the impact of seeing, for example, *Bags' Groove* (Prestige

7109) for the first time, on adolescents who didn't quite fit into their milieu. Those LP jackets were so strange looking that if we took them out of our houses, we carried them in a plain brown paper bag. A Sonny Clark record was really a revolutionary thing back then. These covers were inextricably linked in our minds to the music inside. It didn't dawn on me until many, many years later that these records were the vital connection between, and the intersection of, jazz music and visual art, especially photography and the concept of abstraction; a confluence of the African American and the European American esthetics of modernism. Although we didn't know it, these records were introducing us to art on several levels. We would discuss these covers, and we were actually learning something!

The 12" LP, at least as created by these small companies, was a complete, organic work of art, fusing deep, sophisticated music with creative graphics, photography and typesetting. It was something you could hold in your hand and stare at while you listened to the music. Many years later, digital technology, with the CD and especially the MP3, would render both music and packaging disposable, making this experience impossible today, or at least irrelevant. Now you can hear Sonny Clark or Coltrane in Starbucks, a phenomenon brilliantly described by jazz historian and journalist Mark Miller, writing in the *Globe and Mail*, as "a triumph of context over content."

I started going to jazz clubs, staying up late and not bothering to go to school the next day. Fortunately, in the early sixties Montreal was on the jazz circuit. I got to hear all the great players—the masters—coming through town, performing at the Windsor Penthouse, the Tête de l'Art, and a couple of years later at the Jazz Hot on Ste. Catherine Street East. Monk, Miles, Coltrane, Sonny Stitt, Pepper Adams, Jimmy Heath, Jackie McLean, Bill Evans, Wes Montgomery, Art Farmer with Jim Hall, Sonny Red (with Nelson Symonds), Art Blakey and the Jazz Messengers—the great sextet with Freddie Hubbard, Wayne Shorter, Curtis Fuller, Cedar Walton and Reggie Workman. The Who's Who of jazz. The golden age of jazz was right there before my eyes and ears. And it was like Blakey said: "The music washed away the dust of everyday life." The music was exciting, moving, and it made you think. The more you listened, the more you heard.

Montreal jazz in the early 1960s as advertised in the daily press.

Montreal jazz in the early 1960s as advertised in the daily press.

I also got to hear and meet a world-class jazz guitarist who lived in Montreal at the time, the Belgian René Thomas. The first jazz concert I ever attended was the René Thomas-J.R. Monterose Quartet with Freddie McHugh on bass and Pierre Beluse on drums, at McGill University's Moyse Hall, in January of 1961.The beautiful sound of René's guitar and the intensity with which he played it were an early inspiration to me. Thomas lived in Montreal from 1956 until about 1962, when he returned to Europe.

Advertisement from the 1960s for Billy White's Quartet, The New Jazz Four, at a short-lived coffeehouse on Stanley Street.

I heard Miles Davis at the Loews Theatre on Ste. Catherine Street with Hank Mobley, J.J. Johnson, Wynton Kelly, Paul Chambers and Jimmy Cobb in the summer of 1962. I was especially impressed with tenor saxophonist Hank Mobley, who I had heard on records. He was impeccably dressed, as were they all. He just stood there motionless on stage, and these wonderful lines just oozed out of his horn. Hearing Coltrane with the classic quartet later that year really changed my life. Never had I heard music that powerful or that focused. He played "I Want To Talk About You" with the long cadenza, much longer than the tune itself. I remember that between sets Trane went into the back of the club and practiced.

It was an incredibly exciting time in music. Coltrane's *Giant Steps* and *My Favorite Things,* on Atlantic, were released, followed by the Impulse recordings *Africa/Brass,* the blue *Coltrane* record, and *Live at the Vanguard* with "Chasin' the Trane" on it. Trane was rapidly changing the music. Not just in what he was playing on the horn, but in the way McCoy Tyner, Jimmy Garrison and Elvin Jones broke up the rhythm behind him, which was based on Elvin's permutations of the triplet. They were using fourth interval chord voicings, pan-modality and pentatonic scales and patterns in and out of key, influencing the way all the instruments were played. This was music *no one* had ever heard before. Brand new to the world! It was a time of great development, evolution and change in the music. We were witnessing the last true innovations jazz would know, and experiencing them in real time. We were there! Even if we didn't always hear it "live," almost every new record release contained something of this growth and change. Brazilian music was beginning to influence jazz with its fusion of jazz harmony and indigenous rhythms called "bossa nova," and there were Ornette Coleman, Albert Ayler and "free jazz." At the same time I was led back into exploring the earlier history of the music—Ellington, Charlie Christian, Louis Armstrong, Coleman Hawkins and Lester Young.

I was getting a glimpse of that night-time world I had seen in the "noir" movies years before on television, and becoming very serious about trying to play music. I had no interest in the popular music of the day—when you have been listening to Bird or Trane, Miles or Monk, or Clifford Brown, music on this level, how can you take the Beatles seriously? In 1962 the three of us (Bob, Paul and myself) went to see Shirley Clarke's film of the off-Broadway play *The Connection* at the Verdi, an art theater on upper St. Lawrence Boulevard. It featured Jackie McLean and Freddie Redd with Michael Mattos on bass and Larry Ritchie on drums. Jackie sounded fantastic and was just so *hip*, playing himself, and this really reinforced the romantic myth of the creative junkie/artist. Jackie McLean was certainly a more important figure to me than, say, the prime minister of Canada or the president of the United States. The music from this film, composed by Freddie Redd for the off-Broadway stage play, was released on Blue Note records under Freddie's name.

I heard Monk twice in 1965: at Montreal's Jazz Hot, and later that year at an electrifying outdoor concert on Île Saint-Hélène with Charlie Rouse, Butch Warren and Ben Riley. The music at this concert swung like nothing I had ever heard! I remember watching

Monk's foot beat time. It was like another instrument in the band. I knew it was really happening, because Monk got up from the piano and danced, several times. Monk used to say: "When you're swingin', swing some more!"

The guitarists I listened to were players whose musical depth, intensity and power transcended the instrument—players like Wes Montgomery, Kenny Burrell, Jim Hall, René Thomas and Grant Green. They were virtuosi of the materials of jazz as well as of the guitar. They all had their own sounds and styles. You could hear two bars of music and you knew it was Kenny or Wes or Jim. I was never a "guitar weenie," one of those people who were more interested in collecting beautiful instruments, or in just hearing someone play fast. I just wanted to play music, and I just happened to play the guitar.

I had barely made it through high school and had no thoughts as to the future, of going to college or of how I was going to make a living. I just wanted to learn to play this music, which wasn't taught in the schools back then. I certainly had no motivation in any other direction. I worked really hard at it, practicing, trying to learn tunes, listening to and transcribing from records, and trying to figure out the harmonic systems. Though I didn't go to music school, I had the best teachers in the world—Bird, Miles, Coltrane, Sonny Rollins, Clifford Brown, Bud Powell, McCoy Tyner, Bill Evans—all right there on the recordings. I had a turntable with a 16 RPM speed, which lowered the pitch one octave, and made it easier to hear what was going on. Sometimes if the pitch was slightly off, I would tape coins to the tone arm to slow it down a little. I copied solos from the records and played along with them, trying to learn the musical vocabulary of jazz and its inflections, starting with a few "words," then constructing basic "sentences." Maybe eventually I would be able to tell a story.

It was very difficult trying to figure this stuff out by one's self, but it seemed to be the only way to do it. There were a few hard-to-find books to learn from in Canada at that time, and there was information gleaned from older musicians, but back then every harmonic principle learned was like digging a potato out of the frozen earth with a teaspoon.

During this period I bought a cheap string bass and took some lessons. I never became an accomplished bassist, but learning this instrument and its function in the music was very helpful to my then limited understanding of harmony. Some years later I actually made a few gigs on a borrowed electric bass. In the late '70s someone left an alto saxophone at my apartment. I fooled around with it, took a few lessons, and got to the point where I had to ask myself, "Am I ready to spend eight hours a day on this?" I wasn't. That was that.

I met the brilliant trumpeter and composer Herbie Spanier one night at the Tête de l'Art, and began studying with him, taking lessons in improvisation and theory. Herbie didn't just give you information—he made you think. He had a Zen approach to life and teaching, which kind of fit in with some of the things I had been reading—writers such as Kerouac, Burroughs, and Alan Watts (and other Zen literature). Now, I have never pretended to understand Zen. In fact, not only did I not pretend to understand it, I really didn't understand it! Still don't. But somehow its apparent contradictions were comforting on some level. Occasionally one gets a flash. The poet Gary Snyder has quoted a Zen master: "The perfect path is the easiest one. *Now strive hard!*"

Herbie talked about concepts like "musical gravity," how a harmonic progression gravitated to a point of resolution, and how this gravity could be defied, or at least deceived or extended. At one lesson he told me, "Never let the line interfere with the time or the harmonic structure." Next time it was, "Never let the time or the harmonic structure interfere with the line." It makes perfect sense now. Herbie hired me for my first jazz gig—an afternoon concert in St. Sauveur in the Laurentian mountains, about forty miles north of Montreal. Wayne Hooke was on bass and Brian Emblem played drums. Also at the Tête de l'Art I met the jazz writer and broadcaster Len Dobbin, who was very encouraging to young jazz musicians. He would invite us to his apartment and play obscure records and tapes for us from his vast collection.

I became friends with drummer Brian Emblem and we started hanging out and playing at an after-hours club called L'Enfer (The Inferno), which was in a warehouse building off an alley behind Bleury Street. None of the chairs and tables matched each other, and some were broken —as if they had been picked up at random off the street, or purchased at a job lot at ten cents on the dollar. The place didn't sell liquor, just coffee, sandwiches, and an Italian soft drink called Brio, but there seemed to be a lot of pot being smoked. The clientele was a diverse mix of French and English, Black and White, young and old. L'Enfer was also a hangout for Quebec separatists, revolutionaries and existentialists. It was a wild scene! We younger musicians would play earlier in the evening, and the older cats would come in later after their gigs, get up on the bandstand and musically kick our asses. We never knew who would show up. Trumpeter Herbie Spanier, saxophonists Wimp Henstridge, Doug Richardson, Stu Loesby, P.J. Perry; drummers Norman Griffith, Spike McKendry and Billy Graham and pianists Oliver Jones, Billy Georgette and Norman Zubis were just some of them.

Sometimes visiting musicians from New York would stop by late. One night Roland Kirk (pre- Rashaan), who was working at the Windsor Penthouse, showed up. He got up on the bandstand with his three horns, with Billy Georgette on piano, Norman Griffith on drums, and three bassists—Charles Biddle, Noble Samuels, and Carlton Palmas. He played "Oleo" so fast that the bass players dropped out one by one, until he was just playing with Norman, who kept it together. On another night Jackie McLean arrived after his gig at the Tête de l'Art and sat in. Bob Walker and I would take the bus back to the East End at six or seven in the morning, as the buses were filling up with day people on their way to work. L'Enfer was closed by the police in the summer of 1963.

Brian Emblem and I hung out together all the time, smoked pot, and talked music, music, music. It was like how Eddie Condon had described his early years: "The music poured into us, like daylight going down a dark hole." Brian had an extensive record collection, and taught me how to listen analytically. He had a great ear and could tell you exactly what was happening on any given record—what the drums were doing, the bass line, the comping patterns—all of it! Through Herbie Spanier we met pianist Billy Georgette, who introduced us to some other young musicians. Billy was kind of a guru to us, and he instilled in us a professional work ethic. Be on time for the gig, dress appropriately, and play whatever the job required. He encouraged me by saying, "If you work at something long enough, you'll do it well." We started getting a few gigs. My first real, professional job was a wedding in Montreal North with Norman Shackell, a saxophonist I had met and played with at L'Enfer.

L'Enfer business card, 1963.

We were catching the last years of an era. The era of live music. At that time in Montreal the town was still wide open, and there were many nightclubs employing musicians. Even little neighborhood clubs or bars often had a trio of some kind. The further east you went, the further down the scale they were. You could actually learn your craft on the bandstand, playing dance music and accompanying floor shows—jugglers, hypnotists, dancers, comedians. The working-class French-Canadian patrons of these places were quite sophisticated in one way. They knew all the South American dances. You had to be able to play sambas, cha chas, mambos, meringues etc. This had filtered down by a kind of osmosis from France, where South American orchestras had been in vogue in the Paris of the 1920s and '30s.

There were gigs out of town where you would get a miserable weekly salary and room and board and you would stay in one place for weeks or months at a time. Mining towns, Indian reservations, beer bottles flying: Trois-Rivières, La Tuque, Val d'Or, Baie Comeau, Sept-Isles, Chute–aux-Outardes. Tough! You would see people get beaten within an inch of their lives right in front of the bandstand. Not only had you better keep playing, but you'd better be swingin'. I once saw an inebriated man jump through a glass door—blood everywhere. There was a paper mill town about two hundred miles north of Ottawa where almost everyone in the club was maimed, crippled or had missing limbs.

One experience I remember was in a small town near Baie Comeau, on the edge of an Indian reservation. On the first night of the gig, as we approached the bandstand in our suits, several toughs grabbed the pianist/singer/bandleader and began to beat him unmercifully. After the bouncers broke it up he led us to the bandstand, blood dripping from his face, and opened with Buck Owens' "Act Naturally." ("They're gonna put me in the movies....") A couple of nights later we came to the job and found the club closed, with a police seal on the door. We didn't get paid, and it was a long drive back to Montreal, with barely enough money for gas or food.

These were gigs you did where the sole objective was to get out in one piece, with the money. You learned to play for keeps on those bandstands. I used to carry *The Essential Lenny Bruce* on the road with me back then. The book was a compendium of his best material and I learned a lot from it.

Although there was a lot of night driving, I saw much of the province at this time, including beautiful landscapes in Quebec's provincial parks. I remember dawn on the road, the majestic sight of a moose in the mist by the side of the highway. I also remember having a flat tire in the middle of Parc des Laurentides on the way to a gig in Chicoutimi, with no spare! Hitchhiked to a garage, and returned with a tow truck.

My first trips out of Quebec province (and my first experiences with air travel) were to St. John's, Newfoundland. Less than twenty years removed from being a separate, self-governing British colony (Newfoundland became a Canadian province in 1949), one could immediately feel the sense of isolation of the people. There was an inherent distrust of those from "the mainland." Almost everything (including ready-made pizza crusts) was flown in from the mainland. The basic foods seemed to be fish and chips, and chicken and chips—chips being the British term for French fried potatoes. Good fresh fish—cod and halibut.

Brian Emblem and I worked for a couple of months in a Holiday Inn in St. John's with a pianist from Montreal, Ilene Bourne.

We accompanied singers from Toronto like Dinah Christie and Catherine McKinnon, a week at a time. We met and jammed with a couple of good young American jazz musicians who were in the US army, stationed there.

I had left my parents' home and was sharing an apartment on Park Avenue near St. Joseph Boulevard with a saxophone player, Richard Ashby. I started to learn about survival, and trying to stay one step ahead of the system. You figured out which bills had to be paid, and which ones could slide. I also learned to prepare food and cook. Many musicians are great cooks. It was something learned out of necessity because of the odd hours, or living alone, or trying to save money, which was always tight. I learned the difference between parsley and parsnip. Due to my parents' meat and potatoes background, food at home had been very simple. I didn't know what garlic was until I lived on my own. I picked up recipes over the years. When I prepared a great-tasting dish that was very inexpensive, it felt like you had somehow beaten the system. Anyway, all we were doing was changing the molecular structure of matter by applying heat.

It wasn't necessarily about what you had to do, or should do, but about being aware of what all the different possibilities were in any given situation. It was just like playing music. My life was really about doing what I felt was truly important, what I felt compelled to do as if by some inner urge, rather than what society expected of me. Sometimes you had to break the rules in order to survive. If everyone around you was breaking the rules and you weren't, you were at a disadvantage. Four things that I learned in this period: 1. Mind your own business. 2. Don't volunteer any information—stay under the radar. 3. You can learn something from anyone. 4. Anyone will say anything, especially if they're trying to sell something or promote themselves.

About this time I also gravitated to the black music scene around the famous "corner," Mountain and St. Antoine streets. This was center of Montreal's black entertainment world. Down the hill and under the railroad tracks were Rockhead's Paradise, The Black Bottom, The Harlem Paradise, the Club 99. These clubs were all in the area known as Little Burgundy, which was the black neighborhood. Because of its proximity to the railroad yards, a lot of black Americans who worked on the trains as porters and cooks had settled there. Although Montreal had real diversity, the music world was still somewhat segregated, mostly by language, however, rather than color or race. In the late 1960s the Ville-Marie Expressway was cut through that neighborhood, essentially destroying the character of the area and decentralizing the English-speaking black community.

I heard a lot of great music at the first Black Bottom club which was in a basement on St. Antoine Street a few doors west of Mountain Street. It later moved to a larger space with a liquor license on St. Paul Street in Old Montreal. The amazing guitarist Nelson Symonds was blowing the roof off the place every night, along with Norman Griffith (later Villeneuve), Charlie Biddle, Noble Samuels, Charlie Duncan, Buddy Jones, Clayton Johnson and many others, including Ed Curry, a great singer from Brooklyn. He had a wonderful repertoire of standards and blues—"Day In, Day Out," "In the Still of the Night," "That Old Black Magic," "Polka Dots and Moonbeams," and a fantastic arrangement of "Old Man River." Visiting musicians from out of town would hang out there after their gigs. They would often play until 7 or 8 in the morning.

Nelson was truly an underground legend. Several name bandleaders (including John Coltrane) wanted to take him on the road, but he didn't want to travel, and had previously run into immigration problems in the U.S. Many years later when I met the great drummer Billy Higgins in New York and he heard I was from Montreal, he asked after Nelson.

The original Black Bottom didn't serve liquor, and between sets the musicians would disappear around the corner to Whitey's Bar. When Nelson would play at the Windsor Penthouse, after the set he would go to the bar and ask for a triple *alcool*—the potent cheap liquor, akin to vodka, produced by the Quebec Liquor Board.

Nelson finally recorded much later in the '90s. Although he sounded good on the recording, it was nowhere near the level of his playing in the early and mid 1960s, when he was playing every night in the clubs. He died in October 2008.

Sonny Greenwich was in and out of Montreal then, and used to sit in at the Black Bottom. He was a genuine innovator, with a very original sound and style. He was really the first to bring the innovations of Coltrane to the guitar.

I met and came under the influence of two other wonderful but very different guitarists: Billy White and Ivan Symonds. Billy White, who I had first heard playing with Herbie Spanier's group, was from Verdun—the primarily English-speaking working class community located to the southwest of Montreal and separated from Montreal by the Lachine canal. Verdun produced a number of accomplished jazz musicians in addition to White, including pianist Norman Zubis and the bassists Freddie McHugh and Billy Meryl. Its most celebrated native was trumpeter Maynard Ferguson.

White had a brilliant musical mind, and he always looked sharp in those days, often wearing a white suit. He was also a junkie, and an accomplished burglar. Billy had done time for drug possession and had a rather nihilistic view of life. If he saw spilled gasoline in the gutter, he would be the first one to throw a lit match in it. We became friends. I would go to his house and he would show me things on the guitar. Billy knew all the Monk tunes, and first taught me to play "Off Minor" and "Monk's Mood." I would drive him around in my father's car. I knew what he was into, but he didn't talk about it or offer it to me. A few years later, after I had started using drugs, I met some of his friends and connections, old time junkies and hustlers, and we would get high together. It wasn't so much that Billy was a drug addict (which he was), but that he never wanted to find himself in a position where he wasn't on *something*. Bennies, goofballs, Percodan, alcohol, heroin, codeine cough syrup—whatever.

Ivan Symonds was the cousin of Nelson Symonds, and a great guitarist in his own right. He had an indomitable spirit, and a huge capacity for playing music. I remember hearing him and Nelson and Sonny Greenwich play until daybreak one morning at the Black Bottom. He worked as an auto mechanic during the day, and played at night. He heard me play somewhere, probably at L'Enfer, and invited me to come over to his house with my guitar. This was the beginning of a beautiful mentor/student relationship. We would play tunes and he would stop me and say, "No—try it this way" or "Use this chord here," and show me all kinds of different fingerings and harmonic substitutions. He started occasionally sending me as a replacement on gigs. I used to sub for him in the downstairs lounge at Rockhead's Paradise, and other spots in the area. A couple of times he sent me to sub at the Esquire Show Bar with rhythm and blues acts who had come to town minus a guitarist. The Esquire was a long-established American-style showplace with a horseshoe shaped bar surrounding the stage, and a little bar off to the side, which was populated by suspicious characters.

I was also making forays into the border states—Vermont and upstate New York—around this time, playing with a black rhythm and blues band, guys I had met while subbing for Ivan. I worked regular weekends at the N.C.O. club on the Plattsburg, New York air force base, and spent the winter of '65 (or was it '66?) withan organ group at a ski resort in Vermont. I met and worked with a great blind saxophone player named Jack Todd, who also played good organ. He was originally from Hartford, Connecticut, and lived in northern Vermont. He came up to Montreal to do a couple of gigs. For a Canadian, crossing the border with a musical instrument was always a hassle, because U.S. immigration assumed you were going to work illegally. They were usually correct in their assumption. For the ski resort gig in Vermont, the club had gotten a U.S. work permit for me.

Sometime in the mid-sixties I met a bass player I'll call F.T. He was related to a famous trombonist who had played with Duke Ellington. F.T. was a junkie and a hustler from New York who was around the Mountain-St. Antoine street scene at that time. I worked with his group at the Harlem Paradise (site of the much earlier Café St. Michel) with Bill Kersey on tenor saxophone, and I went on the road with him for several weeks, accompanying strippers with a carnival around northern Quebec. This was a tough gig for very short money, at the lowest end of the carnival circuit. We would set up outside the tent and play a set while the barker worked the crowd. When he had a crowd together, we would move all the instruments into the tent and play for the girls. This was repeated three times a night. Behind the stage the ladies would relieve themselves in a slop bucket in full view of passersby.

It was just guitar, bass and drums, so the load was on me. We had to play a lot of blues, and we did "Watermelon Man" and "Now's The Time" three or four times a night. I don't remember the drummer's name. He was a friend of F.T.'s from the States. He wasn't really a jazz drummer but he laid down a serious shuffle beat. Another learning experience. By the end of that gig I had learned to play some blues and make it mean something!

F.T. was not a great bassist, but he really knew a lot about music—harmony and arranging. Brian and I started going over to his house to play and he would talk to me about harmony and voicing. He likened it to cooking, and told me things like: "Put some spice in that chord—maybe a flat ninth or a thirteenth" or "Lay a fried egg on top of that," meaning put a sharp eleventh or some other altered tone on top of the chord voicing. F.T. was a good cook. One day he made picadillo, a Cuban dish with ground beef and vegetables over rice (with a fried egg on top!), a recipe I still use today.

Being part Puerto Rican, he also knew a lot about Latin music, and played us records by authentic New York latin bands like Ricardo Rey and Ismael Rivera, bands that that we had never heard in Montreal. This was the music that later became known as salsa, which in fact means "sauce." He pointed out how the bass line worked in relation to the various percussion instruments, and what the basic keyboard figures were.

F.T. smoked a lot of pot and was full of incredible stories of things I had only read about: being in the Federal Narcotics Hospital in Lexington, Kentucky (aka the Narcotics Farm), with its great prison band playing Tadd Dameron arrangements; living in the Morris Hotel in LA in the '50s with Ornette and Dexter Gordon; being on the road with Silas Green's minstrel show; boosting car radios on the street in LA, etc., etc. I remember him telling me about the close personal relationship and musical interchange in New York between the pianist/composers Bud Powell, Thelonious Monk and Elmo Hope. He talked about drugs constantly. He described his idea of heaven. There would be heroin running down the gutter and you would just dip your spoon into it, marijuana grew everywhere, and there would be chicken leg trees if you got hungry. No political parties—just a girl party and a boy party. F.T. was something else! At one point on the road he was talking about heroin, and I guess I casually mentioned that I'd like to try it. At that time I only smoked pot, with maybe an occasional Dexedrine. Other than a beer once in a while, I didn't drink.

From the very beginnings of time, from the dawn of civilization humans have always harbored a desire to "get high." In the earliest agricultural societies crops were grown not just for food but for fermentation—to produce drinkable intoxicating liquids, not to mention the cultivation of plants like cannabis sativa and the opium poppy. In Germany in 1898, a chemist in the employ of the Bayer pharmaceutical firm chemically bonded one molecule of morphine with two molecules of acetic anhydride, producing a compound called diacetylmorphine. It was briefly marketed under the name Heroin. The brand name stuck, leaving a terrible legacy.

One day I went over to F.T.'s place, and he was busy at the table with his equipment. He was an old-timer, and instead of a syringe he used an eyedropper with a paper collar to hold the needle in place, and a cooker made from a bottle cap instead of a spoon to dissolve the drug in. There was a myth among old-time junkies that the silver in a spoon "took" the heroin, or rendered it less potent. He prepared his fix and shot it up, and looked at me and said: "You once said you wanted to try some of this." I didn't hesitate more than a few seconds before rolling up my sleeve. So many of my musical heroes had done this. He cooked up some more and quickly found a vein and gave me the injection. I don't remember getting a powerful "hit" that first time, but I sure got high. Maybe too high. I got sick and threw up, but I felt pretty good. I must have felt good, because I did it again a few days later. He must have given me a little more because this time it was incredible—that feeling in the stomach when it hits you. That sense of going up in a fast elevator that stops suddenly. I didn't get sick this time. We sat around nodding and listening to music. I couldn't believe that something this fantastic existed in the world. A high to die for, as the saying goes. And a lot of people did.

I just loved the drug. I remember going home on the bus, high, and looking around at the other people and thinking: "These poor palookas will never, ever feel this good!" Unfortunately, neither would I. One rapidly builds a tolerance. But the drug seemed to give me self-confidence and help me concentrate. Playing music on it somehow slowed things down, making the individual beats of the music and the spaces between them seem wider, so I began to feel and understand the great rhythmic subtleties, nuances and mysteries contained in just one beat of music, and how one could vary the placement of notes within it. Anyway, all I ever wanted to do in life was to be able to phrase eighth notes like Hank Mobley. Even then I realized that there was some kind of mysterious rhythmic infrastructure over and under and around the basic pulse in the playing of the great soloists, especially the saxophonists that our primitive European notation system was incapable of dealing with efficiently. Later I learned that part of it was a matter of subdividing rhythms: for example, subdividing the quarter note triplet and feeling or hearing time in larger units than single beats or even two or four measure phrases. I also learned that one had to make one's own musical "time," not depend on anyone else. In this music everyone had to play their instrument with the rhythmic clarity of a good drummer.

Heroin also seemed to help the periodic bouts of depression I had experienced all my life, which I realized much later were probably symptoms of some kind of borderline bipolar disorder. My friends tried it and some of them, including Brian Emblem and the late Leon Feigenbaum, a great bassist, succumbed to its ravages. I remember pianist Kenny Gross trying it and saying, "This is so good, I'll never do it again." And as far as I know he never did. Smart. After a couple of years, I didn't see F.T. anymore because he was arrested for armed robbery and deported back to the States. I never saw him again.

Logic and reason never interested me, and statistics are notoriously unreliable, and as the great photographer Henri Cartier-Bresson once said, "Facts are not interesting." They were not. I was more interested in legend, lore, rumor, myth and hearsay, which are often more indicative of the larger truths. Accordingly, I kept playing around with heroin for a few years before I developed a real habit. I soon learned to shoot up by myself, quickly overcoming the common fear of needles. When you cooked good heroin in a spoon prior to injecting it, you could smell the flowers from the distant poppy fields. Or you thought you could. I learned also that the needle and its accessories were as much of a habit as the drug. I was an occasional user at this point—a weekend popper.

I continued smoking pot for a while, taking a few pills: amphetamines (good for staying up and driving long distances after the gig), or whatever was around. I didn't drink though, other than an occasional beer. I thought I was a hip junkie, and we looked down on drunks or drinking to get high. I later learned that alcohol has its place. I eventually stopped smoking pot. As hard as I tried I could never really play behind it. I would either get paranoid or forget what tune I was playing. I was rapidly losing interest in cannabis-based drugs. I remember going with a friend to a party in Ville LaSalle, a suburb south-west of Montreal. These were people I didn't know and they had some dynamite hashish. For the windup after we smoked, they passed around a bowl of ether to sniff. Now that's just ridiculous. Talk about "out of it"! However, the ether did mitigate the paranoia that was caused by the hash. To this day I don't know how I drove home that night.

There is a story, apocryphal I'm sure, of three travelers crossing the desert. One was a heavy drinker of alcohol, one was a user of narcotic drugs, and the third was a pot smoker. After wandering in the desert all day, they came upon a walled city with a locked door. Repeated knocking brought no answer. Needing a place to rest for the night, the drunk became very angry, cursing and trying to break down the door. The user of narcotics said: "Well, I'm just going to go to sleep until someone opens the door." The pot smoker said: "I don't know about you guys, but I'm going in through the keyhole!" My wife Sylvia, upon hearing this story mused: "Well, who's to say he didn't?"

I was finding also that I didn't care for the time-wasting social aspects of buying or using marijuana. You would often have to light up with people and sit around listening to their silly bullshit. People who sold heroin didn't want you hanging around, bringing unnecessary heat. You gave them your money, got your product and left immediately. Well, to each his own. I was never into psychedelic drugs. People would say to me: "Man, you've got to do some of this righteous acid. It's like an eight-hour movie in your mind." I would answer: "I've already got the movie. I want something to get rid of it." My few experiences with LSD were like, "Oh, Jesus! Another eight hours of *this*? I've got things to do." People who smoke a lot of pot or take psychedelic drugs tend to be unfocused, go off on tangents, or are easily distracted by bright colors. Not all of them, certainly not the older musicians who smoked.

In the late sixties there was a lot of speed (methamphetamine) around. It was really a low-life chemical kick. I injected it a few times, and although I enjoyed the initial rush, staying up for two or three days feeling like I was inside a pinball machine was not my idea of a good time. Other than the occasional functional use of Dexedrine my pharmaceutical interests definitely lay in the other direction. I was becoming a purist. I have never understood the concept of multiple drug abuse. Why would you take good heroin and dilute or dispel its effects with alcohol or a bunch of other garbage drugs? The one exception was the "speedball," a mixture of heroin and cocaine injected into the vein. In the words of the writer and master addict William S. Burroughs, "If God made anything better, He kept it for Himself."

In spite of (or perhaps because of) all this drug experimentation I continued working in music and practicing, trying to learn. Throughout the 1960s the CBC produced a weekly series of jazz concerts in the Ermitage, a beautiful little hall on Côte-des-Neiges Road, which they recorded and broadcast on French language radio on a weekly program called "Jazz en Liberté." I played on several of these, with saxophonist Stu Loseby, vibraphonist/drummer Cisco Normand, and pianist Pierre Leduc. On one of these my first original composition, "Karensong" (for my first serious girlfriend), was recorded.

There was a little jazz club in Val David owned by the late drummer Richard Robinson who would bring in different musicians to play with him. I played there on weekends until the musicians' union busted me for working at a non-union venue. After fining me, the union hooked me up with an accordion trio with a six night a week gig at a club on Boulevard Henri Bourassa in Montreal North, playing dance music. We wore bright red band jackets and I worked there for several months, until the contract ended.

In July of 1967 John Coltrane died, casting a pall over the entire jazz world. The engineer Rudy Van Gelder, who had recorded Coltrane frequently, told me that Trane as a man was so deep that he was "beyond understanding." Pianist John Hicks once said to me: "We were so lucky to have lived in the time of John Coltrane."

By 1968 I was working on the road with Captain Vann and the Pirates, a rhythm & blues group doing the bar/hotel circuit in Quebec, covering the R&B hits of the day: "Mustang Sally," "In The Midnight Hour," "Show Me," "Who's Makin' Love," "Dock Of the Bay." We played some serious dives. Vann Walls was an organist and heavy drinker who had written the Ray Charles hit "One Mint Julep" and had sold the

The author, Val David, Quebec, mid 1960s.
Photographer unknown.

rights to it for a few hundred dollars. The band consisted of Vann, myself, Joe Conyers (a good rhythm & blues drummer from South Carolina who also sang), and on saxophone, first Richard Ashby, then Glen Bradley.

Vann got us a gig in Halifax, Nova Scotia, and we drove straight through from Montreal, an 800-mile drive. We travelled in his old truck with the four of us, all the instruments, and Vann's Doberman Pinscher, who was none too friendly. The drums were tied to the roof. The Captain carried with him a large hamper of fried chicken, several glass milk bottles of good homemade South Carolina hot sauce, and several bottles of gin. Somewhere in New Brunswick Vann ran out of gin, and we had to leave the highway to replenish the supply before he got the DTs. Suddenly the truck swerved, the drums flew off the roof onto the highway, and one of the glass milk bottles shattered, sending the pungent hot sauce all over the inside of the truck (and us). Between the hot sauce, the dog, and the gin, we really stank by the time we arrived in Halifax. Halfway through the first week of the two-week engagement at pianist Joe Sealy's Club Unusual, Captain Vann got drunk and got us all fired.

Halifax had a small black community, known as Africville, around the Göttingen Street area, and had been one of the last stops on the underground railroad. Nelson and Ivan Symonds were originally from Halifax. We stayed in this neighborhood, and through this community I managed to hook up with Al Cowans' group, which was in residence at a strip club, a tits and seafood emporium called the Lobster Trap, working six nights a week, playing dance music and accompanying the floor show, usually a stripper, which changed every week.

Al Cowans had been, along with Montreal bassist Nick Aldrich, a member of the "Tramp Band," a musical variety/comedy act which had toured with Cab Calloway and appeared in several films in the '30s and '40s. They had been in Montreal since the early 1950s.

Al added me to the group, a good band consisting of himself on drums, a fine organist named Jimmy Slaughter, from Cleveland, who sang in the style of Nat Cole, and a wonderful tenor player named Rashied Ali. Every week the routine was the same. The girls would hand out their music at the Monday rehearsal, and as the drum part was handed to Al, he would reach into his jacket pocket and exclaim: "Goddamn! I forgot my reading glasses." The rest of us would crack up! Al couldn't read music, but he would always nail the show by ear.

Rashied was from Philadelphia, and sounded a little like Jimmy Heath. It was a good band. I was kind of fucked up, doing drugs, and Rashied tried to look after me, inviting me to his house on our days off. His wife would cook. He had a lot of stories of the early days of bebop in Philly—hanging out and practicing with Clifford Brown, the Heath brothers, Trane, Benny Golson, etc., and working in Howard McGhee's big band in the late '40s. It turned out his name back then had been James "Sax" Young, and Jimmy Heath mentions him in his book, *I Walked with Giants*. I was getting to hear a lot of oral history from people who had lived it. The Lobster Trap was owned by a man named Saul Freed, who always used to hassle Al about putting on more of a show. Rashied was funny. When this would happen he used to say, "That JAMF (jive ass mother fucker), he wants to see some uncle-ing". (A reference to Uncle Tom).

After several months in Halifax, this gig ended and I returned to Montreal and began working with another organ group. This, however, was something quite different. Marius Cultier was one of the most phenomenal musicians I ever worked with. He was an amazing pianist and organist from Martinique. The rest of the group—a great drummer, Jean Claude Montredon, conga player and percussionist Jojo Grocavla, and Marius's wife Gisèle on vocals and hand percussion—were also all from Martinique. They all spoke in Creole, a bizarre mixture of French and African. He put this band together as a commercial venture to work the circuit in Quebec. The band played the entire spectrum of Afro-Caribbean music, including some very authentic Trinidadian calypsos. Yet again I was the only white guy in the band.

There was no bassist—Marius took care of that with the foot pedals on the organ. Although I think he hired me for the jazz content of my playing, he had some very specific roles for the guitar. He showed me various latin keyboard figures that he wanted me to play. Marius was a great entertainer and showman and often he would leave the keyboards and step out front to sing and dance, and "work the room." This would leave me onstage alone with the percussionists to play repeated montuno patterns and two or four-measure vamps, while the cross rhythms of the drums and percussion built to an incredible level of complexity and intensity. Trial by fire! At first I would sometimes get lost, but after a while I could do it. This experience also gave me a chance to use some of those basic latin rhythmic things that I had learned from F.T. We opened at the Black Bottom and went on the road in Quebec, playing some of the places I had worked with Captain Vann. The band was well received in these places, but I think it was a little ahead of its time. The Afro-Hispanic and Afro-Caribbean rhythms were somewhat different than the older South American dances popular in Quebec, and it would be another thirty years before they became part of the musical mainstream in Canada. Playing with this group was an invaluable learning experience for me.

I had also begun classical guitar studies with a teacher. I was not well versed in classical music, but it was something I wanted to explore. I soon found that my right-hand fingers, which were used to holding a pick, were virtually untrainable. I stayed with it for a while, but it became obvious that I would never do it well. However, it was good to familiarize myself with that repertoire. Later on I developed a kind of home brew right hand pick-and-three-fingers style, which I used in my jazz playing sometimes. I thought of it as a sort of right hand-left hand piano effect, alternating single note lines with chordal punctuation.

I married around this time, and my wife also became involved with heroin. The junk neighborhood was the "student ghetto," just east of McGill University—Prince Arthur and Milton streets between University and Park Avenue. You could almost smell drugs as you walked down these streets. In the early '70s I found myself in a situation where heroin was around all the time, every day. I was working in a band with someone who was using and had a good connection. In these circumstances it didn't take long to develop a habit. In 1970 or '71 I was introduced to someone I'll call C.R. He sold heroin, but he had a lot of class for someone in his line of work. He went out of his way to help us several times when my wife and I were sick, suffering with withdrawal symptoms. I started going to see him every day. Eventually he got very strung out, did something stupid, and went to prison. Sometimes the bassist Freddie McHugh would come over on Saturday night and we would get high and watch the hockey game on television, if we weren't working.

One day bassist Leon Feigenbaum and I were rehearsing at my place with a musician I'll call G. I won't use his name because today he is a successful executive with a large musical instrument corporation. Leon and I got high, and G begged us to let him try some. We finally did, and he sat there nodding. We started to play, just guitar and bass, and after a couple of tunes, Leon looked over and said, "He's not moving at all!" Sure enough, he was hardly breathing. We put him in a cold shower, clothes and all, to lower his body temperature, and walked him up and down the hall. Up and down. Up and down. Finally his legs started to move by themselves, and it looked like he was going to be OK. But he was pretty fucked up, alternately nodding out and throwing up. My wife came home from work and after getting high herself, drove him home in his car, telling his wife that he had food poisoning. A junkie will tell anyone anything, whether or not they expect to be believed, just like any businessman. (I once had a record distributor tell me, when I went to collect money owed to me, that he couldn't pay me because his house had burned down!) The punch line of this story is that the next day the phone rang, and it was G: "Hey man, can I do some more?" The man had overdosed and almost died, and he wanted to do some more!

I had a guitar student who was a high level drug dealer. I would go over to his house and he would hand me this beautiful Ramirez nylon string guitar, and set out a snifter, a bottle of very old cognac, and a pile of cocaine on the little table beside me. I would play for hours, pausing to sip and snort. While cocaine was not my preferred drug, I enjoyed it once in a while on social occasions like this. He eventually got busted for something big, like importing or conspiracy to import. We went to visit him while he was out on bail. His lawyer was there. Montrealers always had a sense of humor. The lawyer told us: "I'll get him off, if it takes fifteen years." It didn't take fifteen years. And he didn't get off. He later sold me the Ramirez, which I still play once in a while.

But in the meantime, I was surviving by playing music. I had actually become a professional musician by default. I had a nice apartment on St. Dominique Street between Rachel and Marie-Anne streets, where Billy White and pianist Pierre Leduc had previously lived at different times. A nice block, mostly Portuguese and quite affordable before the arrival of well-heeled gentrifiers like Leonard Cohen. The apartment was a great space for a musician. It was above and adjacent to a warehouse, so there were no neighbor problems, and I could practice, play or rehearse there anytime, day or night. Directly across the street was an old decommissioned firehouse which was occupied by an American artist named Don Bonham, and the author and playwright Michel Garneau lived up the block.

Somehow, I always managed to find a decent gig when I really needed it—or at least something that paid the rent. A couple of months in a club, playing in the band on stage for the Montreal production of *Hair* at the Comédie canadienne, and various other stage productions at Place-des-Arts, a run with a show at the beautiful old Monument-National theatre on St. Lawrence Boulevard working out of town with singers, club dates, industrial shows—whatever came along. Club dates were one-night jobs mostly playing dance music for society functions. Industrial shows were big, scripted extravaganzas produced by large corporations, usually car manufacturers, to introduce their new products to their local distributors. They traveled from city to city with their cast and musical director, and hired local musicians. In those days rents were low, food was cheap, and one could live a marginal existence and still live fairly well.

At one point I worked for about six months at the Casa Loma on Ste. Catherine Street East alongside the legendary drummer Claude Ranger, accompanying Marilyn Apollo's girlie show. This was one of the last of the big showplaces in town. A lot of the clubs were run by or controlled by organized crime. As a musician, if you worked in a "mob joint" you knew you would always get paid and be treated well. I was once given a $100 tip by one of these characters for accompanying his wife, a singer who didn't sound too good. Fortunately she had great charts by Vic Vogel.

All during this time I was making occasional trips to New York to hear live music and buy records. I had been fascinated by that city, and all its energy and filth, since a childhood visit with my parents when I threw up in a cab and it didn't bother the driver. Didn't faze him at all. "The cab's going to stink for a while" was his comment.

On one of these visits someone (I don't remember who—maybe drummer Jim Blackley, who Brian Emblem had studied with) arranged for me to have a lesson with one of my guitar heroes, Jim Hall. Jim was wonderful. I spent the afternoon with him, and he gave me enough things to practice, think about and work on for years to come. He even made sandwiches. On another visit I went to Slug's, a lower east side club where the best music in New York was to be heard at this time, and caught Donald Byrd's group with Sonny Red (always one of my favorite alto players), Bobby Timmons on piano, Walter Booker on bass, and a great drummer from New Orleans named Leo Morris, who was to become much better known later as Idris Muhammad. What a band! Serious music. Bobby Timmons was featured on a solo performance of "My Funny Valentine." I also heard another of my guitar heroes, Kenny Burrell, in duo with bassist Major Holley at The Guitar, a short-lived club on Eighth Avenue. We stayed at the Rutledge Hotel at 30th Street and Lexington Avenue. The place was full of roaches, and the desk clerk, a scrawny little white guy, was on the nod more often than not. Needless to say, it was affordable. These days it's a fairly clean Ramada Inn.

In Montreal I heard the Ayler Brothers (Albert and Donald) with Call Cobbs on piano, Lewis Worrell on bass, and Sonny Murray on drums, at The Barrel on Mountain Street between Ste. Catherine and Dorchester (1965 or '66). This was absolutely electrifying! My

Matchbook, front and back, Slugs' Saloon, New York, 1967.

hair stood on end! To this day I've not heard anything like it! I was not a fan of what was known as "free jazz." I still feel that when the disciplines of form and harmony are dispensed with, there is a real risk of having the music sound all the same. Maybe this is similar to abandoning the concept of perspective in visual art. With the Aylers it worked because of the musical personalities involved and their unique sound, and the element of the blues, but much free jazz sounded like bullshit to me at the time. I did enjoy Ornette's music (though he is a very traditional musician), and I did appreciate late period Coltrane, but I found that a little went a long way. The Harlem Paradise had a brief jazz policy in the late sixties, where I heard Grant Green with Fathead Newman, John Patton and Clifford Jarvis (incredible music!) and Donald Byrd's quintet with Sonny Red and Bobby Timmons. It was almost the same group I had heard at Slug's in New York earlier in the year.

Somewhere around this time I began to notice differences in the way musicians played or approached music. Among the black musicians, even the not-so-good ones, there was a sense of the music being a matter of life and death, which it was. With some of these old guys if you played the wrong chords, you might get a trumpet blown in your ear (or worse!). On the bandstand it was serious. With a lot of the white musicians, even though they might be really proficient musicians doing a really great job, you sometimes got the feeling that they were thinking about their mortgages, or dinner, or something else.

This perception was reinforced when I met people like Billy Robinson and Sadik Hakim. Billy was a "tough tenor" from Fort Worth, Texas, where he had grown up with Ornette, Dewey Redman and Charles Moffet. Billy was a monster saxophonist influenced by Sonny Rollins, and he had some intriguing original music. He landed in Montreal after a stay in New York working with Mingus and Freddie Hubbard. He had a Muslim name, but didn't use it professionally. I went to hear him at the Black Bottom, and he had a young guitar player who just wasn't making it—a talented kid, a good player, but he just didn't have the experience to deal with the music that Billy was laying down. Charlie Burke, the owner of the Black Bottom knew me and suggested that I sit in. I did and Billy fired the kid and hired me on the spot. This caused something of a racial flap, as the kid was black. But then so were Billy Robinson and Charlie Burke. I worked there with Billy most of that summer (I think it was 1970) with various bassists and drummers (Claude Ranger, Freddie McHugh, Errol Walters). Charlie, the owner, played drums sometimes. With Billy, the music was up on another level, more serious than anything I had previously experienced.

After the run at the Black Bottom ended, I did some other gigs with Billy, and we became friends. He was a mentor to me, and I learned so much from him. He would often come over to my apartment and we would rehearse his compositions or listen to music. He loved Johnny Griffin's solo on "Rhythm-a-ning" with Monk at the Five Spot, and we would listen to it over and over. He must have known what I was into, but he never mentioned it to me. He didn't use drugs (except for a little pot) and as a Muslim he didn't drink, but I suspect he had his own experiences with drugs in the past.

Pianist Sadik Hakim was living in Montreal then, as was a great drummer from New Orleans by way of Los Angeles named Tony Bazley. Bazley had previously recorded with Wes Montgomery and

Billy Robinson, Montreal, 1974
Photo: © Len Dobbin

Harold Land on the west coast. Through Billy I did some gigs with them, and then Sadik got a record date for the Canadian Broadcasting Corporation (*London Suite*, RCI 378) and asked Billy and me to play on it. I was just blown away—here was someone who had played with Bird, Prez, and other giants, asking me to play on his record date. He didn't really need a guitar player as there wasn't any guitar-specific music. I had to accept that he just liked the way I played. He used the guitar as another horn, and was generous with solo space. Sadik was not a pianist with an overabundance of chops, but had a brilliant musical mind, was totally steeped in bebop, and was one of the best, most swinging "compers"—accompanists—I have ever played with.

Also on the date was a very talented multi-reed player who played alto on this session. He had a Muslim name and was kind of antagonistic to white people. It was all "Brother Hakim" and "Brother Robinson," and bassist Vic Angelillo and I were "Mr. Bass Player" and "Mr. Guitar Player." He asked me why I wanted to play this music when my ancestors were slave owners! I told him: "Fuck you, Russell (using his original given name), this is 1973, and the music is bigger than that, and anyway, they weren't slave owners. Maybe they built the ships." (My Scottish ancestors on my father's side were shipbuilders who landed in Quebec in the 1700s.) I would run into him over the years and never had problems with him again. At one of the rehearsals for the date Billy was late and this alto player lit into him in front of everyone, accusing him of "niggerism," and holding back the progress of the race with his behavior. It was embarrassing. When we did the actual recording, guess who was an hour late? Mr. Alto Player! Billy Robinson showed a lot of class, not saying anything, just continuing to warm up on his horn. The date turned out well, and it was my jazz recording debut. I also played on a record by Billy Robinson for the CBC (*Evolution's Blend*, RCI 375) during this period.

In the early '70s I started to get a few calls to do what is known as studio work: advertising jingles, television shows, tracks for pop singers, that kind of thing. I wasn't very good at it because I wasn't a great sight reader, and wasn't all that versatile. I was getting called to sub by Richard Ring and Tony Romandini, two of the busiest first-call studio guitarists. I was probably the sub that the leaders dreaded to see. But I guess I was adequate, didn't fuck up too badly. It was some funny shit! I played on sessions for a CBC comedy show called *Let's Carl the Whole Thing Orff*. The title says it all! I would often sub on a CBC French language TV show called *Boo Boo dans le métro*, a talk and variety show aimed at French Canadian housewives, which was broadcast live at noon every weekday from a shopping mall in the east end of the city.

Sometimes we would do a recording session starting at 9 a.m. and go all day. We would break for lunch, and these studio guys would drink their lunches. They'd be knocking it back, and I'd be sitting there with coffee, being nervous, trying to make conversation. After lunch, back to the studio and these guys, behind four or five martinis, would nail those charts—just ace them—and I'd be sitting there stone-cold sober, scuffling with the parts. At one of these all-day sessions we recorded the music for a whole season of a children's television show. It was all short cues—not one piece was more than thirty seconds long. I received residual royalties for many years from this one session. Occasionally we would get a call to mime on television, putting on a suit and pretending to play along with music that we had previously recorded.

Montreal, early 1970s.
Photo © Len Dobbin

53

During the summer of 1971 I worked in a band at La Ronde, on the former Expo '67 site, accompanying acts like Trini Lopez and Tony Orlando and Dawn, and sometimes I would sub for Tony Romandini with Paul Notar's group at Ruby Foo's, one of the last of the big restaurants on the Decarie Boulevard strip. Once in a while, I'd get "the talk" from the older studio musicians: "Why do you want to play jazz? Don't you want to have a nice house and a new car, a farm in the country and a jeep?" No, I didn't want these things. I still don't. I don't mean to criticize anyone's lifestyles or choices—I'm just saying they didn't work for me. My main concern then, apart from learning to play this music and just trying to survive, was keeping my central nervous system comfortably adjusted. I had no interest in mundane considerations like having a big car, buying a house, having a family or acquiring wealth. After the gig, I'd go out and get high. I never, in my years of using drugs, let it interfere with the music. I was always on time and never got too fucked up to play. I was a drug user, not an abuser.

Paul Bley once said, "It's all a question of different drugs," and it was. One noticed how a drinking person's sense of humor was different from a pot smoker's, or from a junkie's. As a musician (and a junkie) I learned to traverse and blend in with all strata of society. I performed for the rich, the poor, the working class, and all ethnicities. As a junkie I dealt with anyone from the children of ambassadors to the lowest east-end street criminal types. Here it didn't really matter who you were. In that world all that mattered is who had the bag, and who had enough money to cop.

At this time I put a band together with soprano saxophonist Jane Fair, pianist Fred Henke, bassist Brian Hurley and drummer Brian Emblem, playing original music. I was trying to write and perform music in the style or area of the Mahavishnu Orchestra—high register fuzz tone guitar blended with soprano saxophone, playing music written in odd meters. The band did a couple of gigs and made one recording, the tapes of which have been lost. It was an interesting diversion—something different to explore. I soon became bored with this concept.

By mid-1973 it was time to stop using. I've always considered my ability to see right down to the crux of every issue to be a curse,

JANE FAIR - Soprano saxophone
BRIAN EMBLEM - Drums
PETER LEITCH - Guitar
BRIAN HURLEY - Bass
FRED HENKE - Piano

Poster for a gig at the Rising Sun, Montreal, mid-1970s.

rather than a blessing, but it made me realize that I had to deal with this habit. The pianist Bill Evans once said that being addicted was like experiencing the process of death and transfiguration every day. If one were a thinking person, one could enjoy this process on some twisted level. Evans also said that he had believed the common myth that smoking marijuana led to the use of "hard drugs" and that was why he smoked it. Ha Ha! He smoked it and followed himself.

Although I loved the drug, I had never liked that petty criminal milieu and most of the characters involved in it. On top of this our habits were escalating. We were borrowing money, passing a few bad checks, and the constant chasing the bag and scrambling for cash were starting to interfere with my thinking. I was just tired of it—I was too serious about music and my wife and I decided to kick.

There was more to deal with than just a physical, metabolic drug addiction in which the body adjusts to an opiate metabolism during addiction, and then shifts back to a normal metabolism when one stops using. This shift is what causes withdrawal symptoms. But there is also a behavioral addiction, an addiction of routine and milieu. Fortunately I never got busted. The closest we came to it was when we were shaken down by detectives when we were leaving a notorious drug bar after unsuccessfully trying to cop. There was a lively traffic in methadone from the patients at the local addiction rehabilitation clinic, and we got some of this to help us kick. In those days the clinic gave you a "carry"—methadone to take out, mixed in orange juice so it couldn't be injected. Freddie B. was the king of the junkies at the clinic. As the oldest and most strung-out of addicts he received the highest dosage and he used to sell some of it.

Methadone is a vicious, dangerous drug created by Hitler's scientists during a morphine shortage towards the end of the Second World War. More powerful and longer acting (but less enjoyable in the manner in which it makes its presence known to the central nervous system) than heroin or morphine, the drug and its programs turn people into "lifers." The theory is that it takes the junkies off the street and makes them "functional." It becomes an easy routine—you go to the clinic and get your fix. But a lot of these people want and need to be active and "on the street." Perhaps the methadone clinic should be placed in a truck or a bus. You could keep it moving, parking at random locations, never telling the patients where it is at any given time. That way they could participate in the excitement of the chase, as well as getting their medication. I believe that in order to cure narcotics addiction one thing necessary for the addict to have is a strong motivation in some other direction. Many junkies do not have this, and I think that at least partially accounts for the high percentage of curative failure. Fortunately I had music.

The running joke was that there was an Indian restaurant near the clinic where some of the junkies would hang out. The proprietor wasn't too glad to see them because they didn't eat much. He couldn't kick them out so he prepared them a special dish. It was called "The Curry with the Syringe on Top."

A doctor we knew gave us a book of spiritual philosophy by P.D. Ouspensky and some goof balls (Seconal or Nembutal). "Give me that old time barbiturate! Old time barbiturate! Give me that old time barbiturate! Nembies are good enough for me!" Anyway, at least the Seconal helped. I remember my wife and I taking some and running out to the corner diner for breakfast, thinking we would be back at the apartment before it hit us. We both ended up with our faces in our plates. Barbiturate-induced sleep is all deep sleep. No dreams. This class of drug (Seconal, Tuinal, Nembutal, Phenobarbital etc.) eliminates those pesky rapid eye movements. A peaceful sleep.

The barbiturates don't really alleviate opiate withdrawal symptoms, except for the insomnia. When you eventually wake up, you are still in withdrawal, but also groggy from the barbiturate. The junk in Montreal at that time probably wasn't very pure, so our habits weren't too bad. Withdrawal was like having the flu for a week. There were muscle aches and pains, with alternating chills and fever and diarrhea. No fun, but we got through it. Heroin withdrawal, if one is young and in reasonable health, causes no lasting health problems. In fact, heroin and the opiates are much less physically damaging to the body than alcohol. What is dangerous is the unsanitary milieu: unsterile needles, syringes, eye droppers, spoons etc. In any case, the way to stay quit was to get off the scene, out of the milieu.

Looking at it from the perspective of 2013, the act of "shooting up" is so twentieth century, like bebop or abstract expressionism or street photography. Far more efficient delivery systems exist today. In some suburban areas, heroin is cheaper on the street than Oxycontin. Yet the needle is as much of a habit as the drug, and I guess there are enough people still doing it, apart from the medical profession, to keep syringe and needle manufacturers in business.

By the spring of 1973 I was working seven nights a week at the Hotel Aviation in suburban St. Hubert. I was accompanying floor shows and playing dance music with a trio. The emcee, who was a bus driver during the day, sang country and western tunes in English, and loved to tell jokes on stage about "Les Anglais" (in French). Even I found them funny. I had to, as I was the only English-speaking person in the whole place (or maybe in the whole town). On Sundays we started at 3 p.m. and worked until 2 a.m. On that day we would accompany an amateur show in the afternoon, which consisted of mentally challenged or deficient people attempting to sing the French pop songs of the day, for which they were paid with bus tickets.

In the fall of that year I got a call to go to Quebec City to play on a CBC television show five days a week. I took the gig, happy to leave the Hotel Aviation and be out of Montreal, away from drugs. I already knew and liked the city. It was a town where people ate and drank well, and liked to have a good time. Two restaurants I remember in particular were the Biarritz, serving Basque cuisine, and an Italian place called the San Remo, and there were lots of brasseries serving good food. Both of those places are long gone. I was off drugs, except for a couple of times when my wife arrived on the bus from Montreal bringing me a syringe loaded with heroin. Other people say it with flowers.

The gig was a talk/variety show called *Le Joint*, where we accompanied singers and played the guests on and off the set. I composed the closing theme for the show, which gave me some decent royalties. Having to read new music every day greatly improved my sight reading skills. Suddenly I found myself working all the time: a recording session in the morning, the TV show in the afternoon, jazz and other gigs at night. I stayed in Quebec City for two years. Once in a while I ran back to Montreal to do a gig on the weekend. One of these was an album of Christmas music for the CBC, with organist Buddy Munro and drummer Brian Emblem. I even did a couple of performances with the Quebec Symphony Orchestra, as part of the quintet in Canadian composer Norman Symonds' "Concerto for Jazz Quintet and Orchestra."

This was the only time in my life when I made any real money, beyond mere survival. I bought a used BMW 2002 and it was the only well made, beautifully designed automobile I have ever owned. It was good to have had that experience. Once was enough. When it started to age, the cost of parts and maintenance for it was worse than having a junk habit.

When the TV show ended in the spring of 1975 I returned to Montreal, and went on the road in the province with several local pop stars. Quebec had its own local French language star system. The artists were known as *vedettes* (stars) and travelled with their own bands, and had their own celebrity tabloid publications. I accompanied acts like Nicole Martin, Karo, Patsy Gallant and Ginette Reno and her sister Huguette Rayno. These acts revisited some of the places on the circuit I had worked with Captain Vann and Marius Cultier years before. There was one town less than thirty miles south of Montreal which had been caught in a time warp, where it was always 1955. The women all had huge beehive hairdos and the men all looked like Elvis. They raced souped-up jalopies up and down the main street.

After several months of this I landed at the Stork Club on Guy Street with an organ trio backing up a Sinatra-style singer for a while. It had been one of the large, sophisticated supper clubs with dancing in years gone by, and was now barely surviving. During that summer I relapsed and developed a small habit, which I was able to get rid of before moving to the Café du Nord on Boulevard Pie IX near Fleury Street in Montreal North for the winter of 1976-'77, a very cold winter. It paid the rent, but it was very low-end employment playing dance music. We played seven nights a week; on Sundays we started at 3 p.m. and finished sometime after 1 a.m. A lot of beer was consumed on this gig. On occasion during a slow ballad the drummer would urinate onto the carpeted bandstand while sitting at the drum set, still playing.

While I was at the Café du Nord I became involved in a very unusual group led by Richard Sasnow, a keyboardist and composer from New York, who was probably in Montreal for the duration of the Vietnam War. The band consisted of myself on electric and acoustic guitars; a symphonic percussionist, Paul Duplessis, playing African log drums; a Colombian percussionist, Joey Armando, who I had known for years; a virtuoso classical bassist, Dennis James, who played with the Montreal Symphony Orchestra, and was to become a close, lifelong friend; and the leader on keyboards. The music was all

Richard's and very different from anything I had previously played. It was free-form extended writing, more modal in concept than tonal. The ensembles were played by electric guitar and arco (bowed) bass, in unison or octave unison, over keyboard and percussion. I guess Richard wanted a soloist who could bring a more traditional sensibility to his music, so that was me, coming from the bebop or post-bop esthetic. It was a very interesting band. We did a few gigs and recorded a demo, but nothing really happened with it.

The death knell for Montreal's fabulous night life had been sounded decades earlier by Mayor Jean Drapeau's campaign to clean up the clubs and bars. Places employing live musicians like the Chez Paree, the Café du Nord and the Hotel Aviation, and even the Stork Club were merely holdovers from a previous era, and were on their last legs. Actually, the decline of Montreal as one of the great cities of the world had begun with the opening of the St. Lawrence Seaway in the late 1950s. This was a system of locks and canals that allowed oceangoing vessels that previously could go no further inland, to continue on to the Great Lakes giving them access to many more Canadian and U.S. ports. This had a devastating effect on industry and commerce in the city.

I was making a living, but I was not getting many opportunities to play jazz, and I was starting to think of moving on. The political situation was getting weird in Quebec. Repressive language laws were being passed. French had to be the language of work in large companies and French had to predominate in all public signage, with exceptions for English institutions. The push for Quebec to separate from the rest of Canada was very strong and the provincial government and its leaders were behaving like small-time banana republic fascists. Except that they had no bananas. They did have a corps of special "language police" who went around harassing English people about their signage.

The result of all this was that English-speaking people were leaving in droves, along with all of their money. The fences were going up, and the economy was going down. Quebec has yet to recover economically. The federal government of Canada merely cringed and cowered in the face of Quebec separatism. Besides all of this, I felt I could no longer live in a place where most of the drummers had no understanding or appreciation of Kenny Clarke, not to mention Philly Joe or Elvin. Kenny Clarke, one of jazz's great drummers, along with Max Roach, laid the foundations of modern jazz drumming. He participated in some of the great Miles Davis recordings in the 1950s.

All the drugs and two years in Quebec City had done irreparable damage to my marriage and my wife and I separated. She returned to England. I had begun an affair with Linda, a beautiful Québécoise woman who, oddly enough, was a passionate separatist. My political views were then, as now, pretty much nihilist, so that didn't bother me, although I didn't much care for the idea of repressive or totalitarian government (or any government of any kind, for that matter). We really liked each other, and enjoyed each other physically, but we lived quite different lives, and there was no future in a serious relationship. We are still friends today.

With the exception of the small black American community, because of the cultural and language differences most of Quebec was very far from the socio-cultural roots of jazz. In Montreal at that time it was hard to find a rhythm section that could play four even quarter notes in a row. If you tried to do anything at all subtle with the phrasing—back phrase or do anything with triplets, they just didn't get it, and the tempo would drop. Sometimes this would happen in Toronto too, and I remember Neil Swainson and I would say, "It's headed for the lake!" meaning the tempo was dragging.

Some musicians I knew had moved to Toronto, where there seemed to be a higher standard of musicianship. Also, my old high school friend, the photographer Robert Walker, was there.

PART TWO

Toronto, 1977-82

"No sense of the absurd."
— PETER LEITCH

It has been written that there are two solitudes in Quebec. In Toronto there are two million. I should have known what I was getting into when on my first trip to Toronto, I was pulled over by the police and given a speeding ticket for driving thirty-six miles an hour in a thirty-five mph zone. Nasty cops. The Rule of Law was very strong there. Coming from a large cosmopolitan, sophisticated, and wide open city with a certain bohemian spirit, I was surprised at the small town mentality and the puritan strain that seemed to run through everything. It was all a little too clean and a little too polite. There must have been a whole other level of sleaze and grift going on, say in the restrooms at the bus station, because you sure didn't see any of it on the street. It was as if the politicians had never learned the important lesson of Tammany Hall's Boss Tweed in 19th century New York. If they were really going to loot and plunder a town, it had to be wide open, which was good business for everyone.

It was a very buttoned-down town. I guess there just wasn't enough unorganized crime or graft to occupy the police, who seemed to spend a lot of their time rushing into bars and clubs at midnight making sure the alcohol was off the tables, or pulling over older cars or those with out-of-province license plates. My wheels qualified on both counts. Summonses for jaywalking were often issued. In one place where I lived, the police actually came to my door and gave me a summons for not mowing the lawn. Mow the lawn? I was concerned with much larger issues, like how was I going to survive in this town, and where had she hidden the Percodan?

Shortly after arriving in Toronto in the fall of 1977, my friend Walker took me to The Brunswick House, a large beer hall, where a sing-a-long was in progress. He wanted to show me what I was in for with this move. The place was packed with older people singing World War One songs, led by a dwarf on stage. Culture shock. A tale of two cities. Later on, I worked that room playing with Dixieland bands.

It was more difficult to eke out a living playing music here. Although there was a higher standard of musicianship, there wasn't the nightclub scene employing live music that existed in Montreal, and the cost of living was much higher here. It was harder to find a place to live. In Montreal, a much older city, there were many European-style floor-through flats with outside staircases, at reasonable rents. Nice places. In Toronto, unless you could afford to buy a house (and in my circle of acquaintance who could?) you lived in two or three-story single family houses that had been divided or broken up into smaller rental units. You always felt like you were living in someone else's parlor. Perhaps this explains many of the Toronto musicians' abnormal obsession with real estate. As I advised a young guitarist moving to Toronto: "Be prepared to discuss real estate with real enthusiasm!"

The buying of alcohol was a strange, almost intimidating experience. You had to go to a special store operated by the Liquor Control Board of Ontario, "control" being the operative word. You would fill out a form and take it to a wicket, where an old, red-faced Scotsman behind the glass would look you up and down disapprovingly before handing over your purchase. I expected to be fingerprinted every time. Beer was difficult to obtain, too. It was not sold in grocery stores. You had to go to a special store called the Brewers' Retail Outlet. If you suddenly had a taste for a cold beer, you couldn't just go to the corner; you might have to walk or drive for miles to one of these outlets, and wait while your order was processed and sent down on a ridiculous Rube Goldbergian conveyer belt. If you wanted to drink on Sundays you had better start early, as vestiges of "Toronto the Good's" famous Blue Laws still enforced an early closing of bars and restaurants on "The Lord's Day."

It also seemed as if vestiges of the medieval British sumptuary laws, governing the wearing of different colors and fabrics, which indicated class, rank, position or income, had trickled down to 20th century Toronto, along with the puritan work ethic. "Dress presentably, but never well" was the rule. As Sylvia, the woman who would eventually become my wife, was to say later, "What do they do with their money here? They sure don't spend it on clothes." With the exception of Chinatown, and a few good Indian restaurants on Bloor Street West, it was difficult to get a really good meal, even if you spent a lot of money. We once dined on tough, warmed over duck à l'orange at an expensive French restaurant. Better to go to Fran's or Dirty Louie's.

Toronto's population in the late seventies and early eighties appeared to consist mostly of people whose belief in the financial, social, and political systems was unshakeable, although among musicians many of the jazz and studio players seemed to be involved with various spiritual advisors, gurus, and therapy groups. There was a character called Mr. Mills, who had quite an international following. You gave him a percentage of your income, and if you gave him enough money, you were allowed to wash his feet. There was another one called Bawa, who was supposedly four hundred years old, and had never been seen to ingest food or water. There was a Catholic psychoanalytic commune called Therafields, which allowed you to pick bean sprouts on their farm if you paid them, which they then sold in health food stores. It seemed that a lot of musicians in Toronto were ripe for this kind of con.

My first work in Toronto was with bands that played for society functions—not necessarily high society either: weddings, bar mitzvahs, dances—whatever. You haven't seen anything until you've seen drunk, middle-aged, well-to-do Scottish Canadians "get down" to the tune of the Gay Gordons, a kind of Scottish march. I tried to fit in. I even went out to play softball a couple of times with some of the musicians. This didn't last long because not only was I a terrible ball player, but the following day I felt as if I'd been run over by a trailer truck, and had to take more Percodan. My old friend and mentor Billy White was there. He had just been released from prison (he had served a sentence for burglary) and was totally ruined, the victim of multiple drug abuse. He died in 1978.

I started meeting the jazz players and attended sessions at people's houses. I remember quite clearly attending a jam session and practically being interrogated about whether I was going to buy a house. Neil Swainson, a great bassist, moved to Toronto from the west coast around this time, and we connected immediately. We first worked together with the late tenor saxophonist Don Thompson, who was someone I had listened to for years on CBC radio and television. He was known as D.T., to distinguish him from the bassist/pianist/vibraphonist of the same name. Clubs and bars closed at midnight and Don's girlfriend Betty ran an after-hours speakeasy (they were known as "boozecans" in Toronto) where the drinking jazz musicians congregated after their gigs. There were several illegal after-hours drinking places in Toronto. There was one on Shuter Street, and another on Queen Street West, but Betty's (on Church between Queen and Richmond streets) was where the drinking jazz musicians went.

I was off drugs, and was beginning to drink a little myself. Betty would open the place around 1 a.m. She got busted from time to time, but would always reopen within a couple of weeks. Most of us musicians were chronically broke, but Betty let us run tabs. The clientele was a curious mixture of musicians, petty criminals, whores, rounders and gamblers. Even the low life was polite in this

With Don Thompson (saxophone) and Joe Bendsza (drums). Toronto 1980.
Photographer unknown.

town. I got the impression that the musicians who hung out at Betty's and drank were kind of looked down upon by those who didn't. Sure we drank—wasn't any dope in Toronto, at least not that I could see. (Actually, I wasn't looking for it).

Besides D.T., some of the musicians and people I hung out with there and became friends with were pianist Norm Amadio, trombonist Terry Lukiwski, the late pianist Jerry Inman and his girlfriend Karen Zajac, bassists Neil Swainson, John Forest and Bob Price, the late drummer Joe Bendzsa, guitarist Glen Chadwick and a wonderfully talented pianist/vocalist, Ginni Grant. I developed quite a crush on Ginni, and spent many hours listening to her at her solo piano bar gigs. We had a brief relationship that didn't work out for various reasons, but we have remained good friends. Ginni and I also worked together with D.T. He had a band called D.T. and the Shakes, and Betty had T-shirts made for the band. Betty's became my social life. On a typical Saturday I would work an afternoon jam session at John Duck's Tavern on the Lakeshore, go to my gig—a club date—and end up socializing at Betty's after one a.m.

In those early days in Toronto Bob Walker and I made numerous trips back and forth to Montreal in the old BMW. When we crossed the boundary from Ontario into Quebec, Bob would say, "OK! Floor it!" When we arrived Bob and I would separate, and I would meet my old friend Linda for "happy hour" at the Rainbow Bar and Grill on Stanley Street. From there we would move on to her scene on the Rue St. Denis and continue drinking. While in Montreal, I would occasionally run into old contacts and get high for old times' sake. After three or four days, Bob and I would meet and drive back to Toronto.

I became involved in a romantic relationship with Susan, a lovely, intelligent, unusual American woman from Buffalo, who was living in Toronto. She sang and played percussion. We took a long driving trip to Florida to visit my parents who were wintering there. It was my first real look at the American social, cultural and physical landscape, other than visiting New York City and working in the border states near Montreal. I didn't know it then, but I was to see an awful lot of this landscape in the years to come.

* * *

In the spring of 1979 I was working a steady gig, six nights a week, at a hotel on the airport strip, with a good quartet accompanying a singer and playing dance music. The gig paid good money, and I was paying my bills. One week trombonist Al Grey and tenor saxophonist Jimmy Forrest, with Don Patterson on organ and Charlie Rice on drums, were in town playing at Bourbon Street, the club on Queen Street that featured out-of-town musicians. That Saturday night at Betty's after my gig, D.T. was quite insistent that I go down to Bourbon Street and sit in with them the next night, which was my night off from the hotel. I was trying to make my way in the music scene here, I had a good gig, I was paying the rent, and I was reluctant to plunge into the real world of jazz. Anyway, I did sit in with them, and at the end of that Sunday night, Al Grey asked me, "Can you be in Chicago on Tuesday?" Without even considering the logistics, I answered, "Sure!" I didn't even ask about the money. Let me out of here! I found a replacement for my hotel gig and arranged for my friend Karen Zajac to look after my dog. Al Grey took my guitar and amplifier across the border (they were driving) and I flew to Chicago that Tuesday.

We opened that night at Rick's Cafe American in the Lakeshore Boulevard Holiday Inn for a two-week engagement. One night early on in the gig a big, tough-looking, well-dressed black dude came into the club and seemed to know everybody. After the set, we all went up to Al's room. Al introduced me: "This is Captain _____ of the Chicago Police Department." Being technically an illegal alien, I'm thinking: "Uh oh!" Then the gentleman proceeded to pull a big bag of blow from his pocket and laid out lines on the table for us to snort. The next set was a lot of fun! On the Sunday off, we played a matinee at a club on the south side. On the way I remember passing the burned-out shell of the Pershing Hotel, where Ahmad Jamal had recorded his hit "Poinciana" years before. When we arrived at the club and I was bringing in my instruments, I realized I was the only white face for miles around, and that everyone was staring at me, in a not entirely friendly way. The owner of the club came running over and put his arm around me, saying, "Hey, man, How you doin'? Come and get some food." It was some of the best down home soul food I had ever tasted: ribs, chicken, black-eyed peas, greens. During the days in Chicago, Charlie Rice, who didn't drink or do drugs, walked me all over the place, showing me the town. One day I had a nice lunch in the iconic Wrigley Building with one of the waitresses from Rick's, who happened to be drummer Vernel Fournier's girlfriend.

After Chicago it was driving on to Philadelphia; Wilmington, Delaware; and a jazz festival somewhere in New Jersey. On the drive from Chicago to Philly I rode with Don Patterson in his van with the organ. Don, in addition to being one of *the* great organists in the history of the music, was a really sweet guy. He had so many stories. He spoke of that wonderful trio with Sonny Stitt and Billy James, and pointed out the place on the Pennsylvania Turnpike where the brilliant trumpeter Clifford Brown had been killed. He told me of a drive from Philly to Chicago with the great tenor saxophonist Gene Ammons, a serious junkie who insisted on stopping to shoot up at every rest stop. Don had to go in to the men's room and wake up "Jug" every time. When we got to Philly, I stayed with Don and his wife Joan at their house.

One night at the Flight Deck club in Wilmington (hometown of Clifford Brown) I was sitting at the bar between sets and started conversing with an older black man, who seemed to be quite knowledgeable about the music. It turned out he had gone to school with Clifford Brown. He talked about how serious Clifford was and how much he practiced, and I started thinking about how this music was just not a cultural reality in the places I had been living. What were the chances of having this conversation in Toronto or Montreal? I had learned by now that it wasn't enough to just try to play this music. You had to understand where it came from, intimately know the culture that produced it, and know in whose footsteps you were following.

I was learning so much with this group. These people were masters of the music, and masters of the road. Al and Jimmy had been with the Basie band for years. Don Patterson, in addition to knowing all the traditional organ tricks, was very advanced harmonically and he played hip right-hand lines that were more like what a pianist would play than an organist. Charlie Rice was one of the best drummers I had ever played with. Nothing flashy or loud, just great swinging time, and every accent meant something. And his drums *sounded* wonderful and blended beautifully with the other instruments. I was learning about playing good "time" at some killer slow tempos, blending, pacing, how to build a solo, what *not* to play, how to lead a band, even how to dress on the bandstand and pay attention to one's shoes. This was the true university of jazz.

When the tour ended I decided to go to New York for a few days. When I got there I called a drummer from Montreal that I knew. "Let's go see Ray Draper," he said. We went down to the Lower East Side, to the area known as Alphabet City, but the legendary jazz tuba player wasn't home so we went to visit Clarence "C" Sharpe, an alto saxophonist from Philly who had recorded with Lee Morgan and was an underground jazz figure.

This part of the city was like a war zone in 1978. It looked as if World War Three had happened while you were on the subway: Abandoned buildings, stripped cars, oil can fires, lots of graffiti. C Sharpe lived in an abandoned building on East 11th Street between Avenues B and C. "C" was very resourceful. He bootlegged electricity from a lamp post on the street, and it was said that he could cook a meal on the bottom of a hot clothes iron. (But you had to hold it very steady.) There was no running water and the bathroom was a shit-strewn vacant apartment down the hall, filled with bricks, plaster and rubble. Within ten minutes I had given C some money, and he ran down to the corner and came back with a couple of bags of dope. We shot up the junk and it was good.

Then it was on to visit a pianist/composer, also from Montreal, who lived on Central Park West. He had a large apartment and I think he was writing or producing advertising jingles or something like that. Anyway, he seemed to have a lot of money and was having dope delivered. I spent the next two days on my face on his living room floor, only getting up to do another hit. All right, so I backslid a little. Here I was in New York, the jazz festival was on, and I hadn't heard any music, bought any records or enjoyed the city at all. I will say, though, that this was the last time I ever used heroin. There in New York, I could feel the palpable danger of being pulled down into this world and dragged to the bottom.

I returned to Toronto, and the world of club dates, Dixieland and the occasional jazz gig. The Dixieland played in Toronto was fun, but it was almost a caricature of traditional New Orleans jazz, played by hard drinking old Scotsmen. That summer I also worked weekends at the Canada House Tavern, situated at the corner of Queen and Sherbourne streets, with bassist John Forest. John wore a big cowboy hat and sang country and western tunes such as "Drop Kick Me Jesus, Through the Goal Posts of Life" and Jimmie Rogers' "Waiting For a Train" (All around the water tank...). The clientele was working class, had anyone been working. Their professional aspirations ran all the way from the dole to minimum wage.

I was getting to work with some really good musicians, however. I became a member of Nimmons and Nine Plus Six, a big band led by the brilliant composer Phil Nimmons, who I had listened to for years on the CBC. I had always dreamed of playing with this band. It was very difficult music. Phil often had the guitar doubling the lead with the saxophones, and it was very angular line writing. Still not a great sight reader, I took the book home and worked on it.

I substituted for Ed Bickert in Rob McConnell's Boss Brass (generally considered Canada's best big band) on a television show. While I appreciated the fantastic musicianship of the members and their perfect renderings of Rob's slick charts, I actually found Phil Nimmons' writing more interesting. At the Boss Brass rehearsal a well-known Canadian alto player, a longtime junkie who was subbing for Moe Koffman, gave me some methadone. Contrary to popular belief, you could get high on this, especially if you were clean, which I was. Damn! It was good.

I did some gigs with vibraphonist Peter Appleyard, a few television shows, and played on a CBC recording by tenor saxophonist Art Ellefson, *The Art Ellefson Trio* (LM479). I was trying to get some gigs for my own group, but as usual what jazz gigs there were paid very little money. Finally, at the instigation of Neil Swainson, who was his bassist at the time, Moe Koffman gave me a week at George's Spaghetti House, Toronto's oldest jazz club and the only place in town where you could work a whole week with your own band playing jazz and make decent money. I put together a good quartet with pianist George McFetridge, Neil on bass, and Terry Clarke on drums. Terry is one of the world's best jazz drummers, and I was so excited to be playing with him. We had an instant musical rapport.

When you had your own week at George's at that time, it meant that you had arrived as a jazz player in Toronto. But the fact that you had "arrived" as a jazz player in Toronto meant nothing in terms of the larger picture.

One morning I was relaxing at Betty's in my tuxedo and bow tie after my gig, having a few drinks. I used to park the BMW in an alley across the street next to a police building. Ironically I think it was the parking violations office. There was not much action there at 3 a.m. Betty's was on the second floor, and when the doorbell rang she used to go downstairs to the front door to look through the peephole and greet visitors. That morning she came running up the stairs shouting, "Peter! Your car is on fire!" I ran downstairs and across the street and sure enough someone had broken the window and ignited some flammable material inside the car. The fire was spreading rapidly, and everything was starting to short out, including the parking brake. The alley had a slight incline to the rear, and the car, now an inferno, began rolling backwards into Church Street. My guitar and amplifier were in the trunk. To a chorus of "Run! Get away! It's gonna blow up!" from the onlookers in Betty's doorway, I managed to open the trunk, lift the instruments out and run across the street. By this time the burning car had rolled into the middle of Church Street, but there wasn't much traffic at that hour in Toronto. Eventually the fire trucks came and the police, who gave me a couple of tickets—I forget what for—probably for littering. At least I was dressed for the occasion. I never found out if this was a random act of vandalism or if someone really disliked me. It didn't matter. Fuck 'em if they couldn't take a joke, as the old saying goes.

The car was totaled, but it wasn't a great loss as it was costing me a lot of money in parts and repairs at that point, and I had long ago learned not to be too attached to material things. I didn't get any insurance money. The insurance had run out. I even had to pay to have the burned-out husk towed to a junkyard. After this I acquired a series of old junkers which the Toronto police just loved. I was also piling up a lot of parking tickets. I had actually started to believe that if I was really good at what I did and not making any real money, I shouldn't have to pay for parking. My life was beginning to be lived off the books. Maybe it had been for years. Maybe it had always been.

And the jazz world kept calling. One morning I answered the telephone and it was the renowned guitarist Ed Bickert, asking me if I could cover a record date for him that afternoon. He couldn't make it for some reason. He didn't mention what it was, but I said sure, I would be there. I got to the studio early, which was my wont, and the first person I met was the legendary promoter/producer Norman Granz. I'm wondering, "What's going on here?" and then in walks Oscar Peterson! I was terrified. After talking with Oscar a little, I felt better. He was from Montreal, and we knew some older people in common from the black community there. It was kind of a commercial date and it went well. He sang on a couple of tunes. I remember asking him if there was anything in particular he wanted me to do or not do, and he answered, "No, just do what you're doing." He featured me on a beautiful ballad he had composed, I think for a movie score, called "Theme For Celine." Later he commented very

With the great Toronto guitarist Ed Bickert, Beaches Jazz Festival, 1994.
Photo: Barry Thomson..

favorably about my solo on this track in an article in a piano publication. He called me for two more record dates before I left Toronto: *The Royal Wedding Suite*, a big band date on the Pablo label; and a recording of an original jazz ballet score, which to my knowledge has never been released. Much later Oscar was to do me a great favor that I've never forgotten.

In the summer of 1980 Al Grey called and invited me to do some gigs and a recording in Philadelphia. The band was the same as before except for the addition, on the recording, of Al's son Michael on second trombone. Al asked me to write something for the record date. It was the first time I had written anything for three horns. I composed and arranged "Blues for Ginni," a medium tempo piece in the minor blues form. It came out sounding pretty nice! The LP was released as *'Out 'Dere*, on the GreyForrest label. So far, it hasn't been reissued on CD.

I stayed at Don Patterson's house in Philly again, and one night he took me on a tour of the bars in Camden, New Jersey across the river. A lot of very cheap alcohol was consumed in these places. The ghetto in Camden made New York's lower east side look like Palm Springs: crumbling buildings, boarded-up or barred windows, spray-painted steel gates, graffiti, and bulletproof glass. Buying cigarettes at a newsstand, I asked a man behind the glass if it was bulletproof and he replied: "I'm gonna be awful mad if it's not!" Again I was the only white face to be seen, but everyone seemed to know Don (famous organists were celebrities in these neighborhoods), and he introduced me as being from Canada, so I guess I was cool. Sort of.

We did a couple of gigs in Philly and Redding, Pennsylvania, and on the way home I went back to New York for a quick visit, and this time I behaved myself. I heard the pianist Al Haig playing solo at a bar on lower Fifth Avenue and bought some records. On the way back I left a guitar and amplifier with Susan, my former girlfriend who had returned to Buffalo, in case there would be more border crossing to be done. Our breakup had been amicable, and we had stayed in touch.

In Toronto again, I found that my friend Walker had moved to New York. I continued working here, there and everywhere.

Occasionally I would work at Bourbon Street with visiting musicians. One night I found myself on the bandstand with Clark Terry and Terry Clarke. I worked there with both Red Norvo and Kenny Wheeler (not at the same time). Now there's a stretch, stylistically speaking. I went to Montreal for a week to work with Milt Jackson at Doudou Boicel's club the Rising Sun, which at that time was located at the site of the former Rockhead's Paradise at the corner of Mountain and St. Antoine streets, where I had worked years before. This was a high point of my life, to work a whole week with "Bags," who had always been one of my musical idols.

I had a good quartet in Toronto, sometimes a quintet with trombonist Terry Lukiwski, which I took to Montreal a couple of times, and we used to play a club in London, Ontario. Moe Koffman continued to give me an occasional week at George's, and I also worked there with various other groups, led by Don Franks, Alvin Pall, Phil Nimmons, Jim Galloway and D.T. I also made a couple of trips to Halifax, Nova Scotia, with D.T. and Ginni Grant.

In 1980 the legendary pianist Glenn Gould passed. Although I didn't listen to a lot of European classical music, he had always been one of the artists I most admired. Growing up, I was exposed to him on CBC radio and television, and his playing had grabbed me. I remembered a television show from the early sixties I had seen of Gould and cellist Leonard Rose playing a Beethoven sonata, and being blown away even then by the fire, depth, and rhythmic clarity of the music. Many years later I acquired a video of this performance, and my reaction was the same! Although he was often criticized for his interpretations and choice of tempos, which I never understood, not being well versed in this music, Gould always managed to imbue whatever music, from whatever composer or era that he was playing, with fire, electricity, great rhythmic clarity and emotional and intellectual depth.

He also managed to live his life exactly as he wanted to. He was proof that if you had enough money, you could thumb your nose at society's conventions and live as you chose, even in a place like Toronto. It's too bad his musical thinking was so Eurocentric. We know he liked and appreciated Lennie Tristano, Bill Evans and Oscar Peterson, but one is tempted to wonder if he had ever listened to Bud Powell, Horace Silver, Sonny Clark, Bobby Timmons, Red Garland or McCoy Tyner (not to mention Monk or Elmo Hope), and if so, what he thought.

Over the years I have sometimes fantasized about creating a script for radio based on imaginary conversations between Gould and Howard Hughes. They had certain things in common—both were reclusive, were pill junkies, and were extremely phobic about germs. The Soviet defector Igor Gouzenko could have introduced them. He could have known Hughes through his CIA connections, and could have met Gould at the CBC. It would have to be radio, as these would be long distance telephone conversations. And radio was one of Gould's favorite mediums.

One night in August of that year I was working at Bourbon Street with trumpeter Kenny Wheeler, where I met a woman named Sylvia Levine. She was there with a couple who were visiting her from Montreal. I had known one of them years ago. It turned out Sylvia had lived only blocks from one of the places I had lived in Montreal and although we had a number of mutual acquaintances, we had never met. As we talked between sets, sparks seemed to fly. One of our first conversations was about sharing the cost of a U-Haul truck to move back to Montreal. This was after I told her I had no money, never went out, and was not interested in meeting women at this time. (I had just broken up with someone.) The next night, I went to George's Spaghetti House to hear a friend of mine, and there they were again. They invited me to Sylvia's for dinner the next night. After that, we started seeing each other. Sylvia was from Columbus, Ohio, and had been a red diaper baby. Her father had been a card-carrying party member, and her mother a certified schizophrenic. She has always said that communism and LSD had gotten her through the worst times, and with me it had been nihilism and opiates. We still argue about this today.

Sylvia's friends from Montreal warned her that I was a junkie, and that I was married. Goddamn people couldn't mind their own business—or at least get their facts straight. I was no longer using drugs, and although still technically married, I hadn't seen or spoken to my wife for several years. In fact, she was not even living on the same continent. By November we had decided to live together. A previous relationship of mine had collapsed because neither of us would give up our apartment and we were both spending inordinate amounts of time on the Gardiner Expressway driving back and forth to opposite ends of the city to see each other, and I didn't want this to happen again.

We both gave up our apartments and rented an old house on Dovercourt Road. It was kind of a chicken shack, but it had enough room for us both to work, which we thought was important. Sylvia was a writer and editor, writing for the *Toronto Star* and freelancing. She had worked as an editor at McGill-Queen's University Press in Montreal. We both possessed a caustic sense of humor. Not long after we moved in, I came home from a rehearsal one afternoon, and Sylvia, who is Jewish, told me, "There are Germans in the basement installing a gas furnace!" I didn't miss a beat. I told her: "Don't worry, they're only following orders!" The landlord had decided to change the heating system from oil to gas, and the workmen happened to be German.

Robert Walker visited us from New York, staying at Dovercourt, and suggested we go to see an exhibit of photographs by Andre Kertesz. It was literally an eye-opening experience—a revelation—like hearing Charlie Parker for the first time. This experience stayed with me but I didn't know how important it would be at the time.

I was thinking about recording. I had a good band which was doing a few gigs, I was writing some original material, and the group was starting to sound tight. There were a couple of small companies recording jazz in town, but they weren't interested in me. I would have to do it myself. Now at that time in Toronto, it wasn't considered proper to do anything entrepreneurial or self-promoting. You were supposed to wait until the establishment said you were OK, and then they would help you. The jazz establishment seemed to have a "Who do you think you are?" attitude. Damn! I knew who I was. Who the fuck were they? At least that was what it felt like. In all fairness, radio broadcaster Ted O'Reilly and a couple of others were supportive of my efforts.

We somehow got the money together (my parents helped) and recorded in February of 1981 at pianist/bassist Don Thompson's studio. The group was pianist George McFetridge, Neil Swainson on

4272 Rue St. Dominique, Montreal, 1981. Cover shot for *Jump Street* album.
Photograph © Paul Carignan.

bass, and Terry Clarke on drums. Terry Lukiwski played trombone on two tunes. New York bassist and drummer Art Davis and Freddie Waits were in town, so I contacted them and they agreed to play on part of the record. Art brought an original blues, which we recorded. I think this offended the Toronto establishment because, as someone put it, they had good bassists and drummers right there in Toronto. It wasn't really about that. Art and Freddie brought their own experiences to the music, and made a beautiful contribution to the record.

My friend Linda Tremblay came from Montreal to help produce the record and design the cover. She had both recording studio and design experience. Sylvia wasn't too happy about this, since Linda and I had been lovers, but I trusted her ear and her eye. We tried to make the jacket look like an old 1950s Prestige cover, but we couldn't find the right type fonts. We did get close to that wonderful bilious shade of Prestige yellowish-green. The color was overlaid on top of a black and white photograph of me in front of my former apartment on St. Dominique Street in Montreal. My old friend Len Dobbin, the jazz writer and the voice of jazz radio in Montreal, wrote the liner notes.

But before the record could be released I received a call from tenor saxophonist Fraser MacPherson. He had a government-sponsored 17-day tour of the Soviet Union set up. His guitarist Oliver Gannon had come down with a severe case of tendonitis in his left wrist, and wasn't able to play for a while. I said I would go. Fraser was a really good player in an older sort of Lester Young style. The bassist was Steve Wallace, who I had worked with at the Skyline Hotel a couple of years before. He was a solid, no-nonsense player, with great time and a huge sound, the perfect bassist for this drummer-less trio. We had no rehearsal—Fraser just called standards and blues.

The first stop on the tour was a concert in Birmingham, England, about 150 miles from London. This was my first trans-Atlantic flight and I was a little nervous. A doctor had given me some valium, and believing there was nothing but a warm bed awaiting me in England, I washed them down with cognac on the plane. When we arrived at Heathrow I was quite fucked up. The plan was to pick up a rental car at the airport and drive straight to Birmingham. It turned out that the rental company had no cars with an automatic transmission, and Fraser couldn't drive a standard. Steve didn't have a driver's license. I had to drive almost 200 miles after an eight-hour flight, the interaction of pharmaceuticals and alcohol in my system and on the wrong side of the road, to boot! One of the most difficult things I've ever had to do. Somehow we got there, slept, did the concert and drove back to Heathrow for the flight to Moscow.

Arriving in the Russian capital, the red (pun intended) carpet was rolled out, since we were representing our government. We were assigned an "interpreter," a lovely young woman just full of propaganda. I was reminded of Greta Garbo in *Ninotchka*. We toured Red Square and saw the Kremlin. Soldiers on parade everywhere.

The weather and the overall outlook was bleak. People on the street wanted to buy our western-style clothes or illegally change money. We stayed in an old hotel, which was obviously once beautiful, but was now verging on the shabby and was for tourists only—no Russian citizens were allowed. There were official receptions, where copious amounts of vodka were consumed. The concerts were in a fabulous old rococo hall with great acoustics. Wonderful, enthusiastic, warm audiences. They even acknowledged the musical "quotes" that appeared in our solos. We were showered with flowers after each concert.

Fraser loved it over there. "Look!" he would say, "There's no advertising!" Maybe there were no Coca-Cola signs, but everywhere you looked there would be giant portraits of Lenin or Brezhnev covering the entire facades of the buildings. Looked like advertising to me. The vibe on the street was very strange. One almost expected to see people in suits made of cardboard riding bicycles made of cement. After Moscow, it was on to Lithuania—two stops: Vilna (Vilnius) and Kaunas. Kaunas was what they called a "closed" city. We were even discouraged from looking out the car windows. I think there were some kind of military installations there. We had been

With Fraser MacPherson, Moscow, USSR, 1981.
Photographer unknown.

told before the tour that we couldn't take pictures anywhere, but Fraser had a little spy camera. He never got caught with it. Again the audience response at the concerts was fantastic. The Lithuanians seemed like really nice people, but we got the feeling that they hated the Russians.

We were paid in U.S. dollars for the tour (a good break financially for us), and upon arriving in the Soviet Union we were given a huge amount of rubles (worthless anywhere else in the world) for expense money. Vilna was situated in one of the largest amber-producing regions in the world. Beautiful stuff! Having been encouraged to spend our rubles on amber jewelry, we all bought some. More on this later.

The next stop was Leningrad (now St. Petersburg), a beautiful city, at least the older part was. There was a lot of recent construction, concrete blocks and white brick, but even the new buildings were starting to look run down. We stayed in one of the newer hotels, which looked OK on the outside, in a pre-fab kind of way. Inside, the paint was already peeling, the plaster was unstable, and the hot water intermittent at best. We were taken to a reception where we were introduced to David Goloshokin, an official Soviet jazzman and historian. Lots of vodka.

At one of our concerts Steve and I met an "unofficial" jazzman, that is to say one not sanctioned by the Soviet government. He invited us to his home. We somehow managed to escape our overseers, and took a long cab ride to the outskirts of town through miles and miles of mud flats to a huge grouping of flimsy, falling-down-looking apartment houses. In fact, it was a Jewish ghetto. Even though there was a language problem, we were somehow able to talk about music. He had bootleg jazz records, and seemed to know what was happening. We returned to our hotel, where the telephone rang all night, every couple of hours. No one on the line—just someone checking up on us, I guess. Since the beginning of the tour, I had been inquiring about the possibility of making a phone call home, and I always got the same response: "Yes, of course, certainly, it will be arranged." But no phone call.

We travelled back to Moscow on the storied Red Arrow express train. A long (twelve hours plus) if not unpleasant trip. Tea was served in antique samovars, and again lots of vodka.

Back in the capital we attended more receptions, and an official Soviet jam session. Lots of vodka. I suspected that the real jazz players were not "official." Steve and I met one of these, a drummer, who invited us to a session with his friends. Foolishly we asked our tour guide if we could go, and got the big "Nyet." After Leningrad they were being careful with us. We went to meet him on the hotel grounds to tell him we couldn't go, and suddenly policemen jumped out of the bushes, questioned the drummer, and took his papers. They didn't say a word to Steve or me. Guess they didn't speak English. They let him go and left. He told us that later they would come and arrest him for not having any papers.

We managed to get out on the street again in Moscow, and saw the famous G.U.M. department store. Not much shopping to do there. We noticed lines in front of shops, but this was not entirely due to a shortage of product. Because everyone, even the store owners, were salaried employees of the state, there was no profit motive. They just closed the stores whenever they felt like it, and hung out in the back drinking vodka. Alcoholism was a terrible problem there. In the mornings there were special buses that picked up passed-out or inebriated, nonfunctioning people. It was hard to find beer in Russia. It only seemed to be available in tourist hotels. Vodka was cheap, but I was tired of it. Steve managed somehow to get hold of a bottle of good Georgian brandy, and we got juiced at the hotel.

For almost two weeks I had been asking about my phone call home, and always got the same fake, smiling, positive response. I couldn't see why a single international phone call (for which I was willing to pay) could be such a problem. Finally I had had enough of these fuckers, their vodka, and their bullshit. I told them, and Fraser, that if I wasn't allowed to call home, I was going to the Canadian Embassy to ask them to send me home. The next day I was told to be in my room at a certain time, and the call was put through. A good punchline would have been that nobody was home, but I was able to talk with Sylvia. They had phoned her the night before to say she was going to get the call, and at what time. Now that's bureaucracy! Or at least totalitarian control.

Finally it was time to go home! At the airport in Moscow soldiers searched our baggage. What's this? Amber jewelry? You can't take this out of the country! There was no arguing with these mean-looking motherfuckers with guns and big red stars on their uniform caps, and anyway they didn't speak English. Our Russian had not progressed beyond "Please" and "Thank you." Maybe someone had made a mistake and would be sent to Siberia after this. All the way home on the airplane Fraser said over and over that he would raise hell with the Canadian government about the amber. It would be eleven years and much shaking of the trees in the diplomatic world before we saw that stuff again. When I got home, I told Sylvia about the jewelry, and I don't know if she believed me or not. Maybe she thought I had spent the money on vodka.

The whole experience reminded me of Canada's own Soviet defector of the 1950s, Igor Gouzenko. He had defected with what later proved to be worthless intelligence, and was a drunk who bilked the Canadian government out of millions of dollars. He used to appear on CBC television wearing a paper bag over his head to protect his identity. America would have had him selling used cars, bag and all. As late as 1979 he was regularly calling the *Toronto Star*, trying to peddle worthless information. Back in Toronto, it was time to get the record into production.

I believe that any musician in today's world should have, as part their education, the experience of recording, producing, packaging, and releasing a musical project—not to mention trying to get it reviewed and distributed. We learned about the mastering process, metal stampers and parts (these were the days of the LP), printing, even about different grades of cardboard. We got a crash course in music publishing and about how the business worked, something I had paid little attention to other than the simple act of doing a gig and getting paid for it. I remember being shocked when we found out that the actual physical display racks in the record stores were owned and placed there by the major corporate record labels. The record business, as we found out, was based on a structure of debt. The retail outlets owed the distributors, who in turn owed the record companies, who owed the artists. What was crucial were the terms of this debt. The so-called major labels, who were their own distributors, could afford to extend credit for longer terms in exchange for the above mentioned "racking" and other privileges. The small distributors, who handled jazz and other "niche" music, could not afford to extend this kind of credit. They needed regular cash flow to stay in business. We found that collecting any money from retail sales was like pulling teeth. The basic and essential lesson learned, of course, was that when everyone kept telling you there was no money in jazz, they were right! All this was valuable knowledge and helped us not to have unrealistic expectations when we had to deal with record companies and the business later on.

The album was released as *Jump Street* on our own newly- formed label, Jazz House Productions. We had a thousand albums pressed and packaged and we sent out two or three hundred promo copies to radio stations and print media throughout North America. Len Dobbin helped us get a distributor who actually placed the record into stores. Through a connection at the CBC, we sold them a couple of hundred copies. We never found out what they did with them. We found out that libraries purchased recordings, so we sent out a mass mailing and sold quite a few that way.

We started to receive some reviews in the jazz press and mailings of playlists from all over Canada and the U.S., indicating radio air-play. The local press was not so responsive. Mark Miller, the jazz reviewer in the *Globe and Mail*, the only Canadian newspaper that had a regular jazz critic, refused to review the record because he said he didn't like it. I felt that he didn't have to like it, but he should have reviewed it anyway. The other local publications pretty much ignored it. After a negative review Moe Koffman told me, "As long as they spell your name correctly, don't even read them, just measure them by the inch!" He was right. I continued doing gigs, trying to promote the album. It was nominated for a Juno award (Canada's version of the Grammy) for best jazz album. We attended the awards ceremony, where rubber chicken, clumpy pasta and Ontario wines (Bright's Unleaded?) were served. We didn't win anything.

I had been working a lot with pianist George McFetridge, and we got a duo gig in the Royal York Hotel, Monday to Friday from 5 to 7 p.m. Musically we were very compatible, unusual for piano and guitar, and George had some very interesting original music. We worked out a repertoire on this gig. I remember that Peggy Lee was booked into the show room at the hotel for a couple of weeks, and every night at 5 p.m. she would come down and sit at the bar and listen to us. She never said a word, but you could tell she was digging it. Not having realized at this point that it wasn't considered good form to do this in Toronto at this time— make your own record or be entrepreneurial in any way—I decided to do it again. We planned to record a duet album. But before we could record, towards the end of the Royal York gig I suffered an attack of tendonitis in my left hand and wrist. I had been practicing a lot during the day, doing the duet gig, and playing on other jobs at night. It was just too much guitar playing. I had to stop playing for about six weeks. A combination of physical therapy, ultrasound treatments and anti-inflammatory drugs eventually straightened out the problem. If there is one thing the human body is not designed to do, it is play the guitar.

We recorded the duet album in February 1982 at McLear Place studios, which had a really good piano, a big Baldwin grand, and we released it as quickly as possible. George and I got another steady cocktail hour gig at a place called Jazzberry's. Mark Miller reviewed us in the *Globe and Mail* as "the brothers Grimm of Canadian jazz." That summer we played the Montreal and Edmonton jazz festivals as a duo, and did a short tour in Quebec with a quartet in places like Magog and Joliette. We were driving an old car that broke down somewhere in the sticks, and had to be towed. My father passed away that summer, and I don't think my mother ever forgave me for not coming back to Montreal to look after her although her health was good at that time, and she didn't seem to need much looking after. We would make a much larger and more significant move later that year.

Due to a combination of an overblown sense of my own import-ance, an inability to see the "big picture," and the influence of too much alcohol, I became embroiled in what could be described as a vendetta against Mr. Miller of the *Globe and Mail*. I was drinking more and more and it didn't suit me. Alcohol seemed to exacerbate the periods of depression, anger and frustration I was experiencing, unlike heroin and the opiates. Fortunately, I never became an alco-holic. I just didn't have that alcoholism gene, or whatever it took to have the disease. Later, when it came time to stop, I didn't have a problem with it—I just stopped, and didn't miss alcohol.

I usually drank after the gig or when I wasn't working. I just needed something to smooth out the edges, which I think a lot of people need. Unfortunately, as I drank more I was developing a physical inability to properly metabolize grain spirits. This all culminated when I poured a beer over this critic one evening in Bourbon Street, and then I circulated a petition among the musicians to have him fired from the newspaper. I have always had a tendency toward the obsessive, and when I get an idea it's difficult to let it go before it gets me into trouble. I have long since made my apologies, and we are on friendly terms today. A few musicians signed the petition, but most of them avoided the issue (and me) like the plague. My phone totally stopped ringing.

I had been thinking of making a move anyway, really since the tours with Al Grey. I felt as if I wasn't developing musically the way I wanted to. I knew there was a whole other level out there that I had to try to get to, not just learn to play it, but try to get to the very essence of the music. In Canada, the idea of playing jazz full time, actually making a living, was just inconceivable, but I knew that somewhere people were doing it. I was thinking about New York. Ridiculous! I was thirty-eight years old, hardly the time of life for a major move or lifestyle change. I had been in touch with Montreal pianist Fred Henke, who was living in New York at that time, and he told me about an apartment sublet in Manhattan's East Village that was available. The apartment belonged to the girlfriend of bassist Ed Schuller. That was the impetus that sparked the move. I had always heard how expensive and difficult to find housing was in New York, and here was an apartment at a reasonable rent. Although Sylvia had been born in the U.S., there were bureaucratic and immigration complications for her also so we couldn't just formally move. For me, how to do it? Once again, I would just have to waive the formalities. I had always taken risks, this was just another one. We had to travel light. Very light.

We arranged for Susan, who was then living in Buffalo, and was a U.S. citizen legal in both countries, to take some essential items across the border. We didn't really own anything of value except instruments, records and books. I sold some guitars—at that time I had different instruments for different kinds of work—a

Fender Telecaster, a Gibson 335, a steel string acoustic etc. I kept my Gibson L5, the old Gibson ES175 and the Ramirez, all of which went across the border in Susan's car, along with some clothes and Sylvia's typewriters. The records and books went into storage in Neil Swainson's basement along with a few household items that we thought we might need later in life. We left a huge pile of furniture, boxes of books we didn't want, all kinds of things we didn't need, in the front yard on Dovercourt Road.

The final indignity occurred when we tried to rent a post office box in Toronto without a permanent address. "You've got to have a permanent address. It's the Law of the Land!" the postmaster lectured us in a thick Scottish brogue. He spoke to us as if we were bums or indigents, or scammers. We were just trying to run a business while we were in transit. We had made a deal with a company in California, Pausa Records, to release both albums in the U.S., and we were trying to keep track of loose ends.

It seemed as if everyone here was trying to stuff elephants into shoe boxes, no one seemed to want to leave their particular comfort zones for any reason, and no one had any sense of the absurd, or any kind of ability to see a larger picture. It was a place trapped in its own image of small town respectability. Okay—we were out of there! As well, Sylvia had written a series of articles for the *Toronto Star* which did not endear her to the Toronto jazz establishment, so we burned the doorknobs behind us on our way out.

I was very happy to be leaving what I thought at that time was a socialist bureaucracy with a national inferiority complex, where it seemed that nothing ever happened that had any import beyond its own borders. An American once described Canada as being just like the U.S. except everyone is on lithium. I felt that living in this kind of stasis, with its accompanying cultural and emotional vacuum, was just too high a price to pay for peace, order, good government and good hockey. Americans were at least right up front with their flag-waving patriotism. There was nothing insecure or self-conscious about it. Those Canadians who were patriotic were almost apologetic about it.

Actually, one of the main problems in Canada for a musician or performing artist was a lack of population density, which made it difficult and expensive to travel within the country. Canada as a whole had the population of New York State spread across a country which was geographically larger than the U.S., so there were huge distances between cities. And there were very high domestic airfares due to government regulation of the industry. All of these factors made it prohibitive to tour. Anyway, as far I was concerned I wasn't moving to the United States, which I had no particular affection for: I was going to New York City!

PART THREE

New York, 1982-

'Think you can lick it?
Get to the wicket.
Buy you a ticket.
GO!"

New York, New York: a city so nice they had to name it twice, according to Jon Hendricks. A helluva town. A loud town. A dirty town. A tough town. A crooked town. A cold town. A hot town. But it's a town where people think on their feet. New York is what the French architect Le Corbusier called "a beautiful catastrophe."

We arrived in the fall of 1982. When we visited Bob Walker in his tiny but elegant West 39th Street apartment, the first thing he asked was, "Have you gotten all the feathers picked out, and the tar washed off?"

Historically, New York City's districts, especially in Manhattan, arranged themselves according to commercial trade zones with specific areas for specific goods and services: the flower district, the fur district, etc. So, by extension, were its blocks arranged. Residential blocks outside of the midtown area, especially in the poorer sections, existed almost as independent villages oblivious to, and almost in spite of, the great metropolis surrounding them. Ours was East Thirteenth Street between First and Second Avenues. Only half of the block was residential. The western half of the block was occupied on the south side by a large telephone company building, and on the north side by the New York Eye and Ear Infirmary.

It was a car repair block. Occupied mostly by Puerto Rican families, it was dominated by the activities of Tony, an older street mechanic. He had been a diesel bus mechanic back in Puerto Rico and he was the unofficial "Mayor" of East Thirteenth Street.

The streetscape was one of jacked-up cars, baseball on televisions and music on radios connected to lamp posts, and people playing conga drums on the sidewalk. People on the street communicated with their families and neighbors by shouting back and forth from the street to their apartment windows. In summer the fire hydrant across the street was always open, providing cooling refreshment for kids and dogs. Although it is illegal to keep farm animals within the city of New York, some mornings we would awaken to the unmistakable sound of a rooster crowing somewhere in the neighborhood. Around the corner at First Avenue and Fourteenth Street, you could buy good, inexpensive steaks from the back of a truck.

There was always an abandoned car or two on the street that Tony was cannibalizing for parts. Sometimes when he was done with them, they would mysteriously catch fire in the middle of the night. Tony pretty much controlled the parking scene. There was a lot of double parking and if the traffic agents came, he would yell at them to "Fuck Off!" and they would leave. The social structure was very loose, but there were unwritten rules, sometimes enforced with baseball bats, and somehow it all worked. Those Puerto Rican guys taught me how to park the car in the tiniest spaces, spaces you wouldn't have thought it possible to fit into.

I was driving an old Toronto police car that I had bought cheap from someone I had met at Betty's. This vehicle was built for high-speed chases, and painted a really ugly shade of brown to cover up the original police car yellow. Just the thing for the East Village. Tony fell in love with the huge V-8 engine, and kept it running for me at a fraction of what it would have cost to take it to a garage (which we couldn't have afforded to do anyway), providing a new battery and other parts for almost nothing. I ended up giving him a set of keys to the car and he kept his tools in the trunk.

I was starting to collect parking tickets again, and in New York, they don't fool around. My car was towed and impounded by the marshal. In this town, the sheriffs and marshals are not actual law enforcement officers. They are independent contractors employed by the city. Tough looking Italian motherfuckers who were probably mob connected. After paying a large ransom to retrieve my car, I kept changing my license plates, from Ontario back to Quebec, and finally to New York State, when a local beat cop warned me that the Canadian plates would draw attention to me. When I got the New York plates Tony told me where to go for a very cursory state vehicle inspection. "Tell him Tony from Thirteenth Street." An extra twenty bucks and you got your inspection sticker—no questions asked in those days.

You didn't need a lot of documentation back then, before the post-9/11 paranoia, and what you did need was easy to obtain. I managed to get a New York State driver's license, a social security number and a bank account, even though I was a completely illegal resident in the U.S. It was hard to get a bank account in Canada even if you were a citizen, if you weren't part of the system, or at least the 9 to 5 workaday world. Here the rule was, "Keep the money moving." For the first time in my life, as a freelancer I was able to have a credit card. The city at that time, and up to 9/11, didn't even seem like a part of the United States. In fact, it was disliked by much of mainstream America. Maybe Mayor Fernando Wood had the right idea when he tried to secede NYC from the union in the 1850s. His mistake was that he tried to take Long Island and Westchester County with him, and the United States sent in federal troops. Once when I was returning from Canada, a U.S. immigration officer asked me the standard "Where do you live" question, and I told him New York City. He then asked with a snarl, "By choice or by obligation?" I replied: "Well, both." None of his fucking business anyway. I carried with me for life an innate distrust and dislike of authority, especially if it wore a uniform.

The city was an entity unto itself, a sort of free trade interzone. And much of the trade was in ideas. There were improvisational aspects to living here, especially as an illegal alien, that were analogous to the music and appealed to me.

I was totally exhilarated. New York was the city of my dreams. We would take long walks from the East Village up to Central Park, and down to the Battery, with barely enough money to buy a pretzel from a food cart on the street. I would look up at the buildings and feel as if I owned them. I could sense the energy pouring off them. I was feeding on the residual accrued energy of the Morgans, the Rockefellers, the Fricks, and their slaves, not to mention a million anonymous forgotten entrepreneurs hustling their way up from the Lower East Side, Brooklyn and all of the poor neighborhoods, making fortunes in Wall Street, manufacturing, the garment trade and the entertainment business.

This evil energy had made New York the capital of the twentieth century. The steel, the concrete, the glass and the bricks all sang to me. The architect and urbanist Rem Koolhaas had described the filigreed skyscapes of Manhattan as the "hieroglyphics of the modern American nation...offering the spectator the largest scale self-portrait yet seen in the world." A case study set in stone, as it were. As a musical metaphor, the street grid was like the basic pulse of jazz, with the buildings and people being the improvisations on top of it.

The streets were teeming with people who had played the game and won. And lost. At least there *was* a game here. After five years in a visual wasteland, it was a pleasure to look at a woman on the street—a total stranger—because you thought she looked good, and have her look back with a little half-smile, because *she* knew she looked good. There were (and still are) chop houses where people eat and drink in a manner reminiscent of the excesses of the nineteenth century robber barons.

New York City is first and foremost a resource, in fact a collection of resources. The very best of everything, from music to art to technology, is available, and often quite cheaply. There is a kind of energy, an edge, that one doesn't find anywhere else. Millions of people hustle their ideas, run their own scams and dodges, all packed onto this island, a geographically limited space. In the competition for this space, friction is produced, both physical and psychic, and with friction comes energy. Nowhere to go but up! Or down.

New York in the early 1980s had no chain stores—no McDonald's, Gaps, or Starbucks. The city at this time was still recovering from its disastrous financial crisis of the 1970s. The major approaches to the city—the Deegan Expressway, the West Side Highway, the FDR Drive—presented a surrealistic, almost post Armageddon view. The shoulders of the roads were littered with abandoned vehicles, the burned-out shells of cars stripped for parts. In the driving lanes one had to swerve to avoid loose mufflers, hubcaps, wheels and an occasional trunk lid. The crosstown streets in Manhattan were riddled with giant potholes and craters and resembled the surface of the moon. It was still a coal-based economy. When you put your hand on the side of a building, it came away covered with black grime. I loved it! I had never seen a place where most of the rules were "on hold." As long as you didn't commit a violent crime, no one cared what you did.

Later, the uncontrolled skyrocketing of commercial real estate prices caused the closing and/or displacement of many individually owned businesses and the chain stores began to move in, with the resultant loss of diversity and visual richness and a partial restoration of "law and order." This is a process that continues today, with the post 9/11 construction boom.

New York is still New York, however, in spite of Emperor-for-Life Bloomberg's current attempts to prettify it for the tourists. One thing that makes Manhattan unique is that when the grid plan of its numbered streets and avenues was devised in 1811, the commissioners made no provision for service routes or alley-ways. A result of this is that to this day, *everything* is in the street—garbage placement and collection, commercial loading and unloading, automobile repair, drug dealing, prostitution, the homeless—ensuring that a certain energy, spectacle, and low level anarchy survive. There are rents or tears in the fabric of the new city through which the old continues to seep, or even pour through, especially at night.

In those first few months Sylvia was still doing some freelance writing and editing for the Canadian Red Cross, so she was flying back and forth to Toronto on People's Express, which was a ridiculously cheap airline at the time. I started hanging out and meeting musicians, playing at jam sessions in people's lofts. I was also spending time at Walker's apartment, drinking. He had a great collection of photography books and he tried to show me some things, but the only things I resonated with then were William Klein's tough, gritty New York pictures from the 1950s. Bob was putting together his first book. He worked in color, doing richly saturated New York street scenes. They were very strong compositions, definitely not your average tourist pictures. He needed someone to write an introductory essay. I suggested William Burroughs, always having been a fan of his writing and his humorous depictions of the underbelly of New York. Bob was able to contact Burroughs, and he agreed to do it. But the essay Burroughs turned in was completely nonlinear, and unreadable as a companion to the photographs. He must have used his famous cut-up technique on it. The publisher was not happy. It was given to Sylvia to edit into a more accessible, marketable form. She had qualms about editing the work of a famous American author, but she did and the end result was finally acceptable to the publisher. No one had any money in those days, and Bob's wife Ania, a dress designer, made her a beautiful suede dress as payment for the editing job. I still have a tape of Walker and Burroughs looking at and discussing the photographs over a bottle of cognac. *New York Inside Out* was finally published in 1985, with the edited Burroughs introduction.

I couldn't afford to go to clubs like the Village Vanguard very often, but there were music rooms such as Bradley's, the Knickerbocker, and Zinno where you could hear the greatest pianists in the world with no cover charge. I used to hear Ron Carter and Cedar Walton regularly at the Knickerbocker Saloon. Two of the first musicians I met in New York were pianist John Hicks and bassist Ray Drummond. I first heard them at Bradley's and it was music on the very highest level. I thought, "Wow, these are the guys I want to play with." John and Ray were masters of the music, and had played with everyone, from Art Blakey to Pharoah Sanders to Betty Carter and Johnny Griffin.

Through bassist Brian Hurley, who was from Montreal, I picked up a little weekend gig at a place called the Downtown, on Seventeenth Street, that paid almost no money. There I met the saxophonist Jed Levy, who was to become a close friend and musical partner down through the years.

One of the last gigs I had done in Toronto was outdoors in a downtown shopping mall called The Grange. At the end of the gig I looked around and Pepper Adams (a major league baritone saxophonist, one of my favorite musicians that I had been digging on record for many years) was standing there! I recognized him and said hello, and he said he was just passing through town on his way either to or from Detroit, and something to the effect that he had enjoyed my playing. I told him that I was moving to New York, and he gave me his address and said to let him know when I got there. When I arrived I sent him a letter and included couple of my tunes I thought he might like. I had just landed in the city, and the last thing I expected to hear on my answering machine was a message from Pepper Adams calling me about a gig(!), but there it was.

There is something about my playing that horn players seem to like, which I take as a great compliment. Altoist Bobby Watson once said in an interview in *Down Beat* magazine that it was my phrasing and articulation that made my playing different from a lot of other guitarists. I didn't have that stiff "machine gun" delivery of eighth note lines, and I certainly was not a virtuoso guitarist.

Pepper hired me for a weekend gig in Fort Lee, New Jersey, at a club called Struggles. The name was prophetic. He even played one of the tunes I had sent him, a blues line named "Fifty Up" (titled for a brand of Canadian beer). After this he called me for another gig at a club called the Village West, but he ended up cancelling this, because I think there was a problem with the money. That club didn't last long. Later that year Pepper suffered a serious leg injury in a car accident, which required an extensive recovery, and I didn't see him for almost a year.

I did a few gigs with Al Grey, going to Philly and Redding, Pennsylvania, and a couple of things with him in town. Jimmy Forrest had passed away, and Al was organizing a new band with Buddy Tate. When Al introduced me on the bandstand he would say: "I brought him down from Canada!"

When the sublet ran out, the problem of whether to stay in the city was solved by Mrs. Austin, the elderly widow who managed our building. I had gotten to know her a little bit, helped her with her garbage and her mousetraps, and one day she said to me, "There's an apartment with a lease available. Do you want it?" New York was deep water, and it was sink or swim. Better to sink here than to swim anywhere else. I was determined to stay here, even if, in the words of the alto saxophonist Sonny Red, "I had to eat the bricks."

We moved into our small, empty, one-bedroom third-floor walk-up on New Year's Eve 1982. At night the street below was often used as a wrong-way fire lane as the sirens wailed and the huge air horns blasted, but we had our own apartment, with a rent-stabilized lease at an affordable rent, and no key money to pay. The large living room windows looked out onto a classic New York air shaft. Duke Ellington had composed a piece of music called "Harlem Air Shaft." Ours was an East Village air shaft: narrow, dark, smelly and noisy, with a large pigeon population and outer windows and sills encrusted with their excrement.

The bathroom ceiling would collapse once a year, from the buildup of water from a leaking pipe upstairs. Jimmy the plumber, who had a shop across the street, would come over and do repairs with the plumbing equivalent of chewing gum and rubber bands. Jimmy was an older black guy who had been a vocalist, and had a nice baritone voice, singing ballads in the style of Billy Eckstein. He was a master plumber, but the landlord was too cheap to allow him to do anything but temporary repairs.

The other tenants of our building were an interesting lot. A composer of micro-tonal music lived on the first floor, and a very bad trumpet player lived upstairs. Fortunately he didn't practice very much, which was probably why he didn't sound so good. Larry, a six foot-plus black transvestite lived on our floor. We would see him on the stairs in his tight leather mini skirt and platform shoes late at night when we were coming home from Bradley's. He loved men in uniform, and would often call the fire department with false alarms. They would arrive, sirens and all, and come up the stairs and say, "Hi Larry, How you doin'?" Larry worked nights as a janitor at the police academy.

New York is a recycling (or free-cycling) town. You would see men in three-piece suits and fashionable fedoras rummaging through dumpsters. We picked up furniture on the street, and household items and utensils could be bought for a dollar or two at job lot stores. You could also find interesting books and records on the street in New York. On occasion, if we had a few extra dollars, we would go out for a cheap breakfast at the Burger Ranch, a not overly clean ramshackle diner at the corner of Second Avenue and Fourteenth Street, one of those places where the cooking grease was not changed too frequently, probably not since 1953. The old proprietor stood at the door greeting customers with a twisted grin.

East 13th Street, 1988, with Mona Clarke, Terry Clarke's mother.
Photo: Terry Clarke.

It appeared that every tooth in his head was loose. George, the resident cat, would sometimes join us at the table.

Soon after settling in I received a call to join a commercial group that played weddings and bar mitzvahs, but they wanted a long-term commitment. I couldn't do it. If this kind of work was what I wanted to do, I could have stayed in Toronto.

In the spring of 1983 I went on the road with organist "Brother" Jack McDuff. I got the gig through saxophonist Jed Levy, and the band was Jed, myself, McDuff, and his longtime drummer Joe Dukes. The first gig was in Indianapolis, and we left Harlem in the middle of the night after a stop at the Red Rooster club. We rode in Jack's old white van, which had tires that were almost totally bald. Driving straight through, McDuff was on the citizens' band radio all the way, conversing with the drivers of the big, brightly lit transport rigs that filled the interstate highways at night. His CB "handle" was "White Folks." We arrived in Naptown just in time to move in the instruments, change clothes and hit. After that gig ended McDuff disappeared for three days, leaving the rest of us at someone's apartment in the heart of the ghetto. The local kids thought Jed and I, being white, were cops. Finally, when Brother Jack reappeared, we hurriedly packed and hit the road again, driving straight through the night and day to Fayetteville, NC. He did have a sense of humor, though. Pulling up in front of a barbecue stand somewhere in Tennessee, he announced, "You don't have to be Black to play the blues. You don't have to be poor to play the blues. But you've got to eat pork!" It was good to experience again the loud, visceral response of these audiences to this music. McDuff made those people scream!

But this was not what I wanted to be doing at that time. I had done the organ thing before, the money wasn't very good, and I felt I needed to be in New York. It was reminding me of being on the road years earlier with Captain Vann. And Sylvia was not too happy with our situation in those early days in the city. I left the band after a few weeks and returned to New York. We were scuffling financially. Pausa Records had released *Jump Street* in the States, but probably because of poor sales they decided not to release the second album. I remember squeezing a couple of hundred bucks out of them by getting on the phone and really crying the blues.

The building next door to ours on Thirteenth Street housed the group Air's rehearsal studio. We would see Henry Threadgill or Fred Hopkins sweeping the sidewalk in front. Henry and I talked about McDuff, who he had also been on the road with. The studio was eventually replaced by a laundromat. Fred and Steve McCall passed away, but even today I run into Henry on occasion and we talk about the old days on East Thirteenth Street.

I decided to apply for a Canada Council grant. At that time you needed three letters of recommendation and appraisal with your application. Phil Nimmons and Don Thompson (pianist/bassist) agreed to do the first two. For the third I tried a long shot. I somehow obtained Oscar Peterson's personal phone number (a closely guarded secret). I dialed the number and Oscar himself answered! He remembered me, and when I told him what I wanted, he replied, "You got it!" I don't know what he said in that letter, but I got the grant! Fourteen thousand Canadian dollars! Survival, for a while, anyway. I was writing some music for an octet, and I used some of this money to record it. The music was never released, but still sounds pretty good today. Hopefully I'll do something with these scores someday.

I joined a group called the New York Jazz Guitar Ensemble. It consisted of five guitars, bass and drums. The other guitarists were Bob Ward, the leader, Paul Meyers, Bill Bickford and Scott Hardy, with Steve Alcott on bass, and either Clifford Barbaro or Taro Okamoto on drums. The arrangements were not easy. Bob Ward had transcribed and harmonized Wes Montgomery solos. It was the most difficult music I had ever faced. I remember at the first rehearsal I couldn't read a thing, but fortunately the guys said, "Look, this isn't a sight reading contest. Take the book home and learn it." I did. I wrote a couple of arrangements for the group. We did some gigs at Barry Harris's Jazz Cultural Theatre on Eighth Avenue, and at a club called Sonny's Place on Long Island.

There were so many fantastic musicians in the city doing so many different things. I decided that I needed to become a better guitar player. New York was a whole other esthetic and required an adjustment. Things that sounded great in your hometown didn't sound as good here. You would walk down the street in New York and hear people playing for spare change who were playing so much music that they'd send you right back into the woodshed. I started practicing four, five, six hours a day, sitting at my bedroom window watching the passing scene on the street. My friend from Montreal, Dennis James, had moved back to New York. A Brooklyn native, he was a virtuoso classical bassist and also a good jazz player. He lived in the Village and left a bass at our apartment, and we practiced together a lot.

In 1983 I also began reviewing records for *Cadence* magazine, the most independent and seemingly uncorrupt of the jazz publications. They didn't really pay anything, but there was a weird system of collecting points with which you obtained free records. It was a good lesson and workshop in learning to write coherently, and allowed me to check out different areas of music that I might have missed or ignored. I did this for a while, until I started to receive records with musicians I knew on them. I was also feeling somewhat like the garbage dump of the reviewing staff when the magazine started sending me uninteresting jazz-rock fusion records.

103

The writing that I did for *Cadence* led to some paying jobs writing liner notes for records.

There were sessions taking place in the old Mercantile Exchange building at the corner of Hudson and Harrison streets in lower Manhattan. The caretaker of the building was a tenor saxophone player who lived in the basement and hosted jam sessions there. At that time the building was owned by the DIA Art Foundation. On the main and upper floors were huge conceptual art installations, accompanied by avant garde composer La Monte Young's electronic drones. Bebop in the basement. At one of these sessions I met the alto saxophonist Bobby Watson. Bobby was a great musician who had played with Art Blakey's Jazz Messengers and was now leading his own groups. He called me for a couple of gigs. On one of these I met the drummer Marvin "Smitty" Smith. Smitty and I were to work and record together a lot in the next ten years, before he left New York to become the drummer on the *Tonight Show*.

By 1984 I was thinking about recording again, this time with a New York band. I had sent out demos to record companies, and there wasn't much interest, though the smaller companies would make suggestions. I always liked the combination of guitar and baritone saxophone, and I talked to Pepper Adams about doing a recording project with me. He was willing to participate. I was going to produce this myself when Mark Feldman of Uptown Records, who I had sent a demo to, became interested. Uptown Records was a paradox, or at least a pair of docs. It was run by two doctors who loved the music: Mark Feldman, a practicing gastroenterologist who lived in Kingston, New York, a small city on the Hudson River about ninety miles north of New York that had been New York State's original capital; and Bob Sunenblick, an oncologist living in New Jersey. Mark was a big Pepper Adams fan, and happened to be looking for a guitarist for the label. I had booked a Sunday night playing at Bradley's with John Hicks, and Mark came to the club that night. We talked and he offered me a record date! I asked John and bassist Ray Drummond, who I had worked a few Monday nights with at a club called "Lush Life," to do it, and I really wanted Billy Hart on drums. I remember that we had to change the date for Billy. I had never played with Jabali (as he was known) but I felt

Billy Hart, the Village Vanguard, 1999.
Photograph © Peter Leitch.

I had to have him on the session because I knew he could play the tradition and swing his ass off, and he also had the range and depth to play any kind of material and make it sound natural and good. I was right about that—he is one of the great drummers.

Coordinating the schedules of these busy musicians was easier said than done. I became aware that not only was New York the jazz center of the world, but it is the jumping-off place for the rest of the world. If these guys were not working in New York, they were on an airplane or working in Europe or Japan. Even at the highest level of jazz, the best players had to travel constantly in order to make a living. We set up the date for that November.

In the meantime, I applied to the Canada Council for a renewal of my grant, and was refused. I later heard that they felt I would never return to live in Canada. They got that right! However, their touring office did come up with a travel grant to tour western Canada. I needed a Canadian band for this. I went with Bernie

Senensky on piano, Neil Swainson, and Terry Clarke to Thunder Bay, Winnipeg, Regina, Saskatoon, Medicine Hat, Calgary, Edmonton, Vancouver and Victoria. Terry and I celebrated our fortieth birthdays in Edmonton, Alberta. (We were born a day apart.) Cathryn MacFarlane, the business manager of the Edmonton Jazz Festival, showed up at the club with a big birthday cake.

All during this period, I was selecting and arranging material for the recording. I was determined that it wasn't going to be just a "standards and blues" blowing date. I wanted a group "sound" with those particular musicians playing the material I had chosen, rather than just me playing the guitar with accompaniment. I had originally conceived the idea of an entire album of pieces by Thelonious Monk, but Mark Feldman, to his credit, talked me out of it, saying, "We need more Peter Leitch." I selected two pieces by Monk which had not been overly played: "Trinkle Tinkle" and "Played Twice." I think I was one of the first guitarists, if not the first, to interpret Monk on the guitar. Now everyone does it. On

With John Hicks and Ray Drummond at the Van Gelder Studio, Englewood Cliffs, N.J., The *Exhilaration* session. November 17, 1984.
Photo: © Scott Sternbach

"Played Twice" I transcribed a couple of choruses of Monk's solo from the original recording, which Pepper and I played in unison. Mark Feldman suggested "'Round Midnight," which I've always loved, and I had a couple of originals: "Exhilaration" and "Slugs, In the Far East." They were not easy tunes. We were lucky to get one rehearsal in with the whole band before the recording. I couldn't believe how quickly these guys internalized the music. The pieces had odd section lengths, and a post-bop harmonic context. I didn't write detailed parts for the musicians—just lead sheets (melody and chords). We didn't have to talk about the music at all. They tore up those originals—just peed on them. They sounded just like I had "heard" or imagined them sounding in my head. To me, John's solo on "Exhilaration" still stands out as the best solo on the record. My two compositions had been written several years before in Toronto. We also did an arrangement of Irving Berlin's "How Deep is the Ocean," in 6/4 time.

Pepper and I got together a couple of times at his house in Brooklyn to look at the music and rehearse. Pepper was one of those guys who could read "flyshit," meaning if a fly left a speck on the page, he would read it. When we looked at the music, Pepper pointed out that the sequence of fourth chords descending in minor thirds which opened my composition "Exhilaration" had been used by Prokofiev in one of his piano concertos, which I had never heard. He then proceeded to eat the piece up musically! He had worked with and hung out with Monk so he really knew how that music should be phrased and interpreted. Pepper was so helpful on this, my first recording project in New York.

I was in awe of him. He was amazing. He knew so much about so many things—all areas of music, visual art, literature, you name it—and he could carry on an intelligent, informed conversation about any of it. And Pepper was a hockey enthusiast, frequently attending games at Madison Square Garden. He was a staunch New York Rangers fan. Being from Montreal, with all those Stanley Cups, I had always considered the Rangers to be a bunch of underachieving losers.

The recording was scheduled to take place at the studio of Rudy Van Gelder in Englewood Cliffs, New Jersey. I was somewhat intimidated by recording at this famous studio where 'Trane, Sonny

Rollins, Hank Mobley, Art Blakey—everybody on almost all of the records I had grown up listening to—had recorded. And I had also heard how difficult Rudy could be. But he was cool (he just wouldn't discuss anything technical) and the date came off well. Mark Feldman was a good producer and easy to work with. In the studio, if he saw that the musicians had things in hand, he left them alone. When he did have something to say, he was usually right. We were to work together a lot in the future and we became good friends. We both grew up musically listening to the same things. He had been in the audience at the Five Spot on the night of August 7, 1958, when the Monk quartet with Johnny Griffin recorded "live" for Riverside records.

We did the date in about six hours, live to two track with no overdubbing and minimal splicing and editing. This is the way small-market, small-label jazz records were made then, and often still are. Some of the greatest records in the history of the music were made on a shoestring and a deadline. Due to inexperience and a desire for the "perfect take" I did get into doing multiple takes on a couple of things. I seem to remember having trouble executing part of the melody on "Trinkle Tinkle" but we still got it wrapped up within the allotted time frame. Pepper was aware of my inexperience in the studio as a bandleader, especially at Van Gelder's, and was extremely helpful, guiding me by running subtle interference, and just generally keeping things moving.

In those days recording an LP meant a maximum of forty minutes of music, less if it was at Rudy's, because he liked to keep it to about eighteen minutes a side when he did the mastering. Look at the timings of the early Blue Note, Prestige and Savoy LPs. Rudy not only recorded the music, but in the days of the LP he also did the mastering himself, which was the last stage before pressing at which the sound could be adjusted or tweaked. I always believed that this process was as much responsible for the "Van Gelder sound" as the actual recording. When I asked Rudy about this, he refused to discuss it. I told him that I had noticed that in the early days of his work for the Prestige and Blue Note and Savoy labels, his initials "RVG" were etched in by hand on the masters, in the black space around the label. He later acquired a stamp for this purpose. When I ran down to the old Europadisc pressing plant on Varick Street to pick up the first test pressings of my album, Rudy's initials were scratched in by hand! I was learning a lot of things about the record-making process, mostly by the seat of my pants!

The album was released in early 1985 as *Exhilaration* (Uptown 27.24). It received some favorable, if not rave reviews, and helped to put me "on the map." By then Sylvia had started to work as the editor of a trade paper, so we weren't scuffling so much financially. Uptown wanted to do another record, this time with a quartet. For this date we got Kirk Lightsey on piano, Ray Drummond on bass, and Marvin "Smitty" Smith on drums. I had met Kirk at Bradley's, and we had done a couple of gigs together at a club called Greene Street. I called Billy Hart for this date, but he wasn't available. He let me know that Smitty was available, and that he knew that Smitty was the right drummer for me! Even though we had met and played together before, this was really the beginning of our long musical association.

We recorded *Red Zone* almost a year to the day after *Exhilaration*. At the end of the record date, again at Van Gelder's, Bob Sunenblick decided that he would like us to do an extra tune for an Uptown Christmas album. There was a general revolt, on principle, among the musicians. We felt that if we were going to record a tune which would appear on another album, there should be a little more money. After much discussion, Bob threw us another hundred dollars each, and Kirk and I hastily put together an arrangement of "It Came Upon a Midnight Clear." This track later appeared on the CD reissue of *Red Zone*. There would be no Christmas album.

The New York Jazz Guitar Ensemble recorded for Choice Records that year. This company was owned by a man named Gerry MacDonald, who, interestingly enough, was originally from Montreal. He had been a saxophone player who came up with Maynard Ferguson, Butch Watanabe and Oscar Peterson. We recorded at his studio out on Long Island. Years later this record was either sold or leased to a Japanese company, and no one got a dime for the CD reissue. At least none of the musicians did.

In late 1985 I got a steady duet gig with bassist Brian Hurley at a place called One Hudson Cafe, at the corner of Hudson and Chambers streets in Lower Manhattan, five evenings a week, which lasted several months. John S. Wilson of *The New York Times* came to hear us and gave us a good review. It was a fun gig, and my friend Walker often hung out at the bar.

Even though I enjoyed the outlaw aspect of it, I was getting tired of being an illegal alien. You were cool if you just stayed in New York, or in the States, no one cared, but it took a lot of extra thinking and preparation to negotiate borders. I was still traveling back to Canada now and then, and starting to travel some in the U.S., going to places like Cincinnati, Louisville, Denver, and even San Diego, working with local rhythm sections. On one these trips I stopped in Albuquerque, New Mexico, to do a gig. Sylvia's brother was living there at the time. I wish I had been photographing back then, as it was quite interesting visually. A very flat landscape with long, seemingly endless streets lined with used car lots and one-story alternating liquor stores and gun stores. A good combination of the old and new west. All that was missing were Cisco and Pancho.

Sylvia and I decided to get married. There was just one problem: when I separated from my wife eight years before, we had neglected to get a divorce. Since we had been married in Montreal and my first wife was in England, and we were now in the U.S., a lot of paperwork was flying across three countries and the Atlantic Ocean. Sylvia knew a lawyer in Montreal who took care of it for us. We were married on December 1, 1985, one day after my divorce became final, in a small anarchist synagogue on East 20th Street. We had trouble finding a rabbi who would perform an interfaith marriage, but Rabbi Swiss was cool. His only concern was: "You're not Catholic, are you?" We had the reception at an Italian restaurant in the Village. I wanted to hire the wonderful guitarist Gene Bertoncini to play, but he insisted on playing for nothing—as a wedding gift! He and Neil Swainson, who came from Toronto for the wedding, played. Ray Drummond, who was there as a guest, sat in.

We consulted an immigration lawyer the very next day. It must have been obvious that we had no money because he told us we could do this ourselves, which papers to file, and only charged us a nominal fee. We started immigration proceedings. Around Christmas 1985, Sylvia's best friend Maryclare visited us, and also

Terry Clarke, from Toronto. On Christmas day we all went to the Walkers' apartment, and made ourselves ill drinking a bizarre mixture of vodka and some horrible sweet green liqueur that Bob had concocted.

In 1986 we arranged another tour of western Canada, with the same band except this time Fred Henke was on piano. We went to a lot of the same places we had played on the previous tour. When we returned to Montreal I had to obtain, for immigration purposes, a certificate from the RCMP stating that I had no criminal record. I went to RCMP headquarters and was told that although I had no criminal record, there was some issue with the Montreal Police Department. "Just wait here while we straighten this out," they told me. That sounded funny to me and I told them I would come back later. The sergeant said, "Well, if you walk out of here, we can't stop you." OK. You *know* I was out of there!

I went to see a lawyer I knew about another matter, to have some paper signed or witnessed. I told her what had happened. She did a lot of divorce work and engaged a private investigator. This peeper somehow tapped into the police computer and found bench warrants in my name for thousands of dollars, for parking tickets going back to the 1970s. The amount of these tickets had kept on increasing, with interest and additional penalties, until they reached a certain amount and then they became bench (arrest) warrants. At that time these warrants were non-returnable outside of Quebec. Those Mounties had called the Montreal police to come and get me, although they couldn't hold me because parking tickets weren't in their jurisdiction. Good thing I got out of there quickly. I was screwed. In order to get the certificate I needed I had to pay up. I had just finished the tour and I had some money in my pocket. I went to the police department, and it was like a scene from a Marx Brothers movie. The officers entered my name in the computer and the old-fashioned printer started up. Paper spewed out in a long scroll, off the desk, onto the floor and out the door, on and on, warrant after warrant. The cops cracked up. We all cracked up. At least they had a sense of humor. (In Toronto they would have had the cuffs on me by then, those Calvinists!) One officer told me, in broken English, "I 'ope you can pay, odder wise you go to Bordeaux by da beach." This was a reference to the notorious Bordeaux Jail, situated on Montreal's back river. I paid. They might have had a sense of humor, but they didn't have a statute of limitations on parking tickets. Well, you win some and you lose some. Money comes and money goes.

Meanwhile, back in New York our possessions were slowly making their way to us from Neil's basement with a succession of visitors. Dennis James visited a girlfriend in Toronto and returned with my record collection in his station wagon. I remember Pat LaBarbera bringing a carton of pots and pans and kitchen items. This was good because we sure couldn't afford to eat out much. Pepper Adams brought back a box of things from Montreal. Pepper was diagnosed with lung cancer in 1985 and passed away the following year.

Neil Swainson had begun working with Woody Shaw and would periodically come to New York and stay at our apartment, using Dennis's bass on gigs. Woody was the last of the music's great innovators on the trumpet. Early in 1986 I sat in with Woody at a club in the Village. At the end of the week, he had scheduled a record date for Muse Records at Van Gelder's. I drove Neil out to Rudy's in New Jersey, and I thought: "I'll just throw the guitar in the car." Halfway through the date Woody asked me if I brought my guitar and said he had a tune he wanted me to play on. It was Sonny Rollins's blues "Solid," which ended up being the title tune of the album. Joe Fields of Muse Records even sent me a check! Woody later called me to sub for his piano player. Unfortunately I was out of town at the time, and couldn't do it. One of my great regrets. Sometime later that year Jed Levy and I played at a party for some advertising executives in the penthouse of the Stanhope Hotel on Fifth Avenue across from Central Park. This was the room Charlie Parker had died in. We played a few Bird tunes, but I don't think anyone noticed.

There was trouble at Uptown Records. Mark Feldman and his partner in the venture, Bob Sunenblick, decided to split. Bob would keep the Uptown label, and the masters would be divided between them. Mark received my two masters in the settlement. It didn't seem so at the time, but in the end this was a good thing for me. There was ongoing litigation and my album *Red Zone*, which had

(Top) Neil Swainson, Dennis James, New York, 2002.
Photo: © Peter Leitch
(Bottom) Record producers Gerry Teekens, (Criss Cross Jazz) and
Mark Feldman (Reservoir Music), 338 East 13th Street, New York, 1990.
Photo © Peter Leitch.

With legendary recording engineer Rudy Van Gelder at his studio,
Englewood Cliffs N.J., 1987. Jed Levy's *Good People* date.
Photo: © Joel Mandelbaum

been scheduled for release, was in limbo. We were trying to set up something in Europe and Mark called Gerry Teekens of Criss Cross Jazz in the Netherlands and recommended that he record me if I got to Europe. Gerry came up with a record date and some gigs.

Neil Swainson and I left for Europe in October, starting with a couple of gigs in England, one of them at the Canadian Consulate in London. Then on to the Netherlands, Belgium and France, playing duo or with local drummers. In Holland we recorded a trio album for Criss Cross. Gerry had arranged to have Mickey Roker, who happened to be touring Europe at the time, play drums. What a gas! Mickey was so easy to play with. Once again we did a record in six hours. I remember listening to the session tapes on a walkman on the train from Amsterdam to Paris, choosing takes and deciding on edits. The editing and assembly of the LP were done when I got home, with Gerry by trans-Atlantic telephone.

By the spring of 1987 Mark Feldman had started up Reservoir Music and was recording again. *Red Zone* (RSR 103) was among his first releases. One of the first new recordings he did was a date led by my friend Jed Levy, which I played on: *Good People* (RSR105). Gerry Teekens didn't like to let things sit in the can for too long, and he released the trio record *On A Misty Night* (Criss Cross Jazz 1026). I had two new releases on the market!

That year I received my green card. Printed on the back of it was, "The person identified by this card is entitled to reside permanently and work in the United States." I was now a legal "resident alien." I was so elated! No more of this outlaw stuff, slithering across borders and having to bullshit my way through immigration. Bob Walker and his wife Ania had moved back to Montreal, and when he visited he wanted to see and examine my green card, over and over.

There were a lot of sessions in the late 1980s and early '90s going on at Ron Schwerin's. Ron is a photographer/painter/drummer who had a large loft at Broadway and 19th Street, in the old photography district. Some of the people I met and played with there were alto saxophonist Pete Yellin, bassist Ugonna Okegwo, pianist Allen Farnham, and the Australian saxophonist Dale Barlow. A really diverse bunch of cats used to show up there to jam. Sometimes we rehearsed for record dates there. Ron had been a successful advertising photographer, now retired, and he shot a number of record cover photographs (including a couple of mine) at the loft, which had been his photography studio.

I had joined Jaki Byard's big band a couple of years earlier. Jaki was one of the true geniuses of American music, an incredible pianist and a brilliant composer/arranger. His big band writing was thickly voiced and harmonically dense. The band didn't work as much as it should have, probably because Jaki had a very loose approach indeed to rehearsing and getting gigs. In August of 1987 the band recorded for Soul Note Records, a European label. Jaki featured me on a slow blues tune. In the fall I did another tour of Canada, this time with Neil Swainson on bass and Marvin "Smitty" Smith on drums. Some of this tour was recorded and broadcast by the CBC. Then it was off to Europe again, this time by myself.

I played in The Netherlands, Belgium, France and Denmark, (Copenhagen and Arhus). On most of these gigs I worked with a fantastic Danish bassist named Jesper Lundgaard. In Laren, Holland, one of my gigs was recorded and broadcast by Dutch radio. These tapes recently found their way back to me by a circuitous route, and the music sounds very good. Someday I might release it.

In Copenhagen I did a couple of gigs, and met Doug Raney, Jimmy's son. (Jimmy Raney was one of the most influential guitarists in the history of jazz.) Doug is an excellent guitarist and we did a gig together, which was a lot of fun. I had a funny experience with Danish Jazz Radio. I was scheduled to be interviewed. The format was that I would be taken to the home of one of Denmark's best known painters, Hans Henrik Lerfeldt, who had a huge and very comprehensive jazz record collection. I was to choose recordings from the collection, play a track and we would all discuss it.

Hans Henrik was a weird dude. A lot of his paintings seemed to be of nude women covered with flies or other insects. He weighed between 300 and 400 pounds and was a junkie. He was a good friend of Chet Baker's, and had compiled and published the definitive Baker discography. In Denmark junkies are maintained by the health care system, so he wasn't a bust-out, on-the-street kind of junkie. The interview was supposed to take a couple of hours. I think we had a bottle of Four Roses bourbon. But Hans would keep stopping the proceedings and disappearing into another room, I guess to shoot up. Then he would come back, and his housekeeper would appear with a huge plate of pancakes with strawberry jam. This happened over and over in the course of the evening. Maybe it was something to do with maintaining his blood sugar. Or his weight. We didn't get out of there until after 3 am. I heard a lot of wonderful music, though. Later Hans Henrik and I corresponded when he was working on a René Thomas discography and was looking for information about René's Canadian recordings. He passed away before he could complete this work.

At some point on the tour Gerry Teekens told me he was coming to New York, and asked if he could stay with us. I told him that our apartment was very small, and he replied, "I am not a fat man!" I liked Gerry, we had grown up listening to a lot of the same music, and he had a great sense of humor, so I said OK. We also talked about doing another record for Criss Cross. After this European tour, I went to Edmonton for two weeks at the Yardbird Suite club. For the first of these I led my own group, and I accompanied saxophonist Bennie Wallace for the second

The late James Williams, New York, 1999.
Photo © Peter Leitch.

week. I stayed at the home of Cathryn MacFarlane who I had met on an earlier visit to that city. She later moved to Toronto and was to become a good friend over the years.

When I got back home I did a couple of Monday nights at the Blue Note with Bobby Watson on alto, James Williams on piano, and Ray Drummond and Marvin "Smitty" Smith. James Williams was a great pianist from Memphis Tennessee, and another former Jazz Messenger. The musical chemistry of this combination was truly magical and I wanted to record with this group. Bobby and I played well together—our respective tones blended. When we were playing ensembles, I let Bobby lead because he knew the way. This was how one learned in the traditional way outside of the academy—playing alongside a master. I had been writing some new pieces and I wanted to do an album of original music. Gerry OK'd the project, and he came to New York in December of 1988, staying at the Hotel Leitch-Levine on East Thirteenth Street.

The concept for the album took shape as *Portraits and Dedications,* a series of compositions about or dedicated to people who had influenced me, friends, and people that I liked. (There actually were some!) On December 30th, we recorded at Van Gelder's. I was getting to be more comfortable there; I got along with Rudy, and I thought this was my best recording to date. Jed Levy played alto flute in the ensemble on two pieces, expanding the palette of the music. At the session I also did two duets—a medium tempo blues with Ray called "The Bulldog," and a beautiful rendition of Duke Ellington's "Warm Valley" with Bobby Watson. Bobby invoked the warmth, spirit and sound of Johnny Hodges on this.

Jazz composition is an interesting process. Lacking formal study in this area, what I have always tried to do was to just create an interesting framework for musicians to improvise within. I was using short forms—song forms and blues forms—which are the most basic and common raw materials of jazz. But you try to make each piece a little different somehow. Sometimes I would come up with an idea—say four or eight measures of something, or a bass line, or a melodic fragment—and it would go nowhere. I might put it aside for years and then it would suddenly develop into something. At other times a piece would just write itself in an hour! Of course I wasn't writing on a deadline.

I have always loved the process of making records, any part of it, so I was very happy when Gerry asked if I would produce, or supervise, a few dates for Criss Cross that were scheduled for when he was not able to be in New York. The producer of a jazz record functions differently from a pop music producer, who basically creates the product from scratch, adding tracks and more tracks and mixing and remixing, taking months or even years to create a product that the artist has little to do with.

If the leader and his/her musicians on a jazz date have their act together (and they usually do), the producer doesn't have to do much. His role is to just be another set of ears, make a few suggestions, work with the engineer to make sure everything sounds right, and of course watch the clock. This was an exciting time for me—learning a new role in the music. I have never, to this day, seen anything go down like a Kenny Barron date I "produced" for Criss Cross (Criss Cross Jazz 1044). The band was Kenny, Ralph Moore on tenor, David Williams on bass, and Lewis Nash on drums. They were done in two and a half hours! All first takes, and there was some complex original music. The only thing that needed to be redone was the closing ensemble of one piece, which Rudy Van Gelder easily spliced onto the main body of the take. If only they could all go down like that! Gerry also hired me to write liner notes for several Criss Cross releases, including this one. I was writing notes for some Reservoir albums as well. It made me think of my time spent reading liner notes in the record stores many years before.

During the course of my travels I was learning about jazz education. The promoters of these tours usually booked workshops and clinics at conservatories and universities as a way of making some extra money. I started compiling, on paper, things I had learned over the years and realized there were a number of important aspects of the music that weren't in the curriculum at most of these schools. I made a tape of important historical jazz guitar recordings which I would play for the students and discuss with them. Although I had never studied in, or even set foot in any formal jazz education institutions, here I was teaching in these places!

I prepared and handed out reams of paper dealing not only with the playing of the guitar, but with broader topics like improvisation, rhythm section playing and harmony. At that time many of the people who administered these programs, at least those in the U.S., were white professional educators with academic qualifications rather than experience as professional musicians. They could tell you who played third trumpet with Woody Herman in February of 1953, but never spoke of, say, Kenny Dorham or Donald Byrd. An exception was Paul Jeffery (Monk's last tenor saxophone player), who invited me to Duke University to do a workshop and a performance with his student band. He asked me to send him some original music, which he arranged for big band. Great, great charts! He paid me a compliment later when Jed Levy asked him how it went. He replied "That motherfucker really knows some harmony!"

Portraits and Dedications (Criss Cross Jazz 1039) was released in 1989, and in the fall the journalist-turned-promoter Jon Poses (who had written the notes for the record) booked a two-week tour of the American midwest for us. We managed to get the recording band for the tour, no mean feat, considering everyone's busy schedule.

(Well, I wasn't that busy.) Bobby Watson was only able to do one of the two weeks, so Sonny Fortune did the other one. We played St. Louis, Columbia, and Kansas City, Missouri; Wichita, Kansas, up to Ames, Iowa; Madison, Wisconsin; and Waukegan, Illinois— Smitty's hometown, where we met his family.

We also did a concert at the huge federal penitentiary at Leavenworth, Kansas. Maximum security. This was an eye opener for me. We all had to be thoroughly vetted. On entering the prison you had to go through a series of many doors, all of which locked behind you. If there were any warrants on any of us, they would stay locked. The prisoners were all black (at least those we saw and performed for) and the staff and guards were white. As we left Leavenworth in the van, the guys talked about genocide! I was learning about race in America from the inside (so to speak). One guard in the prison had been particularly obnoxious). One of the musicians explained to me something that a black person has to deal with every day: "Was he a racist, or just an asshole?" A split-second decision that has to be made constantly, in dealing with white society. On the highway in Iowa we stopped for gas and went into a convenience store, and I had never seen such hateful stares as those from the white farmers inside. Back in the van in the parking lot someone said, referring to the Klu Klux Klan, "Let's get out of here, those people be puttin' on their sheets right now!"

I was to learn much more about racial politics in the next few years as I became close friends with people like John Hicks and Bobby Watson and met their families. As an outsider I had always noticed a certain warmth, humor and a strong sense of family and community in the black American world that didn't seem to exist in my stiff, repressed Anglo Saxon Protestant background. As a white person sometimes I felt welcomed into this world. Sometimes I felt uncomfortable, but then I felt uncomfortable with most white people too.

John Hicks was a brilliant, sophisticated, urbane, well-educated man as well as being known as "everybody in New York's favorite piano player." I was hanging out with him at Bradley's, and we were doing some gigs together. I loved John's compositions, and had learned some of them. As we became friends, John kind of took me under his wing, talking to me of history, America, and race, as well as music. Once when we were leaving the apartment on East Thirteenth Street at 2 or 3 a.m. with John and his girlfriend Elise (on the way to Bradley's, probably), John pulled me back and said: "Let the white girls hail the cab." Okay! I was starting to understand. John also taught me the important lesson of "being ready when the motherfuckers call" for a gig or a record date or even a rehearsal— even if they never did call.

I had settled on John, Ray and Smitty as the band I wanted to work with, but they weren't always available at the same time. We managed a few hits together, at Visiones in New York, and a few concerts and a couple of midwestern tours, and the music was fantastic. I was working the occasional weekend, as well, at Zinno with Kirk Lightsey, another wonderful pianist. He and Cecil McBee would work duo through the week, and on the weekends, when the room became noisy, he would sometimes add me to the group. Another great pianist I met, played with and became friends with during this time was George Cables.

I began to realize that I needed to record for a bigger label. Reservoir and Criss Cross were essentially one-man operations. Mark and Gerry were two of the very few honest people in the music business, but they had neither the budget nor the time nor the employees to do a lot of promotion, and thus had to stay small. Mark did buy some advertising in the jazz publications, but it was not enough. I really liked working with them, because they genuinely loved the music, and were willing to take chances. Their decisions were not based on sales, and unlike many record companies they let you keep the publishing rights to your original music. Neil Swainson was now working with George Shearing, and thus had a connection with Concord Records. He began talking me up to Carl Jefferson, the owner of the label. Concord, based in California, was at that time the largest of the independent labels. They specialized in an older style of jazz, more mainstream than bop or post-bop, but Carl really liked guitar players. When I mentioned the possibility of recording for them to Hicks, he said it was a "white man's record label" and wished me luck.

In early January of 1990 John hired me for my first week at Bradley's, with Ray on bass. Bradley's was not just a world-class jazz club, it also served as a clearing house and office for the musicians. It was the only club with a 2 a.m. set, which attracted a lot of musicians who would drop by after their earlier gigs. If anything happened in the jazz world, you heard it first there. Being at Bradley's was breathing rarified air. New York forces you to grow and develop faster than in other places. You would be playing and look up and there's Tommy Flanagan sitting there. Or Kenny Barron. Or George Coleman. Or Ron Carter. Your idols, people you had grown up listening to on records were sitting there checking you out. Scared the hell out of me! It was like going to school every night, and made me work that much harder on the music. I would get up the next day and practice some more. One of my fond memories is of sitting in the office at Bradley's one morning around 5 am with Hicks and Tommy Flanagan, listening to Tommy tell about John Coltrane laying "Giant Steps" on him.

There was always something extraordinary going on. One night (I should say morning) Betty Carter and Cecil Taylor had a long screaming match from table to table. On another night Phil Spector came in and started brandishing a gun! The police were called, but the staff managed to get him out of there before they arrived. Bradley's usually closed around 5 a.m. (sometimes later). Often John would continue on to an Irish bar on Eighth Avenue, a place frequented by postal workers. One morning we arrived there to find the gates down and a man in a white apron sweeping up. John banged on the window. The man looked up and exclaimed, "Oh, Hello Mr. Hicks." He opened the place for us.

We often used to walk home to the East Village from Bradley's at 3 or 4 am, and had to pick our way through a huge thicket of drug dealers and their crackhead customers at the corner of Thirteenth Street and Third Avenue. No one ever bothered us. We minded our own business and they minded theirs. I never sensed any danger in the city. You just needed to be alert enough to distinguish between people with criminal intent, hustlers, crazy people, and harmless old bums with the spit running out of their mouths.

Playing with and being around musicians like John, Bobby Watson, and Gary Bartz , going back to the gigs with Al Grey and McDuff and Sadik Hakim and Billy Robinson—people on that level of mastery and creativity—taught me that you always gave 200% on the bandstand. You never "phoned it in." You might have stayed up drinking the night before, you might have travelled all day and didn't have time to eat, whatever, when you were on the bandstand and the music started none of that mattered. It was another world and the music was everything, and somehow you found the energy.

Hicks told me he'd gotten a little heat from the black community for hiring me at Bradley's. I have always accepted the fact that this music is the creation of black Americans, but I have never bought into the concept that white people "stole the music." There has always been a lot of stealing going on in music or any art, by people of every conceivable race or color. In my own case, I've never felt that I'd stolen something. This music was given to me. And it was given with a lot of love. By a lot of black people. By the happenstance of employment I happened to be thrown into the culture that produced the music, which was such a valuable experience. If you want to really learn about something, you'd better understand the culture that produced it. That said, coming to the United States from Canada, especially Montreal where there was a lot of diversity, I failed to realize that race was still a huge issue in America. Racism has always walked hand in hand with its partner, ignorance. But come to think of it, by the same token so to speak, ignorance and stupidity are two of the few things in our society that know no color line. When you consider the history of four hundred years of slavery and repression, it should come as no surprise that racism (on both sides) exists in jazz, supposedly the most democratic of musical forms. John put it in perspective when we were in the South together. As we got out of the van at a gas station somewhere in Arkansas, John asked, "Where's the colored toilet?"

In the 1950s many cities in America built huge government subsidized housing projects for low income residents. This was probably a delayed reaction to the great migration north of unskilled workers from the south in the 1930s and '40s. Most of them were black, seeking a better economy and a more comfortable racial situation. I believe the government wanted to contain and segregate these people. As these projects were being built, industry was falling off in many cities, and jobs were moving to areas other than downtown. After funding the building of these immense prefabricated ghettoes the federal or state governments failed to provide money for maintenance, repair and upkeep. Draconian welfare laws (no able-bodied males were allowed to live in welfare apartments, no telephone or televisions were allowed) contributed to the shattering of the family unit and a growing sense of isolation. (The 2011 documentary, *The Pruitt-Igoe Myth*, powerfully traces the history of one of these projects in St. Louis, Missouri). The projects were, in effect, concentration camps. It was institutionalized racism from Washington on down through the various state and municipal governments. As conditions deteriorated in these projects the residents were blamed. Later on, in the 1970s and into the 80s many of these buildings were emptied and demolished, literally imploded under the guise of urban renewal. Once, on the way to the airport after a gig in St. Louis, the driver (a young white guy) pointed out such an area, talking about urban renewal. John Hicks immediately translated "urban renewal" into "negro removal" and later at the airport, he said to me: "You see, the shit ain't changed. Not really." Upon reflection, I think that what he meant was although the obvious trappings like the segregated toilets and lunch counters were gone, the attitudes remained.

After a concert in Wichita, Kansas, we went out for a few drinks. John must have been in a confrontational mood because he wanted to go down the street to Denny's for something to eat. Denny's was a chain of restaurants which had been in the news for discriminating against black people. They had refused to serve some brothers who happened to be federal agents and lawsuits were pending. We told him: "John, you don't want to go to Denny's. Fuck those motherfuckers. Lack of business will hurt them more than anything." We talked him out of it. Mainstream America is still very reluctant to discuss race, at least in mixed company, even today with a black president.

In jazz the subtle unspoken racism seems to be tied to a solid economic principle—keep the money in the community. I moved to New York at a time when the music schools in Boston and elsewhere, had begun spewing out graduating classes of competent, technically excellent, conservatory-trained musicians every year. Most of them were white. When I arrived in the city, I was older, foreign, didn't have many gigs, and didn't have that music school old boy network behind me. Oddly enough (or maybe not) the black musicians (not all, but a lot of them) who I met seemed more welcoming and friendly to me than the white ones, a lot whom would look at me funny or just look right through me as if I didn't exist. I guess I hadn't gone to the right schools. Right! Later on when I was working, recording, and touring with that great quartet (Hicks, Bulldog and Smitty), I was shocked when white musicians, names that you would recognize— people I would have otherwise respected— said things to me like, "Why are you working with those black guys? They're not going to hire you." I answered, "Well, you're not hiring me!" Goddamn! If I thought like that I wouldn't even be playing music. If you were serious about music, or about learning something, you couldn't be thinking about that stuff. Anyway, some of "those black guys" did hire me. A well-known publicist told me that the jazz critics and journalists were somehow offended that I had a black band. Why? Did it remind them that their sisters might want to marry one? Well, maybe, as Lenny Bruce had said years ago, they didn't want to marry your sister. I've never been able to fathom this, but it's OK to have one white person in a black band (in fact, people like it), or one black person in a white band, as long as it isn't the leader. Apparently Buddy DeFranco, Pepper Adams, and several other white bandleaders who hired black sidemen experienced this phenomenon to some degree. In fact, on a couple of Pepper's first albums the company wouldn't put his picture on the cover because he was white!

Along with the white promoters the new breed of jazz writers were among the worst of the so-called reverse racists, and you could see in their writing that their attitudes were really all twisted up. Many of them were musically ignorant, lacked a sense of historical or musical perspective and were corrupt, too. They made the somewhat naive Canadian jazz writers look good—even if you didn't agree with them, you didn't question their integrity. A lot of what was written about the music in publications like *The New York Times* in the '90s was obviously bought and paid for by the big record companies.

You would see these "jazz journalists" appear at major label record dates like cockroaches coming out of the walls, anywhere there was a chance of a free drink, or a hot dog or a few crumbs of free food. It gave a new meaning to John Updike's definition of critics: "pigs at the pastry cart." The critics/journalists of an earlier era—the '50s and '60s—seemed to have a greater knowledge of the history of the music and a genuine love of jazz. Some of them, such as Ira Gitler, Leonard Feather, and Gary Giddins, actually played instruments and knew how the music was constructed on a technical level.

I have always felt that musicians should take their own poll of critics and journalists. You could give out awards in various categories such as "Most consistent misuse of musical terminology" and "Best regurgitation of a major label press release" and "Best autobiographical essay in the guise of a review," etc. The awards themselves could consist of dog shit or broken glass. Most musicians, black and white, feel this way, although very few of them will admit it publicly.

All my life it seemed as if I put myself on the wrong side of the fence. Why did there have to be a fence? But I was enough of a sociopath that generally if enough people told me not to do something, I'd go right out and do it! I guess I identified with the words of the song Groucho Marks sings in the film *Horse Feathers*: "Whatever it is, I'm against it! Even when you've changed it or condensed it—I'm against it!" A life of alienation from all cultures, including my own, has allowed me to be myself in any situation, and basically not to give a flying fuck about any of it. The excitement of being in New York, recording, playing with great musicians, and the traveling all worked to keep my episodes of depression at bay, but I could always feel them lurking in the background like cats waiting to pounce.

One of the great bassists I played with during this period was the late Walter Booker, also someone I had been hearing on records for a long time. It was so wonderful to play with superb bassists like "Bookie" and Ray Drummond, especially in an era when there were so many bassists whose technical proficiency far superseded their intelligence, and whose playing ignored the bass function.

Yes, there was a lot of cocaine around in those days. This was a drug I never had a problem with. I could take it or leave it. I took it in social situations if it was offered and it seemed to help overcome my innate shyness. But I never felt that I needed or wanted to use more and more of it, or go chasing after it the next day like some people did. I don't think cocaine is a true physical or metabolic addiction like opiates or nicotine. However, it is a very harmful drug and I think it really compromises the immune system. It wasn't addictive in my experience, perhaps because I didn't use it regularly, or in large amounts. It gives one a burst of energy and does increase one's ability to absorb and metabolize larger amounts of alcohol without getting drunk, providing a sort of balance. It just didn't provide me with the comforting psychological answers that heroin and other opiates had in years past. I saw cocaine and its derivative, crack, destroy a number of lives, and consider myself fortunate that it was never a drug of preference for me. I scrupulously avoided any scene where there was even a hint of heroin use.

In 1990 I signed a three-record deal with Concord. We arranged it so that the first date would take place towards the end of a week at Bradley's in January 1990 with John and Ray. Smitty Smith came in for the recording on drums, and we had a band. Concord didn't record at Van Gelder's studio and my first project for them, *Mean What You Say* (Concord CCD 4417), was recorded at the old A&R Studio in the west '40s. I think it was on Forty-Sixth Street. It was one of those famous old studios where many important recordings and film soundtracks had been made. I think mine must have been one of the last dates done there, because it closed not long after that. We had an excellent engineer, Jim Anderson, who I was to work with often in the future. It was recorded on analog tape with Dolby SR noise reduction, and is a great-sounding record. This was my first CD. The era of the LP was over, and as *Mean What You Say* was being released, my previous LPs on Reservoir and Criss Cross were being reissued on CD.

The way it worked with these labels was that the record company would assume all the costs of recording, manufacturing and packaging, paying the sidemen, etc., and you were paid a non-returnable advance on royalties. You had to negotiate to get as much as you could up front, because you would never see any royalties on sales. This money went towards absorbing the cost of the recording. You did receive royalties from performing rights organizations such as BMI for radio airplay of original compositions, which is why retaining your publishing rights was so important.

Looking back, I see that I was really busy in the late 80s and the early and mid-90's. Back to Europe a few times. Unfortunately, I never got to be a tourist on these trips. I saw airports, train stations, hotels and the venues we played. It was always on to the next gig. I did get to walk around Paris a little, but not nearly enough. People often think that it's a great thing to travel and see all these wonderful places: Paris, London, Copenhagen etc. The reality is that you're working and it ain't no vacation! And you have all these considerations: you're thinking about the rhythm section, the audience, and what you played last night, what worked and what didn't, what you'll play tonight. Maybe there will be a new band tonight. Will you have time to rehearse? Probably not. And mundane

With Terry Clarke, Bernie Senensky and Neil Swainson,
Edmonton, Alberta, 1985.
Photo: © Cathryn MacFarlane

considerations such as can you get coffee in the morning, and a decent meal before the gig. You worry about spending money, so you will come home with some to pay bills. If you are fortunate enough to have a day off, you really need to rest.

We did several more tours of the American Midwest and I went back to Canada for some gigs. There was a club in Montreal called Claudio's, owned by Elda Guglielmin, where I worked several times. After her club closed Elda later moved to Calgary and then to the Vancouver area, and she became a good telephone friend. We would often talk for hours. I played the Top of the Senator club in Toronto a few times and I was working more in New York.

I became the only guitarist in those years to be on the regular rotation at Bradley's. Bradley Cunningham, the owner, had passed away and his widow Wendy was now running the place. She had expanded the booking to trios, instituted a "quiet" policy, and turned the place into a world-class listening room. This was in sharp contrast to the Knickerbocker Saloon down the street, of which it was said by musicians, "They have a *loud* policy. And they enforce it!" I always worked at Bradley's with Hicks, usually with Ray Drummond on bass. That trio was a post-bop update on the classic Nat Cole trio instrumentation, which was very popular in the '40s and '50s.

I also worked at Sweet Basil, one of the major clubs, a couple of times with a quintet. On one of these weeks Sonny Fortune played alto. On the other Gary Bartz (who John had introduced me to) played. This quintet with Gary also worked a couple of times at Visiones, a club at the corner of West Third and MacDougal streets in the Village.

I recorded *Trio/Quartet '91* (CCD4480) for Concord early in 1990 with Neil Swainson on bass, Smitty Smith on drums, and a wonderful young trumpeter from Philadelphia, John Swana. I felt that he could have made a significant impact on the New York scene, but he preferred to stay in Philly, where he remains. I recorded John Hicks's composition "After the Morning" on this date. I had always loved this piece and had played it many times with its composer. I wanted to take it out of the context of the piano and this was the first time the tune had been done this way. When I played it for John, he really liked it. He smiled and said, "Yeah! It sounds pretty good without the piano."

Village Voice advertisement for a quintet gig at Sweet Basil, 1991.

Conducting the guitar ensemble at Domaine Forget,
Charlevoix, Quebec. Late 1990s.
Photographer unknown.

In the summer of 1991 I played the Ottawa Jazz Festival with
John and Ray. Tacked onto this gig was a concert at Domaine Forget,
a music (mostly classical) and dance camp in the Charlevoix region
of northern Quebec, which was beginning a jazz program. After
a series of travel adventures we got there and played the concert,
which was very well received. I was invited to return the following
year as a jazz guitar teacher. I went back for a week every summer for
the next eight years. We looked forward to this annual escape to this
beautiful sylvan setting. Sylvia and I would fly to Montreal and rent
a car there. It was a beautiful drive to Charlevoix County, northeast
of Quebec City, along the north shore of the St. Lawrence, past
Montmorency Falls, past the shrine at St. Anne de Beaupre, past the
Christ-o-Rama (a large open lot where religious icons were sold), up
and down huge trucks-in-low-gear hills with runaway truck lanes
alongside the road. This was a route I had driven thirty years before
en route to gigs in places like Baie Comeau and Sept-Isles.

All of the teachers at Domaine Forget were given private house-
keeping apartments. Although I was paid very good money and
expenses (even enough to rent a car) for this, I had to work very hard.
I had a lot of guitar students to whom I gave private lessons every
day, and also conducted ensembles. It was made more difficult for
me because all the teaching was done in French. I managed with my

broken Québécois French—the grammar was poor, but my accent was okay. The hardest part was using the French musical notation system. It was based on the Do-Re-Mi system of solfeggio—where the notes are identified as syllables instead of their letter names—which I hadn't used before. Sylvia was by this time working in the stressful world of advertising and really welcomed this annual respite from Madison Avenue. For me, there was only one drawback. I have always had an aversion to flying insects. There were black flies, gnats, mosquitoes, wasps and species unnamable by those without a degree in entomology—if it flew and liked to bite human flesh it was at Domaine Forget. Give me that old-time insecticide!

I had joined the International Association of Jazz Educators at the urging of pianist James Williams. During one of their conferences at which I had presented a clinic, I was approached by the director of the conservatory at Edith Cowan University at Perth, in Western Australia. Would I be interested in coming to Perth for three weeks as artist in residence? Certainly. A tour was arranged, and I spent a total of six weeks in Australia. I still was not happy with my guitar playing, and during my three weeks at the conservatory I managed to maintain a rigorous practice schedule in addition to my teaching duties. During my stay in Perth I met Ian MacGregor, Ray Walker and several other fine guitarists who were the founders of the Jazz Guitar Society of Western Australia. This is a society dedicated to promoting jazz guitar, and publishes a newsletter which has a world-wide readership. I was invited to become a patron of their society. During the other three weeks in the country I travelled to Adelaide, Melbourne and Sydney, teaching and doing gigs.

We did several more tours of the American Midwest with John, Smitty and Ray or Walter Booker, and Gary Bartz made a couple of the gigs with us. On one of these in the St. Louis area (actually it was a festival in Edwards, Illinois, I think), we met Mr. Eddie Randall, who had been Miles Davis's first bandleader in the early 1940s. The respect shown him by the guys was amazing.

I had a disagreement with Concord about the ownership of the publishing rights to my original music, and they were dragging their asses about doing the third recording I was contracted for. I finally got them to agree to a sextet date with Gary Bartz and Jed Levy on saxophones, and John, Ray, and Smitty (*From Another Perspective*, Concord CCD 4535). I wanted to get my music out of what I called the "guitar ghetto." There were a lot of people out there who only listened to guitar records, and a lot of jazz listeners who didn't listen to guitar records, and I was trying to bridge this gap. After this date Carl Jefferson told me, "All right, you can keep your damned publishing rights. We don't want you to go away mad." That was the end of my association with Concord.

In the spring of 1992 I received a call from bassist Steve Wallace in Toronto. Incredibly he had the amber that had been confiscated from us in Russia eleven years before. Fraser MacPherson had been unrelenting in his pursuit of it, and his perseverance finally paid off. Fraser had gone to the Canadian government, which made inquiries of the Russians. The amber had been finally located, in little plastic bags with our names on them. It was put on a train from Moscow to Leningrad, and given to a Canadian sea captain, who brought it to Victoria, British Columbia, from whence it went to Ottawa with a Canadian ballet troupe, and then on to Toronto.

At Sound on Sound Studio, New York, with John Hicks, Jed Levy, Ray Drummond, Gary Bartz and "Smitty" Smith. 1992. One of the sessions that produced the Concord CD *From Another Perspective*.
Photographer unknown.

This was all unofficial of course, under the table, as no one would admit that a mistake had been made. Steve brought my amber to New York. Sylvia loved it and still wears it.

One morning I picked up the guitar to begin the day's practicing, when it slipped out of my hands, smashing on the hardwood floor. This was the Gibson L5 I had been using since 1980. Well, time to let go. I was reminded of the scene in *Horse Feathers*, in which Groucho throws a beautiful Gibson L5 guitar into a lake, from a rowboat—the high point of the film, for me. I acquired a Zoller model guitar (built by Hofner in Germany in the 1970s) from Atilla Zoller, the instrument's designer, which I use to this day. It is very clear and even in all the registers, from the bottom to the top. Sometimes the bottom end of the L5 would get kind of "muddy" sounding.

I have never had any kind of romantic attachment to guitars. In fact I never really liked them at all. They were simply a tool, and if they worked well, were fairly comfortable to play, and suited the musical purpose at hand, that was enough. Most good guitars are highly overpriced anyway. I felt the same way about cameras later. I remember playing someone's Benedetto guitar. What a great instrument! But not thirty or forty thousand dollars great.

In the early '90s a superb young guitarist named Russell Malone moved to New York from Atlanta. He was a personable fellow as well as a great musician. He had worked with Harry Connick Jr., and already done a record for a major label. You just knew he was going to be the next major "guitar star." When he arrived in the city, apparently he went around telling people that I was his favorite jazz guitarist. This seemed to really help my credibility in certain circles, and I've never forgotten it.

Living in New York City is an everyday series of challenges, compromises and trade-offs. You trade off a larger living space and certain comforts for the privilege of being "on the scene" and getting your ass kicked, musically and otherwise. Our place became so small and crowded that we eventually rented part of a room in a neighbor's apartment for office space. Drastic changes were taking place on our East Thirteenth Street block. Crack cocaine had hit the area with a vengeance. Children we had seen grow up over the previous ten years had turned into crackheads and dealers. There were a couple of shootings, there were knifings, and crack-crazed prostitutes would scream at each other all night long under our windows. It was becoming violent and getting scary. One afternoon I was sitting in front of my window practicing, watching the activities of Harry, a notorious crack dealer who lived across the street. His apartment was on the ground floor and there was constant action there, day and night. That day I saw two plainclothes cops go into the building, and Harry came bursting out of his first floor window, clearing the stairwell leading to the service entrance below and the iron fence, landing on the sidewalk, and taking off up the street, the officers in pursuit, guns drawn. They had neglected to leave any backup on the street!

The bodega next door had turned into a crack den. I was out of town when the police raided it, breaking down the door with a battering ram. For some reason, along with the crack epidemic came a proliferation of rats—mostly the ubiquitous Norwegian brown rat. We had to get out of there. Years before, we had put ourselves on a list for government subsidized housing, and in 1993 our names came up.

In August 1993 we moved into a much larger two-bedroom floor-through apartment on Morton Street in the West Village, half a block from the Hudson River. The novelist Patricia Highsmith, the pioneering independent filmmaker Maya Deren, and the Rosenbergs (Julius and Ethel, not the Dutch gypsy guitarists) had all lived on Morton Street, named, I believe, for a revolutionary war general (not Jelly Roll). It looked at first as if the living room alone of our new apartment could contain the entire East Thirteenth Street place. After we'd lived there awhile, our new home didn't seem so large! It started to fill up very quickly.

It was nice to be so close to the river. You can see everything from tiny sailboats to huge cruise ships and liners plying the water-way. The best is seeing filthy old barges loaded down with #4 bunker fuel oil being pushed up-river by tugboats. It reminds me of my childhood, near the St Lawrence River. The southern end of West Village Houses (our apartment complex), where we live, is right at the edge of an area zoned as light manufacturing so the neighborhood isn't completely residential. Directly across the street, covering the whole block, was a one-story freight depot with trucks parking and spewing diesel fumes all night. We had a good view of the Lower Manhattan skyline until it was later blocked by a new fourteen-story high-end residential building across the street.

The West Village was much quieter than the east and didn't have a huge crack problem, although there was some evidence of it. The amazing thing was that under the federal Mitchell-Lama subsidy program the rents had a ceiling beyond which they could not increase. Around the corner was a meat-packing establishment, probably mob connected. They had removed the no parking signs from their street, and I thought I would take advantage of the free on-street parking. On one of my European trips I left my car there for a couple of weeks. When I returned, the windshield was totally covered with tomato sauce. That was my warning. The mob owned the street. They could have done a lot worse. New York is, and always had been, a Mafia town.

In the summer of 1993 when my contract with Concord was over, Mark Feldman was ready to record again for Reservoir Music, especially in

Sylvia Levine Leitch, Morton Street, New York. 1999.
Photo: © Peter Leitch.

light of the publicity I had received by being with a larger label. In all the years I have recorded for and worked with Mark, we have never had a written contract. We liked and trusted each other enough that it wasn't necessary—a welcome relief after the pages and pages of legal horseshit I had to sign with Concord. And they had still tried to take the publishing rights to my original music.

The quartet with John, Ray, and Smitty recorded *A Special Rapport* (RSRCD 129) back at Van Gelder's for Reservoir. This group had a special rapport indeed! We had toured and recorded together several times and John, Ray and I had worked at Bradley's as a trio. John and I never experienced any of the problems that can arise from two chord instruments playing together—it just worked with the two of us. John's left hand drove the band. Smitty and I worked hand in glove rhythmically, and he was really aware of the sound of his drums. The drums were tuned in such a way that he was able to play loud, yet the overtones produced didn't clash with the other instruments. It was a great sonic blend. Bulldog laid down a big bottom under the band and it felt like he levitated the bandstand! Playing with this group was like riding a beautiful, powerful wave. I had to either sink or swim. I swam, and the experience made me a much stronger, more graceful swimmer. And at least in terms of important subtleties like phrasing and rhythmic inflections, I didn't sound like the other jazz guitarists. You have to tell your own story, even if you sometimes have to borrow someone else's words.

Marvin "Smitty" Smith is a thoroughly schooled musician, a talented composer and arranger (most of the great drummers were— Philly Joe, Max, Kenny Clarke, etc.). Smitty arranged several of my compositions for his own groups and performed them at Visiones and The Village Vanguard. What a thrill this was for me, to hear these pieces orchestrated for a larger group, with horns, played by great musicians.

In 1994 Sue Mingus (widow of Charles) decided to put together a band of five guitarists and a rhythm section to play arrangements of her late husband's music. At the urging of John Hicks, who played with the Mingus Big Band, I was hired as musical director of Guitars Play Mingus. It was a little intimidating to be sitting in Sue's apartment discussing the project with her, with Charles's bass sitting there and his original scores on the wall. She was trying to keep the legacy of Mingus's music alive and she had a lot of different ideas. One idea was to keep changing the personnel of the band. I never understood why. It is hard enough in New York to have the same musicians at the rehearsal and on the gig, what with everybody working all the time and doing their own projects. There were always a lot of subs anyway without deliberately changing it up. This was difficult music, and it wasn't just a matter of reading it off the page. It needed to evolve on the bandstand nightly by being played by the same people. This was how Mingus had worked and developed the music.

Some of the wonderful guitarists who came through the band were Vic Juris, Jack Wilkins, Ron Jackson, Ed Cherry, the late Ted Dunbar, David Gilmore, Russell Malone, and Peter Bernstein. At one point Sue hired Larry Coryell. Now Larry—whatever else you could say about him, and he's a great guitarist—was not a good fit. He was used to being a leader, and didn't have the experience of playing with this kind of ensemble. He played much louder than everyone else, and had trouble playing the parts. On top of this, he was being paid more than everyone else, which pissed some people off. I remember discussing this with Sue, and she said "Well, he made a record with Charles." Without even thinking about what was coming out of my mouth I blurted, "Yeah, and it was the worst record Charles ever made!" Sue thought about this for a minute, and replied, "That's what Charles said." The band did a string of Thursday nights at the Fez, under the Time Cafe on Lafayette Street, and a few other gigs and a short tour, but it was ignored by the jazz press and never really took off.

I had a final blow-up with Sue Mingus over a short tour in the midwest that Jon Poses and Sylvia booked for the band with Sue's knowledge. She threatened to sue me for unauthorized use of the arrangements, some of which I had written myself. We screamed at each other over the telephone and hung up on each other. That was the end of my involvement with the group. About a month after this I was playing at Bradley's and Sue came in and gave me a big hug, like nothing had ever happened!

I acquired a computer and taught myself to use Finale music notation software, with much long distance telephone help from

Postcard, Guitars play Mingus, 1994.

Andrew Homzy, a professor at Concordia University in Montreal, who I had known since the 1960s. Using this software I wrote a series of arrangements for five guitars and rhythm section, including a couple of my Mingus charts, advertised them, and sold many arrangements over the years, mostly to schools. This was one of the very few ventures I ever attempted which proved to be somewhat lucrative. I also used these charts as teaching material.

In 1993 I played the Montreal jazz Festival with Ron Carter's trio with Kenny Barron, doing a Nat Cole tribute. I was subbing for Herb Ellis, who I had met at a jazz guitar workshop where we were both teaching and performing in Louisville, Kentucky. In 1994 I played the Montreal festival with my own group, and in July recorded the duet CD *Duality* (Reservoir RSR CD 134) with John Hicks at Van Gelder's. This was a beautiful sounding CD. Rudy placed a microphone on the guitar itself, and mixed this feed with that of the microphone on the amplifier, resulting in a wonderful half electric, half acoustic guitar sound. This was something he had first done with Kenny Burrell in the early '60s. When the CD was released, of course people compared it to the Jim Hall and Bill Evans recordings. Wasn't anything to do with them, as much as I loved them. It was

(Top) Playing with the great Herb Ellis in Louisville, Kentucky. Early 1990s.
Photo: Jeff Sherman.
(Bottom) With Jim Hall, one of my guitar heroes, Hull, UK. 1994.
Photograph: Sylvia Levine Leitch.

about Peter Leitch and John Hicks! Russell Malone said that John and I swung more than Evans and Hall, which was a compliment, I guess.

In August I was invited to teach for a week at a summer jazz guitar workshop in Hull, England. This was combined with a tour of England and Wales. At Hull, Jim Hall was also teaching, and I had a chance to hang out, have dinner, and talk with him.

The following year, the British tour was repeated, with a trip up to Scotland added. I also toured Canada that year with an all-star group of Canadians, most of whom were living in New York. The band was called "Free Trade" and was comprised of myself, pianist Renee Rosnes, saxophonist Ralph Bowen, bassist Neil Swainson (the only one of us still living in Canada) and drummer Terry Clarke, who had not yet moved back to Canada. After the tour we recorded in Toronto for Justin Time records. On the CD we did two originals of mine, "Visage de Cathryn," for my friend Cathryn MacFarlane, and a piece called "Guess Again," which I composed on an airplane going from Calgary to Vancouver. The resulting CD, *Free Trade* (Just 64-2), won a Juno award as best jazz album that year.

I continued to travel and do gigs at Bradley's, the Knickerbocker, Zinno, and Visiones in New York, and record regularly for Reservoir Music. In July 1995 we recorded *Colours and Dimensions* (RSR CD 140), giving the first word the Canadian spelling—a small gesture toward my own roots. This was a septet date with three horns: Claudio Roditi on trumpet and flugelhorn, Gary Bartz on alto and soprano saxophones, and Jed Levy on tenor, soprano, and alto flute. The rhythm section was John on piano, Rufus Reid on bass, and Smitty on drums. The use of three horns, with the doubling increasing the range and possibilities of timbre, gave me a chance to do some writing and some small-scale orchestration. I played the Ramirez nylon string guitar on two pieces. It sounded like a jewel resting on a plush three horn cushion! Smitty and Gary each brought an original composition, and we did four of mine, a Mingus piece (on acoustic guitar) and a standard, Cole Porter's "I Concentrate On You." We were given two days in the studio to do it in the multitrack format, and I still consider this to be one of my very best recordings. Beyond the guitar ghetto! This was just good music!

George Coleman sitting in at Bradley's, 1995.
Photograph: © Abigail Feldman.

John Hicks during this period was not taking great care of himself, and shortly before the recording date he was diagnosed with tuberculosis. I felt duty-bound to inform Mark, who said, "Well, at least it's treatable," and we agreed he should make the record, even though there was some question of whether he was contagious. We were setting up at Van Gelder's and Rudy had decided to put Rufus Reid in the booth with John and the piano. Mark took one look at this setup and told Rudy, "I want Rufus out of that booth! Now!" He must have spoken with genuine "doctor's orders" authority because Rudy changed the setup immediately. Rudy did not usually take orders from anyone. John and I went outside for a cigarette and he complained that Rudy was bugging him about something, and I said, "Just tell him you're a tubercular motherfucker!" We cracked up. This was to be the last time I would record there. Mark was getting fed up with Rudy's increasing eccentricity, and there was a final blow-up with him at the mixing session for this CD. I had a gig in Montreal booked around this time that John was supposed to do, but because of his condition he was on a no-fly list. Renee Rosnes once again came through for me and made the gig and played great piano.

I also made a quick trip to Toronto that year to record two tracks for a Wes Montgomery tribute album featuring six different Canadian guitarists for a local record company. Apparently the record did well, and was later released in Japan. One of my original pieces was used as background music on the HBO series *Hoop Dreams*. According to the deal we made at the time of the recording, those bastards still owe me a considerable amount of money! Such is the music business.

1996 started with a tour of Holland and Belgium with the Dutch pianist Rein De Graaff and tenor saxophonist Lew Tabackin. The tour was a tribute to the late Belgian guitarist René Thomas, my early inspiration. We played some of the music from *Guitar Groove*, René's best (and best known) recording. At one of the concerts in Belgium Marie and Florence, René's widow and daughter, attended and graciously signed a poster for me.

From Belgium I went to Germany for some gigs and made a duet record with a wonderful guitarist named Heiner Franz, *At First Sight* (Jardis JRCD 9611). Then it was on to England again, for some teaching and gigs. This was around the time that Mad Cow disease first made its appearance, and my German friends warned me not to eat the beef in England. Of course the first thing I ate on arriving there was a steak, and I became very ill. Damn! And I was already mad! And the hotel room in northern England was freezing. I began to think that once you left London the quality of life in the U.K. had not improved since the time of Charles Dickens. There seemed to be no interest in the basic human needs, like eating decent food or staying warm. I recovered, did my gigs and was glad to go home.

In July I recorded a trio CD for Reservoir, *Up Front* (RSR CD 146), at a midtown studio with Smitty Smith on drums and a young bassist I had met and worked with whose playing I liked, Sean Smith. They are not related. Jim Anderson was the engineer. Smitty had already left New York and moved to Los Angeles to become the drummer on the *Tonight Show*, and was back in town visiting when we did this date.

In the fall of 1996 several significant things happened. In October Bradley's closed. I worked the last full week there, with Mulgrew Miller on piano and Ira Coleman on bass. This closure was to signal the end of late-night jazz in New York. Around this time I got a call from a guitarist named Nick Burns, who had taken a few lessons from me. He was working a Sunday night gig at a place called Walker's in Tribeca. He was also the daytime bartender there, and he asked me if I could sub for him on a few Sunday nights. I said sure, I would do it. It turned out Nick was also a photographer and a good printer, doing his own darkroom work. Something suddenly clicked in me and I told him I'd like to check that out. He invited me over to watch him work in the darkroom, and I was fascinated. I had to learn to do this! I was hooked. I bought an inexpensive Nikon manual focus camera and started walking the streets with it. Nick taught me the basics of film developing and printing. At first, this was nothing more than a way to avoid thinking about the music business, which was starting to depress me. Besides, photography let you do all the things your mother didn't ever want you to do: play with vile chemicals, leave the water running all day, look at pictures of nude women, etc.

Before long, Nick had given me the Sunday night gig at Walker's. The place had a connection with Bradley's, one of the owners having tended bar there years earlier. They had been having quartets and even quintets, but the money was very low. I told them I would do duets there for the same money, and that I would be able to bring in a higher level of music that way. They agreed and I started a series of duos with bassists Ray Drummond, Rufus Reid, Sean Smith, Harvie S and Dwayne Burno, and saxophonists Gary Bartz, Steve Wilson, Jed Levy, and Charles Davis, some of my favorite musicians. Playing with Charles is like experiencing living jazz history. He had played with everyone from Lloyd Price to Billie Holiday and Dinah Washington to Coltrane, Kenny Dorham, Philly Joe Jones and Sun Ra. Charles reminded me of my commitment to the music. Once when I balked at playing a particularly difficult Thelonious Monk composition, he told me: "We are responsible for keeping this music going."

It was particularly exciting playing in duo with Gary Bartz. Playing with him taught me to think more orchestrally. His manager,

With Tommy Flanagan and Jo Ann Collins at Walker's, 2001.
Photographer unknown.

Don Hillegas, who was a friend of ours from the Bradley's days (or I should say nights) wondered if we could sell this duo. For some reason, some great piano players would show up at Walker's from time to time, perhaps because there was no piano there. Kenny Barron and his wife came for dinner one night, and Ray Bryant, George Cables, Richie Beirach, John of course, and Tommy Flanagan (not long before he passed away) all stopped by. I had gotten to know Tommy a little bit, and it is one of my great regrets that we never had a chance to play together.

I was influenced by all these great pianists that I had listened to and worked with more than I had been by guitarists. I was more inclined to voice a seventh chord as a stark "I -VII -III" (from the bottom) like a Bud Powell or Sonny Clark left hand, or use Tyneresque fourth voicings. I tried to voice block chords like Bobby Timmons or Red Garland, instead of using those syrupy symmetrical chord voicings from the Van Epps or Johnny Smith tradition, which I couldn't do anyway. I didn't have those kind of guitar chops and I just didn't hear music that way.

* * *

I did a few record dates as a sideman, but the music business was starting to change. Since the early '90s, due largely to the emergence of Wynton Marsalis as a major figure, both as a great trumpet player and as a symbol of the "Young, Gifted and Black" syndrome, the major corporate record labels had been trying to sell jazz. But instead of selling the music and its rich legacy of in-the-moment creativity, they decided it was easier to sell an image. They bought all the press money could buy, and started signing and recording a lot of very young musicians, most of them black, all of them under the age of twenty-five, and dressed them in very expensive suits. In fact, twenty-five appeared to be some kind of magic cut-off number. To be taken seriously, it seemed that you either had to be under the age of twenty-five, or have been dead twenty-five years. Some of these kids could play, but most were in their early or transitional stages of development, and were about as ready to make a major label record as I am to fly to Mars. Maybe not as ready! These records, made with huge budgets (for jazz) and produced for the most part by people with degrees in marketing rather than a knowledge of the music, were mostly terrible—they mostly didn't sell. When they didn't sell the expected number of units, the CDs were deleted from the

Robert Walker, Morton Street, New York, 2004.
Photo: © Peter Leitch.

catalog, returned to the company and actually physically destroyed, the plastic recycled. This was done so that these items would not take up space in the record stores that could be used for new releases. So much for continuity and back catalog. I called it "disposable diaper music."

A new mindset was beginning where music would be disposable, nonproprietary, and free, except for the few big names they could sell. A false economy was being created. The music began to be surrounded by a lot of peripheral parasitic wannabes—publicists, managers, radio promoters and the like—most of them incompetent. Jazz began to be referred to as an "industry." Why would you try to make an industry out of jazz? There's no real money there. Industries produce things that people really need, like air fresheners or cement blocks, or various kinds of widgets. The industry, that is to say the big record companies, started to subsidize their artists, covering travel costs, accommodations, etc. for tours, and even supplied funds to New York clubs to pay their big name artists. This was a really attractive proposition for promoters, presenters and educators, who previously had to cover these costs themselves. As this trend continued it became much more difficult for midlevel artists like myself to function without this kind of corporate sponsorship. You couldn't expect small independent labels like Reservoir or Criss Cross, essentially run on a shoestring and a love of the music, to come up with tens of thousands of dollars for tour support, artists' fees and advertising. It became a monopoly. And still, no one was making any real money. When the major label jazz bubble burst later and that money was no longer there, the promoters had become accustomed to it. Corporate America had taken a great art form and debased it, by turning it into a commodity. When the mass audience didn't buy it the hucksters folded their tents and moved on, looking for the next "big thing." And where was the jazz audience, anyway? It seemed to be both fragmenting and shrinking at the same time.

* * *

I became more and more interested in photography. My friend Walker, who was visiting New York frequently, working on a thirty-year Times Square project, was not about to let me be just a casual

147

hobbyist. He told me that to learn to see, I had to study the work of the masters, the way I had learned to play jazz before it became an academic study. He introduced me to the work of Henri Cartier-Bresson, Robert Frank, Garry Winogrand, Lee Friedlander, Callahan and Siskind and the Chicago school, and many others. I remembered the fantastic Andre Kertesz show I had seen years before in Toronto. Like many aspiring photographers I was thoroughly impressed with the great work of Cartier-Bresson, and then slammed in the face by Robert Frank's powerful masterpiece *The Americans*. Looking at it repeatedly, I saw that it was a work of great subtlety as well as power. Sort of like hearing Bird evolve into Trane and beyond. Winogrand and Friedlander were analogous to Joe Henderson and Wayne Shorter in jazz. They were wonderful individual voices in the '60s and '70s, continuing and advancing the tradition. New York was the photography capital of the world and there were always great exhibits on view. I had seen a large Walker Evans show at the Museum of Modern Art in the early '90s and was very impressed, particularly with his southern photographs.

In 1996 the Museum of Modern Art mounted a huge retrospective of the work of Roy DeCarava, which just knocked me out and made a lasting impression. Not only had DeCarava photographed many of my favorite musicians (he had been a friend of Coltrane's), but what was really impressive was that he was able to extract a fantastic range of subtle tones from a relatively dark image. Dark grays and rich blacks and almost blacks.

I certainly didn't want to become a commercial photographer, so I figured this was something I could learn by myself, taking my time. I was learning photography "by eye," in the same manner one learns music by ear. It was a matter of reconciling the eye with the ear. I brought the camera everywhere with me—to rehearsals, record dates, clubs, and concerts—photographing my musician colleagues and learning to use available light. With these informal portraits I was trying to capture the vortex, the swirl, and the intensity of the music. Using available light gave you a lot of rich shades of grey and black. I was picking the brains of the photographers whom I knew, and I started buying photography books, studying and analyzing the work of the great photographers, in much the same manner that

I had studied the work of great musicians on recordings. While in Toronto to do a gig, I ran into the photographer Paul Hoeffler, who I had met some years before. He seemed really interested in what I wanted to do, and asked me to send him some work. I did, and he responded with much sound criticism, and became a kind of mentor to me, both on a technical and on an artistic level. The photographers I knew and met during this period were generous with their time and information, and encouraging to me. They told me where to buy cheap film and supplies. I started renting time and space in one of the many illegal darkrooms that riddled the basements of Manhattan, which I discovered by word of mouth. I was attracted to the in-the-moment esthetic of shooting the passing scene on the street, rather than in posed or constructed studio photography. What I really wanted to photograph was the city that I loved.

I developed roll after roll after roll of bad pictures, and then once in a while I started to get a few good, fully realized images. Like in music, I was trying to get to the essence of what I saw or heard— evoke a feeling or a mood rather than trying to create a technically perfect photograph. I made a couple of trips to Quebec City, where I photographed the Quebec Bridge, and back to east end Montreal where I looked at what was left of the oil refineries, which had been closed down decades earlier.

I began to see similarities between the two arts. It's all about telling a story, either with music or with images. On a technical level, you could say that the bright white highlights in a photograph corresponded to the top end of the audio spectrum (the treble), and the dark shadows to the bass, with all the grays in between being analogous to the warm mid-range tones found in audio. Melody, rhythms and forms corresponded to angles, shapes and planes. Shooting pictures on the fly was like playing music in real time, and the darkroom processes were akin to the mixing and mastering processes in the recording studio. Or at least, that was one way of looking at it. I was seeing that the frame, that is the four edges that we put around a collection of information to make a photograph, was similar in concept to the form of a piece of music that a jazz musician uses, that empty shell with a harmonic structure that we fill with our improvisations. That empty vessel could be beautiful or merely

Maison de la culture Frontenac, Montreal, with my
photographs, Montreal, 1999.
Photograph: Billy Georgette.

functional. What counted was what we put, or didn't put, in it. On the
street, I was learning to look for juxtapositions, gestures, similarities
and opposing forms, and to clear the frame of unnecessary, super-
fluous information. Robert Walker was a stern teacher, and all this
took years to digest.

It took me quite a while to realize that the great masters of photography didn't just pick up the camera and go out and shoot a great
image every time. It was said that Cartier-Bresson might shoot fifty
rolls of film before lunch, and Robert Frank shot more than eight

hundred rolls to get the eighty-three images in *The Americans*. Garry Winogrand said that what makes a good photograph or makes the difference between a picture that is alive or dead is the contention of (or the tension between) form and content. A perfect balance of form and content is what Cartier-Bresson found so often, and all the other great photographers too, but especially Cartier-Bresson. Not just in the balance of the graphic elements, but also in the balance of the tones. Winogrand also said that photographing something or someone changes it into something else, something mysterious or unexplainable, just by the act of putting four edges around it. Therefore, you could make a good photograph of anything. Or not.

In street photography, we try to organize and capture a moment selected from a lot of rapidly moving visual information in the same way that a musical improviser negotiates the modulatory jumble that is a piece of music like "All the Things You Are" or "Giant Steps," all of which must take place in "real time," or in the moment. I learned very quickly how difficult it was to create any kind of pictorial order from the visual chaos and flux that was midtown Manhattan, especially in crowded and much travelled areas and streets such as Times Square or Fifth Avenue. It all had to be visualized and executed in a fraction of an instant. Like jazz improvisation, it was something that required a lot of knowledge, practice and experience in order to be effectively spontaneous. One has to take a multitude of photographs and play a multitude of choruses before any of it begins to make sense.

In 1998 my mother passed away in Montreal at the age of ninety-one. I had been visiting her in the nursing home, where she had been placed somewhere between the nonstop yelling ward and the vegetable cooler. She left us a little money, which helped. We worked with the old-time English Protestant funeral director who had also buried my father. Such was the state of English Montreal in the east end that he conducted his business from the back of the hearse, cash only, renting a funeral parlor by the hour when he needed it. There wasn't much left of English Protestant Montreal in the east end by then. The only constant is change, and back in New York, with the closings of Bradley's, Zinno and Visiones, there were fewer places

With Gary Bartz, Walker's, 1999.
Photographer unknown.

to work, although I continued to work various other kinds of gigs, sophisticated club dates and such, and I had my Sunday nights at Walker's. I also continued to travel to Canada and Europe, but I could see the economics of jazz changing—and not for the better.

We managed to get a few gigs on the road for the Bartz-Leitch duo, but even this was a tough sell. It was great music, however. We played St. Louis and Columbia, Missouri; did a week in Toronto at the Senator (a great club where I had played several times in the past); and a concert in Montreal, which was recorded for radio broadcast by the CBC. The concert was in a beautiful new cultural center in the east end of the city called the Maison de la culture Frontenac, and coincided with a group show of jazz photography in which I exhibited a dozen images. It was a great experience with a wonderful Montreal audience.

Playing duo every night with a master like Gary was very inspiring, and pushed me to another level musically. Gary liked to segue from one tune to another, instead of having breaks or spaces between the tunes. As we did more gigs together, the improvisation between the tunes became longer and longer, and more and more interesting. Gary also knew the verses to all the tunes. Now that I

Billy Higgins, Fresno CA, 1999.
Photo © Peter Leitch.

think about it, Gary and I never rehearsed. The music just evolved every night in a completely spontaneous, natural, organic way. Gary really knew how to "comp" behind my solos in the duo format. He would play rhythmic figures like a drummer while outlining the harmony, without ever getting in my way.

In 1999 an old friend, Jo Ann Collins, who was originally from St. Louis (John Hicks had introduced us at Bradley's years before), was working at the University of California at Fresno. She produced a jazz festival there, and arranged to have John and me flown out there to play. We were to play with a "local" rhythm section that turned out to be David Williams, a great bassist we had played with in New York, and on drums, Billy Higgins! He was one of the premier drummers in the history of the music. He had worked with everyone, and played on a lot of important Blue Note recording dates. To use an old cliché, I thought I'd died and gone to heaven (except that we didn't have to accompany God's girlfriend on vocals, as in the old joke). Working with Higgins was incredible. His drumming was very intense without being loud, he played with so much feeling and he swung like a motherfucker! It felt like we'd been playing together for years. A recording was made of this concert, but there were audio problems which had to be corrected. It would be more than ten years before I attempted to clean it up for release.

Among the other artists at this festival were Harold Land, who had always been one of my favorite tenor saxophonists (and a brilliant composer), and Jackie McLean, with Cedar Walton. I met Jackie and told him what an inspiration he had been to me all my life and thanked him for all the music. I can still listen to *Jackie's Bag*, with "Appointment in Ghana," "Blues Inn," and "Quadrangle," and feel the same excitement I felt when first hearing it over fifty years ago.

In June of that year we recorded *Blues on the Corner* (RSR CD 160) for Reservoir. I had been working with vocalist Kendra Shank and I liked her voice and her phrasing. We created a unique ensemble sound with her singing wordless syllables, blending with the guitar lines and Bobby Watson's alto saxophone. Kendra did a great job on this. In essence, she was singing trumpet parts. I was always cautious not to make the same record over and over like some artists did, and I was looking for a unique sound on each project. I tried to choose musicians and match them with material that would produce a unified musical or artistic statement over the course of a recording. I had been inspired by Donald Byrd as a recording bandleader and his great output from the late '50s thru the late '60s. They were all good records, many of them different in terms of instrumentation and concept, but all unified by a depth of thought, musicality and soul.

Renee Rosnes played piano on this date. I was becoming concerned that John Hicks, as much as I loved him, was beginning to define the sound of my records with his distinctive style and touch. I never really had to talk about the music with Renee. Like all the best pianists, she just knew what to play, and what not to play, without any discussion. Dwayne Burno, one of the great young bassists, and Billy Hart completed the rhythm section on bass and drums. It was great to play with Jabali again. We recorded a couple of trio pieces. This record received generally favorable reviews although some critics questioned the use of the human voice, completely missing the point. We played a CD release gig with a sextet with Kendra— two nights at a new club, The Jazz Standard, early in 2000.

I went to the North Sea Festival in the Netherlands that year, playing with Nick Brignola and the Rein De Graaff trio. I was contacted around this time to record one solo piece for a jazz guitar compilation CD for a Japanese Label. I would book the studio time, and they would pay for it. I recorded a solo version of "Alone Together" for them. I was paid and apparently the CD was released in Japan but I never received a copy. While I was in the studio I recorded several other solo pieces which I kept for myself. Gust Tsillis, who had been the manager/booker at Visiones, was the engineer at a studio in the Westbeth artists building in the Village.

With Kendra Shank and Bobby Watson, Avatar Studio, 1999.
The Blues on the Corner date.
Photographer unknown.

155

Back in New York I was spending more and more time wandering the streets with my camera, and a lot of time in the darkroom trying to learn to print. To make a good print you had to know what a good print looked like, and I kept on going to galleries and museums looking at great prints made by the masters. The techniques of printing were easy enough to learn, but like anything else worth doing, they required a lot of practice to do well. It was a slow process, and much of it was comprised of correcting errors I had made while exposing the film. Fortunately today's films give us enough latitude to do this. I was trying to learn it all at once. I would take prints that I made down to Walker's where Nick was the daytime bartender, and he would critique them and instruct me.

I began to suffer from major depression again in late 1999. The following year it got worse. I started to feel that there was no place for me in the music business, and my self-confidence faltered. I was beginning to question whether I could even play at all. On some level I knew I could play, and the musicians knew it, but sometimes it seemed that no one else did. I was always more interested in the pursuit of excellence than in the acquisition of wealth, but goddamn, I needed to make a living. I developed an aversion to going to jazz clubs and "hanging out." I have always tended towards the agoraphobic anyway, so this was easy. I stopped reading the jazz press and gradually withdrew from the scene. There were things about the music scene, particularly the business area of it, that had bothered me for a long time—the unspoken racism on both sides, the posturing, and the out and out jive. And there was the minstrelsy and what Glenn Gould had referred to as the "blood sport" aspect of performing.

Weeks would go by and I wouldn't leave the apartment, or even get dressed, except to do my Sunday night gig, or to go out and photograph on the street. I realized that getting dressed signified a commitment to the day, and a commitment to dealing with a world outside of that in my own head. I just wasn't always able to do it. A liver scare prompted me to stop drinking. A routine blood test told me that the levels of something or other were too high, and that was it. I haven't had a drink since. I was getting to the point anyway that when I drank too much, I would feel ill the next day and it would be a complete write-off. I just knew I had to keep on evolving and learning. I was reading a lot about the history of photography and the history of New York City, and looking at the works of French photographer Atget who was an influence on Walker Evans. I had always related to film noir, and I started to go out and photograph empty parking lots at night. My friend Dennis had also developed an interest in photography, and sometimes we would go out shooting together.

I had played a couple of gigs at Kavehaz, on Mercer Street in Soho. This place was a combination gallery/coffee house, with music at night. The gallery space was fairly large and well lit. One night I was playing there and happened to have some prints with me, pictures of musicians I had shot, which I showed to Michael, the owner. He offered me an exhibit. I was really not ready to do this: I was learning to print, and felt that the prints weren't very good. But this was New York, and a lot of things happen by chance in the city. I had to seize the opportunity, ready or not. I had to try to make some decent prints, and had to learn about hanging a show—mats and frames and editing and sequencing. Deciding the order in which a series of images will be seen—either in an exhibit or in a publication—is much like planning the sequence of tracks on a CD or LP. This was something I had always given a lot of thought to, although in the age of the iPod, and its concurrent or resultant diminution of the human attention span, it seems to be becoming a lost art. The exhibit was called "A View from the Bandstand," and consisted of images of musicians in action or in reflection on the bandstand or in the recording studio.

I hired John Hicks to play solo piano at the opening reception. The piano at Kavehaz was one of the worst in the entire city—a real dog—what we called a "piano shaped object." I warned John and told him I would understand if he didn't want to play it, especially solo. John just said, "I know that piano." He played straight through without taking a break, and he made that monstrosity sound like a nine-foot Steinway concert grand. A lot of people came to the opening, and I actually sold a few prints. I learned a lot from having this exhibit—about gallery lighting and how prints looked under it, about different ways of hanging a show, and hosting an opening reception. Mitchell Seidel, a photographer/writer that I knew, gave the show a good review in the *Newark Star Ledger*, comparing me to the great bassist/photographer Milt Hinton.

Jimmy Katz, one of New York's top jazz photographers, who had photographed me a few years before, came to the opening and was encouraging. He loaned me a Leica and a couple of lenses for two weeks. After this, I bought one and then another. This was the camera that all the great street photographers had used. The Leica was quiet compared to the Nikon single lens reflex camera I had been using—its auto focus mechanism sounded like a tractor. I needed to be more unobtrusive when photographing.

One night in Washington, DC, George Cables and I hit a curb while driving back to the hotel in my car from the gig at the One Step Down club. When we got back to New York I discovered that there was a lot of front end damage that would cost at least $1,500 to repair. We were lucky to get home. The car was almost fifteen years old, and I couldn't see spending that much money on a car that old

With Ray Drummond at the opening of my first photo exhibition
at the Kavehaz Gallery, New York, 1999.
Photographer unknown.

(not that I had the money anyway). I decided to get rid of it because it was old and getting expensive to maintain anyway, and I was sick of the New York City alternate side of the street parking routine. This was probably not a good idea, as a working musician needs a car. I worked even less after dumping the car, but I still had my Sunday night duo gig.

I had been looking at a lot of photographs by Walker Evans, and for several reasons in 2000 I decided I had to see the deep South—the region that produced jazz and the blues. I was realizing that many of our great modern musicians were either born in the south or had southern roots. The music really did come up the river from New Orleans. It sure didn't come down Interstate 95 from Boston! I wanted to see if and how these areas had or hadn't changed since the 1930s. I had dipped into parts of the South on tours, but I needed to see that physical and social landscape in detail with a more developed eye. My friend Dennis James had taken a job as principal bass with the National Arts Centre Orchestra in Ottawa, and he was ready for a vacation.

We bought comprehensive atlases showing all the back roads—the idea was to stay off the interstate highways. Those four- and six-lane highways quickly became a blur of black asphalt, white lines and green highway signs, with their universal language. As John Steinbeck once remarked, it was now possible to drive from "New York to California without seeing a single thing." In June of 2000 we took two weeks and flew to New Orleans, rented a car and drove up highway 61, checking out small towns and cities through Louisiana, Mississippi, and Missouri. Vicksburg, Natchez, Tunica, Memphis, Cape Girardeau, all the way to St. Louis. It rained a lot. Tourism is not the industry of choice in these places. South of Natchez we stopped in Woodville, Mississippi, the birthplace of Lester Young. I made a photograph of some men hanging out, sitting in front of a combination liquor store/garage. When I returned more than a year later, they were still there!

I shot thirty or forty rolls of film, but this trip showed me that I'd only begun to scratch the surface. We flew home from St. Louis. This was merely preliminary reconnaissance for future trips. I was

159

Woodville, Mississippi, 2000
Photo © Peter Leitch.

in search of the ghosts of Robert Johnson and Walker Evans. I saw that the deep South was one of the last areas resistant to the architectural and social homogenization that had taken place in the rest of the country. There were still small towns with downtowns. Part of the reason for this was the grinding poverty I observed. Some places had not changed since the time of Evans. The low-rise architecture with corrugated tin facades and Dutch stepped gabled storefronts from the 1920s remained. These communities were too poor even for the ubiquitous fast food chains like McDonald's or Burger King seen in other parts of the country.

Back home, I processed the film I had exposed and found I had a few good images. I put them aside, and continued to prowl the streets of Manhattan shooting pictures, trying to fight off the episodes of depression. Actually, I couldn't fight them. I just had to let the evil wash through me, knowing I might come out on the other side. My Anglican middle-class upbringing had no place for psychiatry. In that world it was considered to be something for rich people, intellectuals and Jewish people. In the culture of my 1950s boyhood there was no middle ground. You were either crazy or you weren't. If you were, they locked your ass up in Saint-Jean–de-Dieu.

My purist, almost puritanical approach to drugs (if it didn't come from God's own opium poppy or was a reasonable molecular facsimile, I didn't want to know about it) left me very suspicious of what I called the "psych industry" and its side-effect laden medications. Psychiatry is a product of western dualistic thought, and didn't seem to be a holistic approach to mental health, not to mention being a shill for the pharmaceutical industry. I felt I would rather deal with the ups and downs than be "leveled out" by these dangerous drugs, so I did not seek what is known as "professional help." I just could not put my faith in people who had to go to school for years in order to learn things that I had been able to figure out for myself on the street.

I had always had a tendency towards paranoia, which is one reason why I was always so concerned with "staying under the radar" in all aspects of my life. As I once told Rudy Van Gelder, when he accused me of photographing one of his microphone set-ups: "Being paranoid is like playing a musical instrument. To do it well, you have to practice it every day." (He cracked up!) I could have given all the money I spent learning photography to psychiatrists and it would have helped them more than they would have helped me.

My experiences with heroin earlier in my life had left me with a lingering fondness for narcotic painkillers. I had some dental and periodontal issues and a dentist and a periodontist provided me with prescriptions for oxycodone (Percodan or Percocet), and this seemed to help the periods of depression.

* * *

An acquaintance from New York, Michael Skaggs, who was a jazz fan and a photographer, had moved to Cincinnati and opened a photography gallery. He invited me to show my jazz photographs there, sharing the exhibit with a color photographer named Ann Segal. Michael actually drove my framed photographs from New York to Cincinnati and back again after the exhibit. I flew there for the opening. The work got a good review in the local press, but nothing sold.

In black and white silver-based photography I had finally found something even less lucrative and less relevant than playing jazz on the guitar. There was nothing happening for me in music. 2001 continued in much the same way. I had to mentally take inventory of what was happening to the jazz scene and me. I had a dozen CDs on the market, had played some major festivals, toured, showed up on time, looked good on stage, played dynamic music with great bands, and somehow had failed to build any kind of name recognition. People would come up to me at gigs and say: "Man, you play so great! How come I've never heard of you?" They were asking the wrong person. Damned if I knew. Perhaps they should have asked the executives of the bigger record companies, or the promoters, or the reviewers who never even bothered to come out to hear me. Yeah, go ask those nice folks at Blue Note records! Anyway, it wasn't working. To quote Raymond Chandler again: "You just had to get peed on by the right dogs." I could not get to that next level where there would be enough money to travel with a New York band, playing my own music. Sour grapes? Sure they're sour. Why wouldn't they be? I had been travelling as a single working with local rhythm sections. I played with some pretty good players, but it seemed there was never time to rehearse any original music, so you would end up playing the well-known standards over and over, or whatever the rhythm sections knew. And the money wasn't great.

Oh well, I was older, white, and a foreigner to boot. Not saleable qualities in the jazz world. It wasn't like the bottom dropped out of the jazz business, it was more like the middle was dropping out. There was plenty of bottom left—there were lots of musicians working for a hundred dollars a night or less. After giving fifty years of my life to this music, I just couldn't participate in the desperate bottom feeding that I was seeing. I needed to make some reasonable money. But I was definitely having a crisis of confidence. I was starting to believe that no one was interested in hearing what I was playing or writing. Sylvia had been functioning as my manager all these years, but not too successfully. She is actually a nice, honest person, and was unable to come up with that special combination of aggression, insensitivity and insincerity that the music business requires. Maybe I should have completely immersed myself in the pre-bebop repertoire, bought some plaid golf pants, a book of old vaudeville jokes, a cheap-looking hairpiece, only worked with white musicians, taken up drinking again, and never played anything more recent than "Back Home Again in Indiana." This is probably the only successful formula for an older white jazz guitarist in America.

I had another photo exhibit in 2000 at Kavehaz in Soho, this time of New York street photographs. There was another good review in the *Newark Star Ledger*. Someone from the Canadian Museum of Civilization came to the apartment and conducted a long video interview with me, and this is now archived at the museum in Ottawa.

Our West Village apartment faced south, with a good unobstructed view of lower Manhattan. One morning in September 2001, at about 9 a.m. my neighbors across the hall knocked on my door saying, "Look out your window!" I looked and saw a huge hole in the south tower of the World Trade Center billowing smoke, less than a mile away. My first thought was: "What a terrible accident." As I watched, another airplane flew into the second tower. This was no accident. I had an unobstructed view, being situated less than a mile from the towers. I sat rooted at the window all morning watching this horrific scene play out, and shot a couple of rolls of film which I developed and put away. Someday I'll look at them. People had done this in the name of God, and it confirmed all the thoughts and feelings I'd always had about religion. In spite of what Karl Marx had written, I guess the only effective "opiate of the people" is in fact opium or its derivatives. Some Muslim musicians I knew used to say, "Only Allah is perfect." But it turns out he's not perfect. People blow up airplanes or fly them into buildings in his name.

I began to have occasional panic attacks, when I would become dizzy or confused.

Shortly after this cataclysmic event Sylvia and I flew to New Orleans, rented a car and embarked on a second photographic exploration of the South. The country was in full paranoia mode: A Middle-Eastern-looking man in a pilot's uniform was removed from the flight at LaGuardia, and in the south we were followed everywhere and occasionally stopped by security people in white pickup trucks, and watched closely by state troopers and sheriffs.

Louisiana is a Roman Catholic state. It is divided into parishes rather than counties, and has a long history of corrupt government

163

reminiscent of Canada's province of Quebec. It is an incredible cultural and ethnic mix—a veritable melting pot—Spanish, French, Black, Native American, Cajun, Creole. A mix responsible for the creation of Jazz. We bought Cajun red bean, jambalaya and gumbo mixes made in Metarie, a suburb of New Orleans. We still order these goodies from them today.

We travelled south on Rte. 23 from New Orleans into the actual physical delta of the Mississippi River, a flat fan-shaped alluvial formation extending fifty or sixty miles south of the city. We drove as far south as the road went, until the Gulf of Mexico stretched before us. Port Sulphur, Jesuit Bend, Boras, houses on blocks, oil and gas rigs, shotgun shells, plywood, huge white water birds, seafood stands, religious shrines. We turned around and continued north on the west side of the river. A lot of refineries, gigantic mounds of coal, and at Hahnville the Holy Rosary cemetery, beautifully tended, with large crypts and huge statues, all in the shadow of a massive oil refinery: a wonderful accidental juxtaposition of ostentatious Roman Catholic iconography and the anonymous sculpture of industry. Again, reminiscent of Quebec. Christ on the cross with a rooster weather vane on top. Sugar cane and "Hallelujah Jesus" signs all along the roadside. The light was poor at the Holy Rosary cemetery that day. When I returned the following year to photograph on a good day, we were kicked out by security and cops before I could take one picture.

In a coffee shop in the mostly deserted downtown of Baton Rouge, the state capital, we heard Sarah Vaughan's original recording of Tadd Dameron's "If You Could see Me Now." We crossed the Mississippi River there and continued north on Highway 61 into Mississippi. At the state line the road surface immediately improved. All that oil and gas and heavy industry money in Louisiana, and the highways were like the surface of the moon.

Driving north, we headed for Yazoo City, Clarksdale and Oxford, stopping in small towns along the way. Clarksdale is in the heart of the mythic Delta region of Mississippi and had been an important railway town, one of the jumping-off places in the great migration north in the 1930s and '40s. It is the site of Robert Johnson's famous "Crossroads" (Hwys 61 and 49) and has an impressive blues museum. President Clinton was photographed there in

1999 in front of the shuttered New Roxy theater, as part of his tour of the poorest places in the country. If Clarksdale was poor, Tutwiler, about twenty miles to the south, was "po", beyond poor. It had been another railroad town, and was, according to legend, where W.C. Handy first heard the blues performed by a lone singer-guitarist on the railroad platform. It was also where Emmet Till's body was prepared for burial. (Till was a young black man who was murdered by white racists in Mississippi in 1955 for whistling at a white woman.) The trains no longer stop in Tutwiler.

Oxford, thirty miles to the northwest of Clarksdale, is a university town, the site of "Ole Miss," the University of Mississippi. It was the home of William Faulkner and has a good bookstore, Square Books, on Courthouse Square, with real cappuccino! Cartier-Bresson's portrait of Faulkner hangs on the wall. Milly Moorehead, at that time the owner of the Southside Gallery next door to the bookshop, directed us to the town of Taylor, about fifteen miles out of Oxford on a back road. It was just a crossroads junction with a post office, a few houses and a ramshackle restaurant called the Taylor Grocery. The hand-lettered sign outside proclaimed: "Eat or we both starve!" There we dined on the best, freshest catfish I had ever tasted. The BBQ was good too! We met a blues guitarist and scholar named Steve Cheeseborough, who gave us a copy of his book "Blues Travelling." We also met the mayor of Taylor, Jane Rule Burdine, who is a photographer as well. Then north on Highway 61 to Memphis, where we dropped off the car and boarded a flight home.

Upon returning home I played a couple of small festivals, Cape May, New Jersey, and Oswego, New York, with a sextet with alto and tenor saxophones, something I wished to do more of, but there just weren't any more gigs. Later that fall Gary Bartz and I had a short Canadian tour playing duo. I remember having a panic attack on the flight to Vancouver, and having to walk it off, up and down the aisle of the airplane. In that city someone had booked our gig on the same night as a Chick Corea concert. Brilliant booking. Leaving Vancouver, airport security singled out Gary and gave him a real going over—emptying his pockets and his saxophone case. I said, "I've never seen that before!" He replied, "If you were black, you'd see it all the time!" I had heard from several black musicians that Canadian customs, immigration and airport agents were among the most racist in the world. We played gigs in Edmonton and Calgary, then home.

In 2002 a small record company in Canada, DSM Records, wanted to release the CBC radio recording of the duet concert that Gary and I had done in Montreal back in 1999. It was great music, well recorded, with a very responsive audience, but the record company didn't want to pay us very much money. Gary named an astronomical figure, and I had to agree with him, and the record company just laughed at us, and that seemed to be the end of that. I shared an exhibit of jazz photographs with a painter named Sonia Lynn Sadler at the WBGO gallery in Newark, New Jersey. WBGO was the local jazz radio station—24 hours of jazz every day. The station had a fine, well-lighted gallery space.

Sylvia and I made another photographic field trip to the South in 2003. Since 9/11 I had been warned about flying with photographic film by several photographers who had had their film fogged by the increasingly powerful airport X-rays. You could ask them to hand inspect a few rolls, but when airport security sees forty or fifty rolls, they balk. I had the film shipped (ground) to New Orleans, where we began the trip. This time we headed east and north, checking out the gulf coast and the eastern part of Mississippi—Gulfport, Hattiesburg, Columbus, Aberdeen, and then west to Edwards and north to Clarksdale and the delta.

I certainly don't mean to romanticize the American South. The history is horrific—slavery, the KKK, lynchings, and the state of Mississippi even had a travelling electric chair to carry out executions in local county courthouses. And the vestiges of institutionalized racism remain—the Confederate flag was openly displayed, and in fact is part of the Mississippi state flag. Billy Robinson had told me many years earlier that the South had really won the Civil War, in that the U.S. government was controlled by southerners, no matter who was in office. Just 1960s rhetoric? Maybe not. I couldn't understand the South. At a gas station and convenience store near Tillatoba, Mississippi, there were three huge confederate flags on the wall for sale under which a black woman sat calmly drinking coffee. We didn't stay around there too long because there was a mean-looking sheriff checking us out.

In Edwards, Mississippi, another decayed former railroad town (Evans had photographed there in the thirties), a fucked-up black man drinking beer at eleven o'clock in the morning in front of an abandoned store told us: "They got all that cotton 'round here, all that money, it don't have to be like this. The train don't stop here anymore and we don't even got a bus station." The local bank manager, an older white lady, blamed forced integration by the federal government for the place's descent into a ghost town. She actually used the word "nigra." The new plantation owners are giant agribusinesses and multinational corporations, and nothing comes back to the community. In the past, even the old time local slave-owner had to build himself a nice house. Mississippi's state prison, the notorious Parchman Farm, was run as a forced labor cotton plantation until the 1970s, making millions of dollars for the state. I believe it was the only state penitentiary in the country that wasn't a money-losing operation. No photography was allowed there.

We did see and photograph the Dockery cotton plantation, still in operation, where the seminal bluesman Charley Patton had worked in the 1920s. When he began recording and playing gigs, he was fired from the plantation for not working hard enough. Recently a

Tilatoba, Mississippi, 2001.
Photo © Peter Leitch.

Jackson, Mississippi; 2001.
Photo: © Peter Leitch.

surviving member of the Dockery family said: "We just didn't know that these people were important."

A transcendental experience: driving on a deserted dirt road in search of a ghost town called Rodney, we turned the car radio to Mississippi public radio. What did we hear? Robert Johnson? Sonny Boy Williamson? Charley Patton? No! Beethoven's "Grosse Fugue." We pulled the car over and stopped, and for the next fifteen minutes anyway, all things were one. The perfect music for this beautiful sylvan setting, in spite of the history. Then it was back on the road with Bird, Brownie, and the blues.

Back in New Orleans we visited with the late, great jazz photographer Herman Leonard. A mutual acquaintance, Maxine Gordon (widow of Dexter), called him to say we were coming. He was very gracious, showing us fabulous prints over coffee. The only advice he had for me was: "Never let anyone else tell you how to make a photograph." We managed to get on the last flight out of New Orleans before the airport was closed down due to an approaching hurricane. A couple of years later, Herman Leonard's beautiful house was destroyed by Hurricane Katrina, along with many valuable prints. Fortunately his negatives had been stored elsewhere.

I had another thirty or forty rolls of film exposed. The Sunday night duo gig continued, but not much else was happening musically, although I continued to practice and stay in shape. I started to print and edit the photographs from the South, and a project began to come forth describing the physical, social and cultural landscape. I was learning about the statement a group of pictures could make, rather than a string of unrelated images, whether they were good or not. Images could be linked by little visual cues, as well as by their narrative content. The idea of sequencing these photographs was cinematic. I didn't realize it, but this was a first step towards filmmaking. I exhibited the first group of Southern photographs at Kavehaz in February of that year, and I sold a couple of prints. The deep South of America is such a huge subject, and I realized I would have to keep going back there and next would be Alabama. The name alone was frightening. I thought of the four little girls killed in the church bombing, and John Coltrane's deep and beautiful tribute.

Finally, after much prolonged negotiation with DSM records we agreed on a price, and *The Montreal Concert*, the duo CD with Gary Bartz, was released in 2003. It wasn't well distributed outside of Canada but it got some good reviews and the music was on the very highest level, inspired by the very responsive Montreal audience. It was the freest I had ever played on a recording. I felt like Gary had me playing way over my head. When I listen to this recording today, I still can't figure out what some of the things were that I played! The whole experience of playing duo with Gary was one of the high points of my musical life. Although we were using traditional structures (mostly), it was very free, pure, improvised music.

Mark Feldman and I began discussing another recording for Reservoir Music. This was to be a quintet with my old friend Jed Levy on tenor and flute, George Cables on piano, Dwayne Burno on bass, and Steve Johns on drums. I composed four new pieces for the date.

My friend Patricia Taylor, an artist I had met at Walker's, bought a broadcast quality digital video camera and began documenting some of the music there. The camera had an amazingly sensitive built-in microphone. We didn't know enough at that point to even turn off the air conditioner or try to eliminate other obtrusive background noises. It was a learning process, and I was intrigued by it. Film or video occupies real time and space in the same way music does, unlike painting or still photography. In spite of our inexperience we did get some good footage, although we didn't know at the time what we could do with it. She came over to the darkroom and shot some footage of me printing there, and also taped an interview of me at home.

The Reservoir recording took place in January of 2004 at Avatar Studio in Manhattan. The CD was called *Autobiography* (Reservoir RSR CD 160), and would be released in the fall. We recorded it in one day. One of the things I find noteworthy on this date is the blend of guitar and tenor saxophone that Jed and I achieved in the ensembles. We always had this great ability to phrase together and blend our tones, going back to our earliest days of playing together in New York. We were always striving for a "sound," not the sound of a tenor saxophone and a guitar, but just the two instruments creating one sound.

In addition to the four original compositions we recorded Charlie Parker's "Segment," and a version of Albert Ayler's "Ghosts." Free jazz? This piece is built on a simple three-chord pattern that is the basis of many traditional calypso and West Indian songs. We played it over a loose calypso rhythm.

Overall, I was happy with the record, though there were a couple of things I would have liked to have had time to take another crack at. I wrote the notes for the booklet. Patricia videotaped the rehearsal and the recording session.

In March I did a Canadian tour with a trio, funded by the touring office of the Canada Council for the Arts. Terry Clarke played drums and Neil Swainson was supposed to play bass, but George Shearing, who he had been working with, came up with some gigs and he had to cancel on my tour. We had a bit of a falling out over this, but fortunately Sean Smith was able to come from New York to do the week at the Top of the Senator in Toronto, a world class jazz room managed by Sybil Walker, where I had played several times in years past. We also made a studio recording for CBC radio's *Jazz Beat* program hosted by Katie Malloch.

Toronto in 2004 had changed for the better. The liquor laws had loosened up, there were some good restaurants and the Calvinist, puritanical strain seemed to be less evident. And it was still home to many of Canada's best musicians. Steve Wallace did the rest of the gigs on bass—Vancouver, Victoria, Edmonton and Winnipeg. I really enjoyed playing with him again. In Vancouver I rented a car and drove to Abbottsford to see my old friend Elda Guglielmin, who was recovering from surgery. It was a good visit, and it was the last time I was to see her.

I had always been interested in film on some level, and a couple of people had commented on a filmic quality in my photographs. I began watching a lot of film noir, revisiting the "B" movies of the 1940s and 50s as they became available on cheap DVDs, such as *The Shanghai Gesture, Detour, Kiss Me Deadly,* and *Out of the Past.* We decided to try to make a promotional documentary DVD in time for the CD release, using footage Pat had shot at the record date and the rehearsal, combining it with darkroom and interview footage. At that point we had no way to review the mini DV tape footage, so we transferred it all to VHS so we could look at it. We selected the best scenes, figured out a sequence and a narrative, and found someone to edit it. We produced a DVD called *Autobiography: The Making of a CD,* but no one seemed to know how to use it as a promotional tool. I think it was still too early on in the game for DVDs. Some people thought it was the CD itself. It was frustrating and time consuming not being able to edit the raw video footage ourselves.

Sylvia and I went to California in July to visit her parents who had just moved into a nursing home in Sacramento. We flew to Los Angeles, rented a car and stayed in a cheap motel near the airport for a week. I had been there to play a couple of times in the 90s but I really hadn't had time to look around on those trips. We didn't do

West Hollywood, Los Angeles, 2004.
Photograph © Peter Leitch.

any tourist things, although we did see the La Brea Tar Pits. I would have liked to see the L.A. storm drains, but didn't know where to find them. Anyway, they probably weren't accessible to tourists, post 9/11. The light was so different in California from that in the east. It was very bright and contrasty, even with all the smog. We mostly drove up and down Broadway from the airport to the old downtown area, the garment district, back and forth, taking pictures in what seemed to be a mostly Mexican neighborhood, with no real center to it.

The city is set in a dry basin pockmarked with over one hundred thousand swimming pools. Environmental damage to the surrounding areas has left the entire region susceptible to wildfires, flash floods and mudslides. Due to the ever present danger of earthquakes, before 1956 there was a height limit on buildings which was lifted after the introduction of new construction methods. Because of this there were very few buildings in the classical architectural styles, with the exception of the Los Angeles City Hall. The concept of the skyscraper had been unknown here, and the city had a decidedly low-rise look as it spread outward rather than grew upward. There were a few exceptions to the generally drab architecture, such as the art deco Oviatt building on Olive Street and Bullock's on Wilshire Boulevard.

Trying to conjure up the 1950s L.A. of Raymond Chandler's novels, Robert Frank's photographs, and films like Robert Aldrich's *Kiss Me Deadly* and Kubrik's *The Killing*, I searched for the old Bunker Hill neighborhood, but it had been razed in the 1960s and was now filled with tall, box-like office towers, although the little funicular railway seen in the movies was still there. We did see the Bradbury building at Broadway and Third. It was referred to as the Belfront building in Chandler's *The High Window*, and the interior was featured in the films *Dead On Arrival* and *Marlowe*, among others. This 1893 eight-story structure looked pretty nondescript from the outside, as did most of the city. Yeah, Raymond Chandler. He lulls you with a long series of adjectives or similes and then finishes you off with a rabbit punch.

Los Angeles had something of the feeling (or lack of it) of Toronto about it. There was some basic absence of spirit, or humor. There was "no *there* there," as Gertrude Stein had written about California. Was it merely coincidence that both Toronto and Los Angeles began as agricultural communities situated on large bodies of water, while Montreal and Manhattan were founded on commerce, on islands in important rivers leading to the interior? Unlike New York, no one walked anywhere in Los Angeles, except maybe the tourists. The natives seemed to spend all their time in cars, sitting on freeways, precluding the kind of random "on the street" interaction among strangers that happens in New York. Even the poorest Mexicans had cars.

It is a city with virtually no cultural history, other than the boorishness and unfettered greed of the motion picture industry; the perpetuation of a system of cheap (and often illegal or undocumented) immigrant labor; and the billy-club justice that was the legacy of the dust bowl Okies and Texans who came there in the 1930s, and whose offspring became law enforcement officers.

On the other hand, there is the great black musical legacy of South-Central L.A. The Central Avenue scene—Charles Mingus, Buddy Collete, Sonny Criss, Eric Dolphy, Hampton Hawes, Dexter Gordon, Harold Land, the list goes on and on. The Central Avenue scene was a hotbed of creativity and innovation which is often over-looked or forgotten in the annals of jazz history. The other side of the coin, so to speak. Until 1953 the musicians union in Los Angeles maintained separate black and white local offices. The white local controlled most of the lucrative recording work for film, radio and television. The phenomenon known as "west coast jazz"—a watered down, sanitized version of bebop in which the emphasis was more on arranging and composing than on soloists and improvisation, was created by alumni of the Herman and Kenton bands, and other traveling bands who had settled in L.A. in the early 1950s, and worked in the recording studios.

One day we drove up into the Hollywood Hills. Here the architecture became more interesting with bizarre zig-zag creations built into the sides of hills half on stilts, and gated mansions and estates with long winding sidewalks and driveways. Frank Lloyd Wright. Richard Neutra. These were wealthy neighborhoods with private police forces on patrol. It was more frightening than any ghetto. Well, I guess it was a ghetto of sorts.

We drove north on Route 1, the Pacific coast highway, as far as Carmel (Edward Weston country), a beautiful drive with breath-taking scenery. We visited the Weston Gallery in Carmel, but unfortu-nately the road to Point Lobos, where Weston had taken many of his famous photographs, was closed that day. Then it was east to Sacramento, the state capital, a very depressing town. Something about it reminded me of Ottawa with more homeless people, even if it was quite different visually. On the way back we visited Sylvia's cousins in Berkeley, and got a flight home from San Francisco.

Sylvia gave me a wonderful 60th birthday party at the apartment. Among many others John Hicks, Smitty Smith and Jed Levy and his family were there—didn't know I had so many friends!

When *Autobiography* was released in September we did a CD launch at Sweet Rhythm (formerly Sweet Basil) on Seventh Avenue South with the quintet. It was a poor turnout, although I feel we did our best to promote it, with little help from the club or the record company. It was also the evening of a televised presidential debate. Why would people waste their time listening to these lying, corrupt, racist assholes on television instead of going out to listen to music?

I was developing a fear of performing to just tables and chairs. People would sometimes ask me if a noisy room bothered me, and I would always reply that "there's nothing louder than an empty room." One needs that communication with the listener. I was practicing every day, maintaining my ability to play, and composing some new pieces. The Sunday nights at Walker's continued.

My depression also continued. I would occasionally have suicidal thoughts, but they were nothing serious as I couldn't find an efficient, painless way of doing it. Sometimes the bottom of the Hudson River looked inviting. The "up" phases were OK. I was able to channel them into creative, or at least useful pursuits: writing music, practicing, working on the computer, cooking and cleaning the apartment. It wasn't like I was out there mindlessly shoplifting, or up all night dropping things and yelling. There wasn't much sleep at these times though. I used to say, "I haven't had a good night's sleep since 1973!" Sylvia sure had to put up with a lot of bullshit from me. Nothing much happened for the rest of 2004. I was starting to feel

With Sylvia at Jezebel's Restaurant, New York, 2001.
Photo: Jo Ann Collins.

like a legend in my spare time and a rumor in my spare room. I was also beginning to feel what I can only describe as "disconnected from reality." All I could do was to try to keep believing in what I was doing.

I got to the point at which the only time I would turn on the telephone answering machine was when I was at home. Not that the telephone rang much anyway. I had always hated the sound of the telephone. More often than not it brought bad news, or at the very least something that would waste time or interfere with my thinking. If I was practicing, sometimes I might be thinking some measures ahead of what I was actually playing, and the telephone really shattered that particular thought process, and then it would be difficult to get it going again. One of the rudest things one can do is to commit an act which will cause a bell to ring in the home of a stranger.

In February of 2005 I worked a week at a new club called Dizzy's Club Coca-Cola. It was part of the new corporate jazz world, part of Jazz at Lincoln Center. I worked the after-hours set. Wynton Marsalis sat in with us one night for several tunes and sounded wonderful. He played a version of "Skylark" that was one of the most beautiful things I've ever heard. But even with all that hype, money and corporate sponsorship the gig didn't pay enough to hire a respectable trio. The more things change... I played duo with bassist Sean Smith, not being able to afford a drummer. My feelings about the music business were turning to disgust. I need to pay the musicians who work with me a reasonable amount of money. I can't be going around asking for favors, and I can't be *losing* money on a gig. It always seemed that the more money there was, the less likely it was that the people or organizations in charge would give it up for music or art. I think they had some idea that they could exploit one's "artistic integrity," whatever that is, and use it against the artist. Anyway, there was never enough money! When you do a gig for a government organization, they are always particularly cheap. Governments spend fortunes putting young men and women in uniforms and giving them guns and sending them all over the world to kill, but spending money to pay accomplished, experienced professional musicians? Forget it!

I continued to photograph on the street around the city, sometimes with a friend, sometimes alone, shooting at night and hanging out in empty parking lots. Perhaps the empty or unattended parking lot or garage at night is the contemporary urban equivalent of the medieval black forest where witches, goblins and trolls lurk.

I made a couple of trips to Coney Island to photograph with Dennis and his friend Tina, a photographer from Ottawa. I became fascinated with Lower Manhattan's financial district, which contained the oldest streets in the city, some of them going all the way back to the first Dutch settlement.

There was an area on the north side of the Brooklyn Bridge known as the "Brooklyn Banks." The Brooklyn Banks was a skateboard park along the north side of the bridge approach. There were fabulous three-story 19th century stone and brickwork arches over vaults built under the bridge itself, with bricked up or locked doors and windows. Some of the arched brick work reminded me of that in Vermeer's painting *The Little Street*. I could practically feel the 19th century seeping out between the bricks and the granite. I half expected to see Leo Gorcey and the East Side Kids appear out of the shadows. These vaults had originally been commercial warehouse spaces and then were used as storage by the city, and then abandoned and forgotten. Apparently in the early '80s homeless people had lived in them, and car thieves had operated a chop shop in one of them, bootlegging electricity for light and to power their tools. This activity was all long gone by the '90s, and all that remained was the original architecture. By the 2000s the park had become world famous in the sub-culture of skateboarding and dirt biking. In addition to the history and architecture, it was just a fabulous-looking place—all curves and angles and ups and downs and bumps. Not a true right angle in the place. The kids had built ramps and jumps, and sprayed everything with graffiti.

I was determined to document the area, and the skateboarders and dirt bikers who hung out there. I seriously considered acquiring a large format view camera to do this, and then rejected the idea on the grounds that I was too old; too old to carry the large camera and all the peripheral accessories such as film holders, a huge tripod etc. I stayed with the 35mm format, using the slowest film I could find for sharpness and resolution, and tried as best I could to avoid the converging verticals, sometimes tilting the easel when printing.

I was to regret this decision later, when the whole area was shut down by the city in 2010 and became inaccessible. Today I see kids skateboarding in the streets and on the sidewalks, alongside the tall chain link fences closing off the "Banks."

Since 9/11 it has become a little more difficult to photograph on the street. New York City is finally becoming a part of the United States. People taking photographs on the street are often questioned or harassed by police or security. One afternoon I was photographing the arches under the Brooklyn Bridge with the camera on a tripod, when I was approached by cops who wanted to know what I was doing. I was told that I was photographing a "sensitive area," and they would have to make a report and put me on file! I showed them my driver's license and they asked me a lot of stupid questions and filed a report. Goddamn! Were they kidding? A sensitive area? The Brooklyn Bridge is one of the most photographed icons in the world! Patricia surreptitiously captured this encounter on video.

The city's past and its mythology has never really stayed dead and now I began to study the history and architecture in earnest— Lower Manhattan in particular. New York was changing rapidly in the post 9/11 construction boom, but if you looked for it you could see the 19th century in the cracked masonry, pitted brick and the verdigris of oxidized copper. These were coded messages which, if you knew how to read them, indicated that something of import had happened here: something beyond the world of money—the world of ideas. I saw myself if not as a latter-day saint, then at least as a sort of latter-day Atget, although unlike the grand old Frenchman I had neither an outlet nor a market for these photographs.

In the meantime Patricia, who was beginning to have filmmaking aspirations, bought a video editing system. It was a freestanding unit which worked on computer principles. Neither of us had the slightest idea how to use it so we decided to make a short non-narrative experimental film as a way of learning the technology. We shot footage in the city at night, of a sidewalk evangelist in Times Square, and a man dancing with a life-size doll in the 42nd Street subway station. We shot in Lower Manhattan on the streets and in the "Banks," and from the twenty-second floor of my dentist's building. We just told security we were going to the dentist, and made straight

Arch #9, Brooklyn Bridge, (Brooklyn Banks) New York, 2005.
Photo © Peter Leitch.

for an open balcony that I had discovered while looking for a place to smoke. It gave us a wonderful view of the west side, especially at night.

We slowly figured out the editing process while making a short film called *Urban Fantasy.* We used original music from some of my recordings. I was learning to create a soundtrack, mixing and blending music with street sounds from the camera microphone, placing them on separate tracks. I learned to cut music precisely to fit scenes. Not that different from mixing an audio recording, except that we were coordinating sound with visuals. I had been influenced by William Klein's first film *Broadway by Light* and an underground German non-narrative film of the New York subways *Stations On the Elevated,*

Skateboarder, Brooklyn Banks, New York, 2006.
Photo: © Peter Leitch.

a minor masterpiece which used the music of Charles Mingus. We weren't interested in learning standard filmmaking formulae. Hollywood tries to make what is unreal seem real, and we were trying to make what is real seem unreal. None of my friends could understand or make any sense at all of the film. Patricia entered it in a small film festival at Long Island University in Brooklyn. Imagine our surprise when our little film was chosen to be screened!

There weren't many gigs, and I felt that I had no place in the music and especially in the music business. As John Hicks used to say: "If you're not appearing, you're disappearing." Though John and I weren't playing music together much, we remained friends. He would always come over at Christmas, and we would go to his place at Thanksgiving. In July 2005 Paul Hoeffler died. I had stayed in touch with him by telephone, and we would hang out when I was in Toronto. He had continued to advise and teach me. That August my old friend and mentor Billy Robinson passed away. He had been living in Ottawa, and we had not been in touch, but I often thought about how much I had learned from him, and what a monster player he was. A year of loss.

The digital revolution was rapidly taking over photography, but I still believed in the silver print as an actual object to be displayed, held, admired, criticized, or whatever, rather than a photograph as a collection of virtual information to be disseminated electronically and then forgotten. There is a certain depth, texture, tactility and plasticity, almost an explosive quality, to a good black and white silver print even if the ability of most people to distinguish such subtleties was becoming a thing of the past. In a digital print the inks lie clumped on the surface of the paper while in a traditional silver print the image actually becomes an organic part of the paper. It works for color, but from what I've seen I don't think digital or inkjet printing is there yet for black and white.

I continued photographing and working in the darkroom, print-ing, making mostly 11"x 14" and 16"x 20" prints. I was making better prints by now and had several series going which were beginning to show some degree of stylistic continuity. I had jazz musicians, the American South, New York on the street, New York at night and a lot of buildings, facades, graffiti and signage.

The Kavehas gallery had closed and in October of 2005 I had an exhibit of my jazz photographs, *A View From the Bandstand,* at the Living Room gallery at St. Peter's Lutheran church in Manhattan. This church was known as the Jazz Ministry and had a big, well-lit gallery space. It was a much larger space than I had previously shown in and hanging over forty photographs really required some thought. I couldn't just "eyeball" this one. Patricia showed me how to mathematically calculate the spaces between the pictures, making them even, and we had a lot of compliments about the exhibition and the way it was hung. I played at the opening, in trio with Sean Smith on bass, and Steve Johns on drums. Bob Walker continued to visit New York often. He came to the opening and even though he was a severe critic, he was starting to encourage me a little in my photographic endeavors. Pat shot some video at the opening.

Sylvia was not happy about my friendship with Patricia but to invert an old saw, you can pick your relatives but you can't choose your friends. Unfortunately when you invert old saws you risk exposing their teeth. Nevertheless hanging out and working with Patricia seemed to help me negotiate the mental and emotional "black holes" I was experiencing. I was encouraged and was becoming motivated to get dressed, shave, and actually leave my apartment. We would sit around in her Fulton Street apartment working on videos surrounded by paintings, photographs and art books. Her knowledge of the city and background in art were inspiring. She was encouraging me with my photography and music at a time when few others were. We would hit the streets of Lower Manhattan together, I with my Leica and she with her video camera. We went to museums and galleries and I was learning more about visual art. I had a very limited knowledge of painting and she had me taking a closer look at the impressionists and other European masters and introduced me to the Hudson River school—fantastic 19th century American landscape painters. I showed her the work of photographers such as Roy De Carava, Robert Frank, Cartier-Bresson and Garry Winogrand.

Sometimes we went to Central Park. Patricia was a landscape painter and had an affinity with the natural world. I was beginning to get glimpses of color and flowers and nature after a lifetime of being mired in steel, concrete and urban noir. I should have known better. She was an attractive woman in her fifties, a free spirit, not in a relationship, had been twice divorced, and was a woman of independent means. But at this point in time it worked. We were just friends and had a good creative working partnership. "A wise man may sit on an anthill....only the fool remains there."

The inevitable occurred. Patricia and I became lovers, giving in to a strong mutual attraction that we had both resisted for years. We convinced ourselves that it was OK because we were somehow "different"—we were artists living in the moment. But it wasn't OK, and it became an awfully long moment. I don't know what made me do this. I still loved Sylvia and was not unhappy in my marriage.

I had never been a woman chaser and I had not been unfaithful before. Being with Pat was like stepping off the edge of the earth into another dimension. I had never known anyone who lived their life so totally "day to day, moment to moment." In theory, on paper, this would seem to be a commendable thing, something we all try to do. In practice it was difficult. For example, living "in the moment" made her constantly late, for everything and anything.

When we were together the very air between us buzzed and crackled with an intense personal and sexual energy. I learned later that everyone who saw us together, even strangers on the street or in the subway noticed this. She saw herself as a muse in the classical sense of being an artist's muse. Needless to say I was flattered by this and I became totally infatuated and obsessed with her, photographing her incessantly out on the street, in cafes, in the city, and at home. She had become a colleague I respected and we worked very well together. There was no competition or jealousy. Her free-spirited thinking complimented my more methodical approach to art, and vice-versa.

I have always tried to conduct my life with a modicum of integrity and discretion. Believe it or not, I have never been a dishonest or duplicitous person and I was having a lot of guilt about this affair. One hears about Jewish or Catholic guilt, but Protestant guilt is underrated. I believe in free will, but I have learned from film noir that sometimes circumstances just conspire against you. As the character Al Roberts says in the film *Detour*: "Fate, or some mysterious force can put the finger on you or me for no good reason at all." I'm not trying to create excuses or justify what I did, but I am trying to figure out reasons for it or motivations behind it. Perhaps because I had been performing in public for many years I had become accustomed to attention and applause. Now that this was not happening on a regular basis—I was hardly working—I was missing this, and it needed a replacement in my psyche. Maybe it was the appeal of being around someone who had a connection, no matter how tenuous, to an older New York. Maybe it was some kind of unexplainable, irresistible physical chemistry, or even alchemy. Or all of the above. Sometimes you have to do what feels good, even if on another level you know it's totally wrong and you hurt other people in the process. At this point I think I was having difficulty distinguishing fantasy or fiction from reality.

Looking back on it I see that my behavior was a kind of sickness—an obsession—the behavior of an addictive personality.

I decided that I needed another record release. I was feeling confident enough in my playing to try a solo recording, which is all I could afford to finance myself anyway. In fact I couldn't even afford to do that. I worked out a deal with Patricia. I would compose and record a piece of music to accompany a slide show of paintings on her website, and she would pay for the recording studio time. She had recently had a financial windfall due to the sale of some inherited property. I began practicing, choosing material and preparing, and in March I did the recording in one day at Eastside Sound on the Lower East side. Patricia shot a lot of video at the session, some of which we used later. I decided to record the guitar on five separate tracks with two microphones on the acoustic guitar, one on the amplifier, a room mic, and a direct line from the amp. I would mix these tracks later, producing a combination of acoustic and amplified sound. I wasn't totally satisfied with everything I did that day, so I returned to the studio and re-did a couple of things. The mixing really turned into a can of worms, or as Mark Feldman would have called it, a "science project." All those tracks probably weren't necessary but it was a good learning experience. I finally got it mixed, and took it to Allan Tucker at Foothill Digital to be mastered. "Tuck" did a fantastic job, greatly improving the sound of the finished product. I had not been happy with the final mix, but I couldn't afford any more studio time to remix.

I see a recording of music as being analogous to a book of reproductions of visual art—paintings or photographs. Attending a concert is like going to a gallery or museum and seeing the actual painting, sculpture, or print. A live performance of music and an exhibition of art share a certain temporal limitation: in the gallery, concert hall or nightclub, the work exists only while we are viewing or listening to it. Each situation presents for the artist/listener/viewer its own set of compromises and trade-offs. In the case of live music, the sounds are diffused into the air, never to be recaptured. When we perform live we have an interaction, a feedback with the audience, a give-and-take of energy. In the spirit of this valuable intangible we are more inclined to take chances, and be somewhat less concerned with so-called "mistakes."

In the recording studio there are different concerns. Music becomes product, and we try to make it as perfect as possible. Anyone can take home a book or a recording, and the work is preserved for all time, to check out at our own leisure. This, along with the lack of audience interaction, and the constant budget-driven fight with the clock, can be somewhat inhibiting. However, there are advantages: for example, we can control the sound of the instruments to a much greater degree, we can correct mistakes, edit and splice together different takes, and if we are still not happy with the performance, we can just do it over. (I should mention that the kind of recording I'm talking about here is the documenting of music performed in real time, and not the kind of multilayered pop production in which instruments are recorded separately and one track alone could be tinkered with for months.)

There are several major concerns in making a solo recording. We have to control the basic elements—that is, create an interesting melodic line while maintaining (and conveying) rhythmic integrity, harmonic structure and emotional depth. We have to make sure the recording contains a minimum of flawed action—you know—mistakes. All of which should take place, ideally, in that almost zen-like state of non-thinking when musician, instrument and music become one. It is akin to Cartier-Bresson's decisive moment, but stretched over time, producing a work where all these elements are integrated into an organic whole. We try to find the essence, the song beyond the ego, beyond the instrument, of what the music has to say and the ways in which it marks and divides that particular chunk of chronological time that it occupies. The musician's medium is actually the space, or silence that surrounds the music rather than the wood, metal or wires of an instrument.

I came up with a basic design for a cover using a self-portrait I had taken of myself reflected in a store window on Amsterdam Avenue. The studio at the advertising agency where Sylvia works did the art direction, and I wrote the notes for the booklet. The solo CD would be called *Self Portrait*.

Our housing complex converted from rental to co-op. The politicians had decided to make our buildings a showcase for affordable housing, and we were able to buy our apartment for a ridiculously low "insider" price. After a twelve-year period we would be able to sell it for market value. I didn't particularly believe in the concept of owning property, as I had always been a renter. We had always believed in the idea of being ready to cut and run if necessary. But I could see that this was a fantastic opportunity, and that in Mayor Bloomberg's New York renters would become the new pariahs. The middle class was being eliminated. Just by pure luck, by being in the right place at the right time, we owned a two-bedroom apartment in the West Village for a fraction of the market value.

In May of 2006 John Hicks died. It was a profound shock although we had known that he had not been well for a couple of years. He had come to Walker's two days before he passed, and looked terrible. We went to the funeral and the viewing, and I played, along with many other musicians, at the big memorial service at St. Peter's Church. Some people had been critical of John's drinking, some of them quite severely self-righteous about it. As he would have said: "Fuck those motherfuckers!" John did what he had to do. In the twenty plus years we worked together and were friends, I can think of only two instances when he was really drunk on the gig. And on one of those occasions he proceeded to drink himself sober, and play his ass off. He never "phoned it in," and always gave 200%, drunk, high or sober. John used to say: "Nobody said it would be easy ... and nobody was right!" I still think about him every day.

Self Portrait was released in early 2007 on my long dormant Jazz House label. Mark Feldman helped us get a distributor. In April I had an exhibit of the southern photographs at the WBGO gallery in Newark, New Jersey. The show was called *Mississippi and the South*. I played at the opening reception with Dwayne Burno on bass and Steve Johns on drums, and spoke a little about the pictures. The people who attended the opening were mostly black, so maybe it was interesting for them to see the American South from the perspective of a white foreigner. We shot some video of the opening. I was planning another trip to photograph in the South, and Dorthaan Kirk, the special events director of WBGO (and Rashaan Roland Kirk's

John Hicks, Sweet Basil, NY, 1999.
Photo © Peter Leitch.

widow), told me: "Be careful down there, You're a northerner, and they don't like *you* anymore than they like us in that part of the world." By "us" she meant black people. And I'm *really* a northerner, more than they would know.

I have always liked to "just get in the car and drive." Anywhere. Dennis James and I rented a car and left for Alabama, driving through New Jersey, Pennsylvania, Maryland, Virginia, and Tennessee. In Bluefield, a town which straddled the Virginia/West Virginia state line, we stayed overnight in a cheap motel with beaverboard walls. Didn't get much sleep. An out-of-it woman was banging on all the doors and yelling all night, looking for her boyfriend: "Billy Bob,

I know you're in there!" And some kind of car-moving activity with flatbed tow trucks was going on in the parking lot at 3 a.m., accompanied by a loud clanging and scraping of metal, and a lot of shouting. Hillbillies on methamphetamine! We were glad to see that morning sun and get out of there.

We moved through Tennessee on the interstate highway (to save time), with a detour to Johnson City. Another dead, empty downtown. Boarded-up buildings and nothing but secondhand clothing and furniture stores. The new downtowns or community centers in America were the junctions of local roads with the larger highways, away from what used to be the town—a collection of ubiquitous fast food joints, used car and truck lots, chain motels, and heavy equipment dealerships. Everyone drove, no one walked anywhere anymore. Back on the interstate, I had never thought I would be happy to see a Starbucks franchise but there it was! Most coffee is awful in the South.

We stopped in Moundville and Demopolis in Hale County, Alabama, two of the towns Evans had photographed in the thirties. They didn't seem to have changed that much in the ensuing seventy years. Outside of Mobile we decided to get off the interstate and take another road into town. We stopped at a traffic light on the outskirts and were approached by old, frog-faced crackers wearing Shriner's caps, collecting money for something or other. The conversation:

"Where you boys headed?"
"Into Mobile."
"Y'all better get back on the highway. This road'll take you right through niggertown."

The light changed and we took off. Could this be America in 2007? Dennis, who is biracial but very light-skinned, asked me: "Did I really hear that?" We stayed on that road into downtown Mobile.

From Mobile we headed west towards New Orleans. All along the gulf coast we saw a lot of evidence of the damage hurricane Katrina had done two years before. Main highway bridges were still down, buildings turned to rubble, boats strangely beached on dry land, signs of poverty. We did find some delicious barbecue at a gas station outside of Biloxi. They sure know what to do with a pig down there in the South. There's something good to be said for a food forbidden by two of the world's major religions.

Post-Katrina New Orleans looked terrible. Filthy streets, broken lamp posts, and shuttered businesses. Tourism, the main industry, had fallen off. Some of the good restaurants had closed, although the cheap bars still seemed to be doing well.

We kept heading west through southern Louisiana, ending up in Port Arthur, Texas, an oil refinery town where the worst features of America had drained down and concentrated. Not too interesting. On the way back to New Orleans we drove through Cajun country, stopping in Morgan City and Lafayette, Louisiana, where we had wonderful crawfish etoufée from a street vendor, and saw actual vultures parading on one of the main streets. We dropped off the car at the airport in New Orleans and got a flight home.

I was always glad to be back home in New York. I processed the film and printed more pictures. Pat and I continued trying to make short films or videos. As a filmmaking exercise she decided to make a documentary about me, my music and photography and my relationship with New York City. We gathered up and looked at all the footage she had shot over the last couple of years and selected scenes from interviews, performances, gallery openings, and street footage, and started to piece them together. As an establishing scene we used shots of the west side taken from the 22nd floor of my dentist's building, a pan with a pullback from the Hotel New Yorker's sign in the background, and added a voiceover. I found some video footage taken at Bradley's in 1996 with John and Ray and we used some of this. I learned how to mix music, voiceovers, and ambient sound to create a soundtrack. We came up with a twenty-five-minute documentary called "The Artist and the City." I thought it could be useful as a promotional device, if I could figure out what I had to promote, and who to promote it to.

In the meantime, we started to work on another experimental non-narrative video about New York. I had continued to compose music during this period, and I had come up with several interesting new pieces, but I felt these videos needed something other than bebop, or post-bop. I was thinking of scaling the music down harmonically, looking for something more minimal.

I borrowed a Korg portable digital mini studio from Chad Coe, a former student of mine, and started experimenting. I worked from the low open E string, just trying to avoid the bebop harmonic system, coming up with various fragments of dissonance and blues, three-chord shuffles, one- or two-chord vamps, montunos (repeated one or two chord "vamps", associated with Latin music), combining them, sometimes overdubbing, fitting them to the different scenes. If you were going to limit music to three or four simple chords, as pop music did, you might as well limit it to one chord and see what you could come up with. The Korg was a tough learning curve for me, but somehow I managed to make it work. Patricia was spurring me on to come up with original music for these videos. On a couple of the bluesier things, I overdubbed a track with a slide. Through the technology known as modeling I was able to radically change the sound of my instrument, making my hollow-body archtop jazz guitar sound like a Fender Telecaster with distortion, for example. I also took advantage of the built-in drum samples on a couple of pieces.

I had always avoided the use of electronic effects, although I did use fuzz boxes, phase shifters and pedals years ago in the course of doing studio work. To me, in a lot of cases these effects took away one's individual voice and personality. Listening to guitarists like Pat Metheny or Mike Stern, for example, I thought "If you are going to use that much digital reverb or delay you might just as well have a lobotomy!" The digital effects, especially the delay, seemed to obscure the attack of the note, which somehow impeded the forward motion of the music. In the words of Duke Ellington, "It don't mean a thing..." However, I could see using this sort of thing in a non-jazz context to bring some other colors to the music. None of the music I was putting together for these short films sounded anything like the kind of music I was known for, but it seemed to work with the visuals. Our short film *Urban Fantasy* was screened at another independent festival, The Big Apple Film Festival, at the Tribeca Cinema.

* * *

I was starting to take oxycodone more often, and it helped to relieve the stress caused by my affair. It takes the edge off the day, as it were. I have discussed with my dentist the possibility of producing an oxycodone-based toothpaste. We could call it Percodent. It would be available by prescription only, and would guarantee him a lot of repeat business, if not a lot of jail time.

I was getting a fairly regular prescription, and friends were mailing me pills from all over the continent, from as far away as Vancouver. A friend had a lot of Oxycontin left over after hip replacement surgery. Also, there were "222s." These are a combination of aspirin and codeine which is sold over the counter in Canada. You cannot buy codeine or any form of opiate over the counter in any amount in the United States. I attended the International Association of Jazz Educators' annual conference that year (2008) in Toronto, where I did a jazz guitar workshop. When I went to the pharmacy to buy 222s, the woman behind the counter remarked, "I wonder what's going on? I must have sold twenty bottles of these in the last couple of days." I didn't tell her that the jazz conference was in town, and the American visitors were stocking up. No one from up north visited me in New York without bringing me one or two bottles. Of course these drugs had a hook attached to them, a hook which had to be very carefully managed. Mostly I managed it, but the problem is that sometimes we don't want to manage it.

Over the years I would receive telephone calls from the late, legendary Canadian photographer John Max. He was a jazz fan and seemed to know my music and was a friend of Bob Walker's. He had seen some of my photographs at the group show in Montreal in 1999, and offered to trade me one of his prints for a print of my portrait of Bertha Hope. We traded prints, with Bob actually doing the transaction. John Max and I never actually met, but he was always very encouraging to me when he phoned and he caught me at some very depressed moments. Bob must have kept him informed as to what I was doing.

Patricia and I were bothered about the limited time we had to spend together and I was becoming increasingly stressed by the double life I was leading. We just hadn't thought it through. We kept on working with video and music, and finished a piece called "City in Balance," about different facets of New York from dawn to dusk, using some of the new music I was composing. This included footage shot all over the city, including Central Park. This segment used music that I later developed into a kind of "walking ballad" called "In Central Park," which I hope to record someday. We shot footage of Lower Manhattan at night and discovered some tango dancers under the Brooklyn Bridge. Using this as a beginning, we put together a short film called *Tango Noir* with more original music. These videos can now be seen on YouTube.

Self Portrait had gotten some really good reviews, but it certainly wasn't a bestseller. We're still waiting for it to go porcelain. The record business had changed drastically. Retail stores and distributors were going out of business, and everyone was burning copies of CDs for their friends, in spite of built-in serial copy management software. In a small market like jazz, even burning individual copies hurts everyone—the artists, the distribution systems, the record companies, and the stores.

I made a little money teaching and had a few students. Every now and then a visiting European guitarist would call me for a lesson. Several of them arrived with transcriptions of my recorded solos that they had made and learned to play. This was very flattering. At least someone was out there listening. I really wasn't interested in teaching which scales to use over a II-V-I progression or how to voice a G13b9. Any Berklee College of Music graduate will teach you that stuff for $20 an hour. I was more interested in teaching the esthetics of jazz—the rhythmic aspects, phrasing and articulation, vocabulary and its use in different contexts, the integrity of the line, and how it related to and interacted with the rhythm section—the kind of things you learn on the bandstand and that jazz academia didn't seem to teach. If you are serious about this music you have to see it as a calling, not a career. You can't expect to play this music and live the American Dream. One of the first things I tell my students is "Keep a low overhead!" This is the music of the unemployed. I don't have too many students.

We began reviewing the footage shot at Walker's, and found some good music. Some of it had audio flaws like too much background noise and had to be rejected, but we found enough useable performances to think about making a DVD. We shot some night time footage of the exterior of the club and the street corner—handheld, cinema verité style—for an opening and closing, to bracket the music, and Patricia did an introductory voice-over. After much editing, we had a DVD! We sent out some promotional copies and it actually got a couple of good reviews, and we sold a few at Walker's.

A photographer friend, Michael Putnam, had put me in touch with the May Gallery at Webster University in St. Louis, and they wanted to do an exhibition of my photographs. I had come up with the concept of "New York to New Orleans," for an exhibit. This would incorporate images of New York and those from the South, contrasting the city's verticality and busy crowded streets with the flat, deserted landscape and low-rise architecture of the South. The visual concept also had a musical parallel, with jazz coming from New Orleans up the river to St. Louis and Chicago, and then to New York, becoming more sophisticated and more complex all along the way.

I was feeling that I needed to get out of town, so I discussed making another trip South with my friend and former guitar student Chad Coe. Chad was originally from Mississippi, and also had an interest in photography. We decided to go in November. I needed to meet with people at Webster University in St. Louis anyway. I got a cheap flight to St. Louis where I rented a car and stayed with my old friend Jo Ann Collins, who was back in her home town working in real estate after her university job in California had been eliminated. I had my film shipped to her place.

I had a good meeting with the people at Webster University and my exhibit was scheduled for the following February. The gallery was large and well lit. The university would pay the cost of shipping the exhibit from New York to St. Louis and back. I would ship matted prints, not framed, and the gallery would use sheets of plexiglass over the matted prints for the show. These were much easier to ship than framed prints. I would play a short concert at the gallery the day after the opening reception. For all this they paid me very well in addition to airfare and a couple of nights in a hotel. Exploring St. Louis I discovered an old industrial area near the Mississippi River that was pretty much abandoned, which I photographed, and Jo Ann drove me around the city and across the Mississippi to East St. Louis at night.

After several days I left St. Louis and drove to Memphis, a pleasant four or five-hour drive, where I met Chad and we went on to Mississippi. We mostly stayed in a cheap motel on the outskirts of Clarksdale, and explored the small towns of the Delta region from there: Lambert. Marks. Vance. Tutwiler. Sumner. Lula. Holly Springs. Chad knew all the back roads. We were in Clarksdale on Thanksgiving Day, and the only place open for dinner was McDonald's. You could barely call it food, and it wasn't even fast. But I was feeling better just from the act of driving on those good roads, and being away from my "situation" in New York.

I rarely talked or interacted with people who I photographed, either in the south or in New York, preferring to be like "The Phantom." Just take the picture and disappear. I rarely thought about music on these trips, except in terms of the historical context of the area, and I always found a few interesting CDs at the Delta Blues Museum in Clarksdale. Chad had brought some great Trane, Sonny Rollins and Clifford Brown discs for the car, and I had Glenn Gould playing Bach's French Suites. I was becoming more aware that I still had merely scratched the surface of this part of the country, photographically speaking, and that I would have to keep coming back. We drove back to Memphis, shipped my exposed film home, dropped off the car and flew back to New York. This was getting to be a routine. Chad had brought a small video camera and shot some footage of me photographing. We later used some of this footage with some original music to make a short video called "4:56 in the Mississippi Delta."

I now had to edit down a lot of photographs into a sequence that would fit both the New York to New Orleans concept and the gallery space. Since I was continuing to photograph and adding new material all the time, it was all easier said than done. Bob Walker helped me with this on one of his visits to New York. We came up with forty images for the gallery in St. Louis.

I was not neglecting music during all of this. I was practicing, doing daily maintenance and trying to write new music. The short film *Tango Noir* that Patricia and I had made was shown at the Big Apple Film Festival at the Tribeca Cinema. I wasn't really expecting anything to happen with these films, but I enjoyed the learning process and the creative collaboration. Now, when I see a film, I pay attention to the musical score and how it works (or doesn't) with the visuals; and the sequencing of scenes and the kind of cuts or transitions that were used. And it forced me into some new musical thinking.

After all the talk of being a free spirit and living in the moment and of a non-grasping, non-possessive love, Patricia was feeling that she wanted this to be a more permanent and more exclusive relationship and that she wanted us to spend more time together. I knew this could never happen and I had told her so. We were starting to have arguments, one of which culminated in me being locked out on the balcony of her fifteenth floor apartment. I thought I would have to leave the quick way. Never try to argue with a literalist. We had tried to end our romantic relationship several times and continue collaborating as friends and colleagues, but this didn't work. The attraction was just too strong. It had become an obsession. An addiction. The situation was becoming untenable, the guilt was tearing me up and I had to find a way to extricate myself.

Patricia was involved with environmental, political and social activism, and many of her friends and acquaintances were activists involved with some movement or other. She spent a lot of time video-taping meetings and protests. While on one level I agreed in principle with these worthy causes—the closing of nuclear plants, sustainability, organic farming, clean renewable energy, global warming concern—I saw that a number of these activists were ego-driven, and poorly informed. Even on a local level these various small factions were unable to work together or even communicate with each other, let alone present a united front. This has always been a problem with the left. The only way to fight big money is with bigger money, and you know that's not going to happen. There's no percentage in dressing up in a hazmat suit and trying to deliver a letter to the president of an oil company.

As I was printing, editing and putting together the exhibit for St. Louis a photographer acquaintance, Dwight Primiano, suggested

I submit some work to the Soho Photo gallery in New York. At that time Dwight and I worked in the basement of a building on East Eighteenth Street, where our darkrooms were located. The Soho Photo Gallery was a cooperative gallery on White Street in TriBeCa, which in addition to showing the members' own work, featured guest photographers once a month. I showed them the "New York to New Orleans" photographs, and was given an exhibition as a guest photographer for the month of July.

I flew to St. Louis in February for the opening at Webster University. The reception and the little concert were well attended and the exhibit was enthusiastically received. I met with the photography students and did a Q&A with them. Two of our videos were shown continuously at the exhibit. I stayed at a hotel for two nights, and a couple more days at Jo Ann's (more shooting in St. Louis) then home. After the show, the university shipped the prints back to me, at their expense!

In the meantime, the Tribeca Performing Arts Center, as part of their Lost Jazz Shrines series, was presenting a three-night tribute to Bradley's in June and I was contracted to put together one of the nights. In addition to playing some great music in a beautiful venue, this gig allowed me to reunite with some old friends and colleagues—Bobby Watson, who had moved to Kansas City to accept a professorship at the university there, my old friend the pianist George Cables, Dwayne Burno on bass and guitarist Peter Bernstein. And it paid really well! I was getting busy, and receiving a couple of much needed infusions of cash!

The Soho Photo Gallery exhibition went up for the month of July. The opening reception was well attended and the show looked really good. By the end of the run I actually sold a couple of prints! We videotaped the installation and created a promotional DVD, "New York to New Orleans."

Jo Ann Collins had taken some of my work to an arts conference in St. Louis where she had met Samantha Musil, the director of a gallery at Mississippi State University in Starkville, MS. Samantha wanted to do an exhibit of my Southern images, especially those of Mississippi. I had hundreds of photographs and I put together a sequence of about forty images under the title A Landscape for the

Blues. This was scheduled for January through March of 2010. She needed framed prints for the gallery, and the only economical way to get them there was to drive them to Mississippi from New York.

It is interesting to consider how a vague notion evolves or coalesces into a definite idea. I had been thinking that perhaps a soundtrack of blues-informed original music would complement the photographs. I had already put together something I called "Mississippi Collage" on the Korg mini studio. It certainly wasn't pure Delta blues but it was evocative of the blues, had the flavor with some modernist tinges. Someone described one of the pieces as "John Lee Hooker meets Bartok!" I took this and some of the guitar pieces I had created for video soundtracks and added some overdubs with a slide and combined it all. Chad helped me create the transitions on his computer, and we came up with a seventeen minute "Soundtrack for the South." I mentioned it to Samantha and she loved the idea and assured me that it could be played in the gallery on a loop repeatedly during the exhibition. The university would pay all the expenses, and give me a sizable honorarium. I realized that in the academic world there was a lot more money for the visual arts than there was for jazz.

This was a very creative time. I began carrying a mini-disc recorder into the street and the subway, recording traffic sounds, sirens, and bits of conversation. The fidelity was not great, but it didn't have to be. In fact, the more low-fi the better. I had the idea that these sounds could be faded in and out of music, creating audio collages. These recordings could be played in a gallery to accompany an exhibit of photographs. I also took the recorder on a southern trip, and recorded some black southern fire-and-brimstone preachers from the car radio for use in a Southern audio collage. Projects for the future.

I was also thinking about a photography book of the New York to New Orleans project. I decided to construct a maquette, or "dummy" book of the project. I printed a lot of 5" X 7" JPEG images from my computer with my cheap printer, which did not even give a true black and white, and pasted them onto sheets of cardboard stock. I started to create a sequence, which changed constantly. Bob Walker helped with this. Someone at WBGO had a connection at the University Press of Mississippi. I spoke with them, and they seemed interested in the idea and we agreed to meet in Jackson, Mississippi, when I brought the photographs to Starkville for the exhibition at the beginning of January, 2010.

Sylvia and I had made arrangements with Craig McGill and his wife Wendy, old friends from Edmonton, to stay in our apartment while we were away. We left on December 29, and by the afternoon of the 31st we had reached Tuscaloosa, Alabama. There we received an email. Craig McGill had fallen early that morning on Grove Street in the Village in front of Arthur's Tavern where Bird used to sit in with a borrowed horn in the last years of his life. Craig had hit his head on the cobblestones, suffered a brain injury and died. There was nothing we could do. It was New Year's Eve and we were in Alabama with a car packed with forty framed photographs which had to be delivered to Starkville, MS, in two days, and an appointment with a publisher in Jackson later that week.

We called our next door neighbors at home and made arrangements with them to feed our cat and continued on. On New Year's Day we drove through Hale County, Alabama, stopping to photograph in Greensboro, Moundville and Demopolis. No sign of life in these towns except for the sound of gunfire in the distance. Celebrating the New Year? On to Starkville. The campus was large and beautifully landscaped, with modern state-of-the art buildings. Right down the road from the hotel was Petty's, a barbecue shack of the first order. Catfish and slow-cooked pork. Barbecue beans. We took it all back to the hotel and ate it in the breakfast area.

The gallery at the university was large and modern in design and concept. We hung the exhibit, and the soundtrack was played in the gallery on a loop, controlled from a sound booth somewhere else in the building. It sounded great, and complemented the images effectively. Samantha had sent me specifications and the dimensions of the gallery, so there were no surprises. On to Jackson with the book.

I had a good meeting with the editor at the University Press of Mississippi. He seemed to like the concept and spent a lot of time going over the photographs, which I had brought JPEGs of on a flash drive, along with the "dummy" book. But the project had to go to committee, and in the end it was rejected as not having enough sales potential. It seemed just like the record business. Oh well, my first experience with book publishing. We hauled ass back to New York in two days. I returned to Starkville two weeks later for the opening reception of the exhibit, this time flying to Jackson and renting a car. I was certainly spending a lot of time in Mississippi. I was to drive back again at the end of the exhibit, to collect the photographs and bring them home.

People say New York has changed with the proliferation of chain boutiques and ubiquitous fast food, and the pricing out of the middle class, but the changes are only on the surface. One day during the bitterly cold winter of 2011, I ducked into the lobby of an office building on Fifth Avenue to warm up for a minute. There was a pianist playing on a grand piano, anonymous ricky-tick lunch time office building lobby music. Suddenly he started playing, in a rubato style, Jerome Kern's "The Folks Who Live on the Hill," with all the right hip harmonic substitutions, Tatumesque flourishes, and superb pedaling. He stayed close to the melody and really conveyed the meaning of this beautiful piece. Cocktail piano as high art. The man was a master of the genre. By the end I was literally moved to tears. You will not hear a performance like this in the lobby of an office building in any other city. One good reason to stay here.

At the end of March I had planned to drive back to Mississippi to pick up the photographs with Dennis James. When the time came, Dennis wasn't able to make the trip. I didn't want to make the long trip alone, and Sylvia had seen quite enough of the American South for the time being. She found the atmosphere of Mississippi and the South to be quite oppressive, not just the history but something elemental, a miasma in the very air and the earth possibly due to the low lying topography of the delta region. I had always found the landscape itself strangely attractive. Somehow, it just didn't look or feel like anywhere else.

My old friend Cathryn MacFarlane, now living in Toronto, was feeling quite stressed by her government job and needed a break. She decided she would like to make the trip with me. She said it was okay with her husband if it was okay with Sylvia. I managed to find a cheap flight to St. Louis, where I rented a car, had dinner with Jo Ann Collins, and drove to Memphis, where I met Cathryn. From there we drove on to Mississippi. The state line is less than an hour from Memphis. We criss-crossed the state, eventually arriving in Starkville where I ate some more great barbecue. Before we took down the exhibit Cathryn shot some video of the installation. Perhaps we could use it later.

We packed up the photographs and instead of driving straight home, we headed south to Meridian (another dead former railroad town and the scene of more civil rights horrors in the 1960s), east to Alabama and Georgia, and then north through Tennessee on Route 411, stopping often to take pictures.

On this return trip I began experiencing severe pain in my left hip every time I got out of the car. It would take five or ten minutes to walk it off. I had a supply of painkillers which would get me home, and I would have to deal with this when we got back to New York.

Back home, at the beginning of April, the hip condition became worse, and all kinds of people with no medical knowledge at all were suggesting that I needed a hip replacement. I had a horror of being put through the medical system—endless hours wasted filling out forms and sitting in overheated waiting rooms to see practitioners who out of sheer greed, didn't keep their appointments. When you finally did see them they thought they knew it all without even listening to your symptoms and they just ran with the insurance card, ordering all kinds of unnecessary tests. I am very fortunate to have good medical insurance.

In the meantime, Dennis, no longer able to deal with the music business, had become a licensed massage therapist and a practitioner of something called ortho-bionomy. His opinion of my hip problem was that everything was just out of line from all the driving and needed stretching. He worked on my hip at regular intervals and gave me a series of exercises to do, and the results were amazing. The pain eventually stopped, although I still have some discomfort from time to time. But it's not serious and I can deal with it.

The winter of 2010/11 was a brutal one. The cold was unrelenting. When the temperature dropped, it was as if our apartment was made of cardboard. All the heat was turned on all the time, and the place was never warm enough. I was ill all the time—a seemingly endless series of colds, dental trouble, digestive problems, prostate issues, and I was feeling nauseous and chilled every morning. Pat and I finally ended the affair in March 2011 and wished each other the best, agreeing that we would have no further contact with each other. And we haven't. I confessed everything to Sylvia, and wonderful woman that she is, she forgave me and took me back. (She had suspected anyway.) Immediately after this all my stress related physical problems and illnesses cleared up, and I have generally felt fine since.

I am recovering from the terrible thing that I did, realizing the enormity of it and we are trying to rebuild our marriage. I was still suffering from bouts of depression. At these times the world looked and seemed flat and everything in it pointless and it was almost impossible for me to initiate any contact with the outside world.

When the depressions passed I looked forward to summer in the city: the stench of rotting garbage and urine in the streets mingled with the smell of sewage and overheated electrical wiring wafting up from the secret city of pipes, conduits and tunnels beneath the sun-baked asphalt and concrete. I remember the sight and smell of the renderer's truck surrounded by a cloud of flies in the old meatpacking district before the area became a gentrified playground for the celebrity rich.

I had been looking at a lot of William Eggleston's color work. And Robert Walker's. I bought a digital camera and slowly started to explore the medium of color. I was attracted by Walker's use of deeply saturated blocks of color as graphic elements in a photograph, influenced by the color field painters of the 1960s. But digital technology has unleashed upon us such a massive assault of undifferentiated, disposable images, sounds and information that I was starting to feel desensitized. An acquaintance of mine, a highly trained, highly successful, high-end commercial photographer, recently said to me: "Any punk with a digital camera is a photographer now!" Now everyone is also a musician, song-writer, artist etc., operating at the lowest common denominator. Excellence no longer matters, having been democratized by easy access to user-friendly technology. Information, much of it useless and transitory, has replaced ideas and the experiences they generate as the intellectual currency of the day. A high level of mediocrity has been achieved. In the face of this deluge I find it difficult and challenging to create interesting color photographs.

Susan Kismaric, a curator of photography at the Museum of Modern Art, said recently in *The New York Times*: "A lot of photography at this point in time is about decorating. It's not about taking the time to look." Again in the *Times*, the photographer Henry Wessel: "People don't pay much attention these days to the descriptive, expressive and suggestive facts found in a good photograph."

The digital post-modern world has become a post-literate, post-linear world: a world where one's life and art have to be condensed into thirty seconds on Facebook to be relevant. A world where attention deficit disorder is a way of life. The norm. What we have now is not Gen X or Gen Y, but Gen ADD. Today I see everyone on the street using handheld devices—iPods and smart phones. Music today often functions as a kind of "white noise" to block people's vacuous thoughts or their disturbing sub-vocal speech. The technology has promoted an instant gratification syndrome that has resulted in a drastic shortening of the human attention span. We have become a culture of abbreviation, which really began in the 1960s, when people became too lazy, stupid or too stoned to spell out things like "Lysergic acid diethylamide" or "Federal Bureau of Investigation." We have also become a culture of impermanence. Excellence and permanence seem to be inextricably linked.

This is happening globally with whole cultures leaping directly from the rice paddy to the mouse pad. We seem to have thrown out the baby with the bathwater of the industrial revolution, bypassing or disregarding things we had learned from it—linear thought, literacy, the ability to see or hear beyond the obvious, the ability to determine cause and effect, consequences and ramifications, and the art of memory, both personal and cultural. We are moving into a new feudalism where only the very rich will be literate in the traditional sense.

I guess I'm just an old-fashioned modernist, feet planted firmly back in the twentieth century. The more contact I have, however peripherally, with the contemporary world of visual art, the more I perceive a world driven by academia that is insular, elitist, entitled, and eurocentric. There is almost no traditional "straight" photography being shown in the commercial galleries, unless it is the work of a designated "old master." Much of the postmodern or conceptual art that I see seems to require pages and pages of pretentious curatorial text to explain it. A proliferation of emperors with very little clothing? We make art or create music to describe things for which there are no words. When asked what jazz is, Louis Armstrong replied: "If you have to ask, don't mess with it!" John Cage once told a student: "If you don't know, why do you ask?"

Every year the jazz programs in the universities spew out a new crop of accomplished young jazz players, few of whom display any musical personality or individuality. The academy has given us an inundation of self-conscious virtuosity, resulting in a music largely devoid of atmosphere, mystery, humor, romance or surprise. At the same time I see young kids playing in a pre-1962 style, even to the point of wearing retro suits and skinny ties. I call it "bebop under glass." The unsuccessful ones do one or two gigs at Small's and then disappear. I watch the few successful ones turn into cynical, grizzled old road rats before my very eyes. New York is tough. So is jazz.

Perhaps playing straight-ahead jazz on acoustic instruments is becoming something akin to playing baroque or so called "early" music on period instruments. I guess there's a niche for it somewhere. Certainly not at jazz festivals. I think that jazz is essentially a small venue music. It belongs in nightclubs or concert halls, not in arenas or stadiums—in fact, not anywhere out of doors. The music is in trouble. It hasn't had a large following since the 1960s, when it lost the black audience to rhythm and blues, and much of the white one to rock. How can a generation raised on stiff music like Radiohead, or rappers like 50 Cent talking about getting shot in the ghetto, relate to the music of say, Gary Bartz, Hank Mobley, Bird or Trane? Or Bach or Schoenberg, for that matter.

The other night on the way to the airport, I locked into a radio station playing contemporary African pop music from Ghana, Sierra Leone, and Nigeria. The guitars sounded like they could have been recorded in Nashville, the horns in Memphis circa 1965, and the songs used simple chord progressions reminiscent of country and western music. The African rhythmic sensibility and the call and response concept were retained, but with nowhere near the level of rhythmic sophistication of the traditional West African music brought to North America by Michael Olatunji and others in the 1950s and early '60s. This was African music filtered through the prism of American pop before being beamed back to Africa. I have also noticed these all-pervading American influences in the music of the Middle East, the Indian subcontinent and Asia. Like the pervasive spread of Coca-Cola and McDonald's, this dilution of valuable indigenous musical cultures is analogous to the American government sending operatives into other countries to destabilize their political regimes. But this is worse because we are talking about music here! With politics, people get what they deserve, and deserve what they get.

I am not photographing much these days. I am still trying to deal with and organize the thousands and thousands of images that I have taken and printed, editing the work into various portfolios, going back through my archive and making better prints from some of the earlier negatives, etc. Fortunately, I have kept a consistent filing system for my negatives right from the beginning. Even with this, it's difficult to keep some kind of order with hundreds and hundreds of prints in boxes piling up. In view of a burgeoning Collyer situation, we have rented a storage unit, something that eventually becomes a necessity for anyone in a small New York apartment. (The Collyer brothers were wealthy world-class hoarders and recluses who lived in a Fifth Avenue mansion and eventually died there amidst 140 tons of garbage. Police and firefighters still refer to dangerously out-of-control accumulations as a "Collyer situation.")

Now, looking all these prints I have made over the last fifteen years, I am able to see them as a body of work. Certainly not all great or even good photographs, but I am able to see how they work together in different series, in the larger context.

I have been getting my images scanned at the advertising agency where Sylvia works, so I now have thousands of digitized photographs in the computer, which also have to be organized—a seemingly endless, thankless task. I am learning about files and folders and how to organize them, name and rename them, and move them around, and how to back them up in an external drive. All of this is new to me. Digital bookkeeping is not my strong suit, but I keep working on it. Maybe this is the 21st century equivalent of the farm work that William Burroughs wrote about as being the best cure for an addiction.

Yes, the days of the freak show at Hubert's Museum, Professor Ray Heckler's Flea Circus, and the peep shows on Forty-Second Street and in Times Square are long gone, but there are certain intersections, corners where there are survivals, recurrences or holdovers from previous decades and eras, no matter how upscale the surrounding neighborhoods have become. First Avenue and East Fourteenth Street, Fourteenth and Eighth Avenue, Varick and West Houston, and Sixth Avenue between Eighth Street and Father Demo Square, with its concentration of tattoo parlors, adult video stores and "pushcart row" of street vendors, as well as various corners in the East Village, the Lower East Side and Hell's Kitchen, are all places where visual sleaze and behavioral oddities survive.

Recently I visited my friend Dennis James in Inwood, at the very northern tip of Manhattan in a totally Latino neighborhood. We went to a Dominican restaurant with Dean Crandall, another retired classical bassist, had some wonderful roast chicken, and afterwards stood around talking on West 207 Street. This is the main drag—salsa music blaring, housewares for sale on the street, cuchifrito wagons, junkies nodding on doorsteps. In the midst of all this the conversation ranged from Mahler's "Ninth Symphony" to the jazz scene in south central Los Angeles in the early ' 60s (Dean is from L.A.). Dean and I shouted lines at each other from "The Connection." Having this conversation in this context was another "only in New York" moment. One more reason to stay here in the city.

In April 2012 I had an exhibit consisting of 38 jazz photographs at the WBGO Gallery in Newark, New Jersey. Once again there was good feedback on the photographs but no sales. Ray Drummond and I played at the opening reception. Bulldog and I hadn't worked together for a while, and it was wonderful to play with him again.

Over the years I have been photographing various parts of the city at night. I have printed and organized these pictures into a series of almost 200 images. Informed and influenced by film noir, Edward Hopper's night time tableaux, and cartoonist Chester Gould's use of strong rich blacks in his Dick Tracy newspaper strip, some of them

Two women in a bar, Ninth Avenue, 1999.
Photograph © Peter Leitch.

look like stills of scenes or sets from an imaginary film noir—you almost expect Robert Ryan to step out of the shadows! I want to place the viewer in a space that he/she would not normally be. Other nighttime images are of New York's mythic skyscrapers and iconic bridges. I submitted some of these to the Living Room Gallery at St. Peter's Church, and was given an exhibit for September and October 2013.

I am preparing for release the 1999 California concert with John Hicks, David Williams and Billy Higgins. The music is so damned good it needs to come out. Working with Allan Tucker at Foothill Digital, we have improved the audio to the point where it's releasable. We didn't know the concert was being recorded and John Hicks plays at what I call "Level III" on this concert. Level III is when you think it just can't get any better, and then John bumps it up another notch! Given the current state of the music business, releasing this CD with no track less than nine minutes in length is almost an act of defiance.

I am now sixty-eight years old, and I never possessed the social skills necessary to become a truly productive member of mainstream society. Society in general, and New York in particular, has little use for the old. Artistically speaking, I'm not going to go quietly. I keep my eyes and ears open, and I ain't going to miss much. As my friend Dennis James says: "We're at the coda now." We just have to hope that there is a long open vamp, or at least a lot of repeats indicated in the score. I'm playing better than ever, and I have a lot of new music that I have to get recorded. And I have a lot of photographs that need to be seen—exhibited or published.

But my frame of reference has shifted. Thirteen years into the 21st century we are in an age of globalization, corporatization, green-washing and "branding." Manhattan's iconic skyscrapers, bridges and pavilions are beginning to appear as old coal-burning relics of the "American Century." Broadway, Wall Street, Times Square and even some of the surviving jazz clubs have become mere simulacra of what they were.

In the end, after all this, the words are not important. As in listening deeply to a piece of music, or looking into a photograph, what is important are the intuitions, the perceptions, and the feelings. And the silences.

......'cause when we're old and wasted,
the dues for what we've tasted run so high,
that we pay 'till we die .....

© Jon Hendricks "Four."

Lower Manhattan, Brooklyn Bridge, 2010.
Photograph © Peter Leitch.

West 42 Street, 2003.
Photograph © Peter Leitch.

Discography

AS A LEADER

Self Portrait, Jazz House, JH 7003, 2007, solo.

Autobiography, Reservoir, RSR 179, 2004, quintet w. Jed Levy, George Cables, Dwayne Burno, Steve Johns.

The Montreal Concert, DSM 3037, 2001, duo co-led w. Gary Bartz.

Blues on the Corner, Reservoir, RSR 160, 1999, sextet w. Bobby Watson, Kendra Shank, Renee Rosnes, Dwayne Burno, Billy Hart.

Up Front, Reservoir, RSR 146, 1997, trio w. Sean Smith, Marvin "Smitty" Smith.

Colours and Dimensions, Reservoir, RSR 140, 1996, septet w. Gary Bartz, Jed Levy, Claudio Roditi, John Hicks, Rufus Reid, Marvin "Smitty" Smith.

Duality, Reservoir, RSR 134, 1995, duet w. John Hicks.

A Special Rapport, Reservoir, RSR 129, 1993, quartet w. John Hicks, Ray Drummond, Marvin "Smitty" Smith.

From Another Perspective, Concord, CCD 4535, 1993, sextet w. Gary Bartz, Jed Levy, John Hicks, Ray Drummond, Smitty Smith.

Trio/Quartet '91, Concord,CCD 4480, 1991, trio w. Neil Swainson, Smitty Smith (+John Swanna, 3 tracks).

Exhilaration, Uptown 27.24, 1985, Reservoir 124CD, 1991, quintet w. Pepper Adams, John Hicks, Ray Drummond, Billy Hart (+2 duo tr. w. Drummond, 1988).

Mean What You Say, Concord, CCD 4417, 1990, quartet w. John Hicks, Ray Drummond, Smitty Smith.

Portraits and Dedications, Criss Cross 1039, 1039CD, 1989, quintet w. Bobby Watson, James Williams, Ray Drummond, Smitty Smith (+Jed Levy, 2 tracks).

Red Zone, Reservoir 103, 1987; 103CD 1988, quartet w. Kirk Lightsey, Ray Drummond, Smitty Smith.

On A Misty Night, Criss Cross 1026, 1987, 1994 CD, trio w. Neil Swainson, Mickey Roker.

Sometime in Another Life, Jazz House 7002,1982, duet w. George McFetridge.

Jump Street, Jazz House 7001, Pausa 7132, 1981, quartet/quintet w. Terry Lukiwski, George McFetridge, Art Davis, Freddie Waits, Neil Swainson, Terry Clarke.

California Concert, JH 2004, quartet w. John Hicks, David Williams, Billy Higgins, 2013.

DVDS
The Walkers' Duets, Pamorama Productions, 2008, with Gary Bartz, Ray Drummond, Jed Levy, Harvie S, and Sean Smith. 58:00.
The Artist and the City—Peter Leitch: A Video Profile, Pamorama Productions, 2006. 28:00.

WITH OTHER ARTISTS
With Chad Coe; *Sympatico,* Sympatico Records 1066, 2010.
With Pete Yellin: *Mellow Soul,* Metropolitan 667961111123, 1999.
With Various Artists: *The Art of Solo Jazz Guitar.* Paddlewheel, Anthology, 1 track (Japanese release).
With Dominique Eade: *When the Wind Was Cool,* RCA Victor 09026 68858-2,1997.
With Various Artists: *Portraits in Jazz,* Radioland RACD 10006, 1996
With Heiner Franz: *At First Sight,* Jardis Records, JRCD 9611 (Germany),1996.
With Chris Mcnulty: *A Time for Love,* Amosaya, MC-4545, 1995.
With Renee Rosnes: *Free Trade,* Justin Time 64-2, 1994.
With Jeri Brown: *Unfolding the Peacocks,* Justin Time 45-2, 1993
With Various Artists: *The Concord Jazz Guitar Collection,* Vol. 3, Concord CCD 4507, 1991 (1 Track).
With Jaki Byard: *Phantasies II,* Soul Note 121175-2, 1991.
With Jaki Byard: *My Mother's Eyes* (Japanese Release) 1995.
With Jed Levy: *Good People,* Reservoir 105, 1988.
With Woody Shaw: (Guest Appearance) *Solid,* Muse 5329, 1986.
With The New York Jazz Guitar Ensemble: *4 On 6 X 5,*Choice 6831, 1986.
With Oscar Peterson: *Royal Wedding Suite,* Pablo Today 2312-129, 1981; *The Personal Touch,* Pablo Today 2312-135, 1980.
With Art Ellefson: *The Art Ellefson Trio,* Radio Canada International 479, 1981.
With Al Grey & Jimmy Forrest: *Out 'Dere,* Greyforrest 1001, 1980.
With Buddy Munro: *Winter Wonderland,* RCI 415, 1975.
With Sadik Hakim: *London Suite,* RCI 375, 1973.
With Billy Robinson: *Evolution's Blend,* RCI 375, 1973.

Photography Exhibitions

1999: Kavahaz Gallery, New York
      Maison de la culture Frontenac, Montreal (group show)

2000: Kavehaz Gallery, New York
      Roho Photo Gallery, Cincinnati, OH

2001: Kavehaz Gallery, New York
      Sweet Basil, New York

2002: WBGO Gallery, Newark, NJ

2003: Kavehaz Gallery, New York

2005: Living Room Gallery, St. Peter's Church, New York

2007: WBGO Gallery, Newark, NJ

2009: May Gallery, St. Louis, MO
      Hudson Guild Gallery, New York (group show)
      Soho Photo Gallery, New York

2010: Colvard Gallery, Mississippi State University, Starkville, MS

2011: Hudson Guild Gallery, New York (group exhibit)

2012: WBGO Gallery, Newark NJ

2013: Living Room Gallery, St. Peter's Church, New York.

Bibliography

Cadence: Peter Leitch interview with Bob Rusch, 1983.

Coda: Peter Leitch interview with Bill Smith, 1987.

Cuademos de Jazz (Spain): Peter Leitch interview with Don Hillegas, 1995.

Down Beat: Peter Leitch profile, 1987.

DownBeat: Article, "Compatibility and Chemistry," 1998.

Hot House: Peter Leitch profile, 2003.

Jazz Improv: Peter Leitch interview, 2004.

Jazz Times: Article, "The Widening World of Peter Leitch," 1989.

Jazz Times: Article, "Peter Leitch's Many Faceted Swing" 1994.

Jazz Times: Article, "Picking and Clicking" 2007.

Journal of the New Jersey Jazz Society: Interview, 2010.

Stacatto (Germany): Article, 1998.

ENTRIES IN:

Alexander, Charles. *Masters of Jazz Guitar: The Stories of the Players and Their Music*. UK: Miller Freeman Books, 1999.

Feather Leonard & Ira Gitler, eds. *The Biographical Encyclopedia of Jazz*. Oxford University Press,1999.

Cook, Richard and Brian Morton. *The Penguin Guide to Jazz on CD, LP & Cassette*. Penguin Group 1994.

Gilmore, John. *Who's Who of Jazz in Montreal: Ragtime to 1970*. Montreal: Véhicule Press, 1989.

Kallman, Helmut, Gilles Potvin and Kenneth Winters, eds. *The Canadian Encyclopedia/The Encyclopedia of Music in Canada*. Toronto: University of Toronto Press, 1981.

Miller, Mark. *The Miller Companion to Jazz in Canada: And Canadians in Jazz*. Toronto: The Mercury Press, 2003.

Summerfield, Maurice J. *The Jazz Guitar: It's Evolution and Its Players*. UK: Ashley Mark Publishing, 1998.

Yanow, Scott. *The Great Jazz Guitarists: The Ultimate Guide*. Milwaukee: Backbeat Books, 2013.

Index

www.peterleitch.com
www.peterleitch.zenfolio.com

www.vehiculepress.com

Véhicule Press